THE TEMPEST

A Medieval Romance

By Kathryn Le Veque

The BlackChurch Guild: Shadow Knights Series

England's most elite training guild.

Knights of the highest order.

Numquam dedite. Never surrender.

THE HISTORY OF THE BLACKCHURCH GUILD

St. Giles de Bottreaux was a knight who had been disgraced for using unconventional tactics. Having served the Duke of Normandy, he was present at the Battle of Hastings. Unfortunately, he caught wind of a Norman lord who was about to betray the duke, and he tortured the lord to gain valuable information about the Saxon resistance.

He was vilified for it.

St. Giles was released from the duke's service because the rebel Norman was both a rich man and a distant cousin of the duke's. With no means of income, St. Giles and his brother, St. Lyon, wandered England, unable to find a suitable position. In desperation, they were forced to become part of a Saxon pirate group out of Watermouth, Devon.

Realizing that piracy was lucrative and putting their knightly skills to good use, the brothers quickly rose in the ranks and ended up commanding their own ships. St. Giles eventually formed his own pirate crew with the help of his brother, men known as Triton's Hellions. Their ships were the *Argos*, the *Mt. Pelion*, the *Pagasa*, and the *Athena*. St. Giles' specialty was in recruiting disgraced knights and giving them a new and rich career. Those knights began training other knights for a life of piracy at an abandoned church on the shores of Lake Cocytus in the Exmoor Forest. The place was called "Blackchurch" because it was a black, burned-out shell of a former sanctuary.

But such a place, hidden from the world, was a perfect staging ground for a warriors' guild.

More trained men meant more ships and more wealth. The pirate ships sailed the known world, bringing back men as well as treasure. As the years passed, those same ships brought diverse warriors from all over the world to the shores of Devon. While St. Giles settled in to manage their growing empire in the Exmoor Forest, St. Lyon assumed the pirate enterprise. All of the trained warriors he brought to Blackchurch combined with other elite trainers to create the most complex and comprehensive battle-training system in the world.

England, who had always dismissed Blackchurch as a pirate training ground, gradually became aware of the quality of those who had completed the course. They were the best-educated warriors in the world. The Earl of Wessex was the first to come to St. Giles and ask him for some of the fine men he'd trained. Soon, fully trained knights with good reputations began asking for admission to the training grounds to learn the "Blackchurch way" of life and warfare. It became lucrative and prestigious. St. Giles' grandson, St. Andrew de Bottreaux, was granted the title Earl of Exmoor by Henry I because St. Andrew gifted the king with an elite group of specialized knights who saved the king on more than one occasion. Soon, the Crown got behind this extraordinary training ground.

Blackchurch's reputation was cemented.

These days, Blackchurch is far less about piracy and far more about training the most coveted and skilled warriors the world has ever seen. Men and women are accepted as long as they are qualified and can pass the entrance test. Every trainer has a specialty—new classes of recruits are formed monthly from qualified applicants from all over the world, and each group of recruits spends at least six months with every trainer. To pay for their training, they either pay the fee once they pass the entrance test or they pledge a portion of their salary once they graduate and find a position. Training is harsh and intense. It is expected that even out of the vetted recruits, most will fail. Those few who succeed become forever known as Shadow Knights, a coveted title denoting their superior status.

As graduates say, you simply don't survive Blackchurch.

You *become* Blackchurch.

The Family Tree of de Bottreaux and the Trainers of Blackchurch

De Bottreaux tree (Lords of Exmoor, who run Blackchurch):

St. Giles b. 1040 – was part of the conquest of 1066, died 1100. Brother, St. Lyon, served with him as a pirate, and it is St. Lyon's descendants who continue to run the pirate conglomerate known as Triton's Hellions. Now run by St. Abelard de Bottreaux.

St. Simon b. 1070 – d. 1135

St. Andrew b. 1094 – d. 1160

St. Paul b. 1119 – d. 1195

St. Denis b. 1147

St. Denis has two sons—St. Gerard (died 1212) and St. Sebastian, a.k.a. "Sebo," b. 1171 and 1173 respectively. Both trained at Kenilworth and Warwick Castle. Veterans of the Third Crusade.

Current list of trainers (moniker is listed after ancestry):

Tay Munro (Scottish/Greek) – the Leviathan – Teaches endurance, physical fitness, structure, and discipline. He's the boot camp, the gateway to the rest of the training.

Sinclair "Sin" de Reyne (Norman) – the Swordsman – Sword training, warfare, military history, how to command an army, etc.

Fox de Merest (Norman/Saxon) – the Protector – Teaches men how to defend and kill using daggers and other weapons. He's the "MacGyver" of Blackchurch. His class is about defense and thinking outside of the box.

Payne Matheson (Scottish) – the Tempest – Teaches offense. Instructs men on how to size up enemies and figure out their weaknesses. How to fight battles from the ground up.

Kristian Heldane (Dane) – the Viking – He is sea-bound. Everything he does is on water—fighting on water, instruction on boats, etc.

Creston de Royans (Norman) – the Avenger – Interrogation, treatment of the enemy, anything underhanded. How to handle torture and difficult conditions. (Sometimes works in tandem with the Conquistador)

Aamir ibn Rashid (Egyptian) – the North Star – Military history (global) and tactics from other armies. Understanding different cultures and how that dictates their fighting techniques.

Cruz Mediana de Aragón (Spanish) – the Conquistador – Conquest and diplomacy, politics, and the art of negotiation. Bribes, coercion, and leverage. (Sometimes works in tandem with the Avenger)

Ming Tang (Chinese) – the Dragon – Former Shaolin monk. Name means "bright water." Fighting kung fu, using hands, feet, and staff only. Fighting with the mind and not a weapon. Meditation for a warrior to calm the mind and the spirit.

Bowen de Bermingham (Norman/Irish) – the Titan – Warrior etiquette and responsibilities, discipline, hand-to-hand combat, using the landscape/land to one's advantage, living off the land, concealment, stealth. Sometimes works in tandem with the Leviathan and the Tempest.

Assistants (second-level trainers assisting the first level):

Axton Summerlin (The Protector and The Swordsman) A trainer eventually known as **The Medusa**.

Anteaus de Bourne (The Swordsman and The Tempest) A trainer eventually known as **The Eagle**.

Rhodes St. James (The Leviathan, The Viking, The Avenger) A trainer eventually known as **The Centurion**.

Pirate Factions (mostly centered around Cornwall and Devon coastlines, or the Irish Sea):

Triton's Hellions: Led by St. Abelard de Bottreaux, based in Minehead, control most of the northern Cornwall and Devon coast

Demons of the Sea: Led by Santiago de Fernandez, based at Fremington, Cornwall and also at Lastres, Castilian coast

Medusa's Disciples: Led by "Bloody Maude" Kilkenny Matheson of Coll Island

Kraken's Horde: Irish faction mentioned in *The Swordsman* out of Dublin

The Sea God/Titans of the Deep: Aragon pirates with bases in Tarragona, Palma, Ibiza

Location Map for The Blackchurch Guild

Exmoor Forest, Devon, England

The Blackchurch Guild

You haven't seen an enemies-to-lovers story until you've read THE TEMPEST!

Medieval mayhem and rollicking adventure has arrived for the Blackchurch Guild knights as a legendary pirate tries to storm their fortress… only to discover the legendary pirate is the most legendary buccaneer of all.

And no one knows the buccaneer better than Payne Matheson!

Payne is the Highlander of Blackchurch. Big, tough, and with a mouth he can't control, he's an excellent warrior with a supernatural gift for fighting. There is no better combatant at the Blackchurch Guild, but there's a reason for that. Both of his parents were warriors.

But he's about to step onto the fighting platform of a much-larger world stage.

Astria Julia is the daughter of Sancho I of Portugal, a royal princess by blood. She also happens to be a rebel, a lass with a mysterious past, and when she ends up at Blackchurch as a spoil of war, it's Payne who is assigned to guard her.

But he gets much more than he bargains for with the fiery Portuguese princess.

When an immovable force meets with a permanent object, it's a battle of wills to see which one breaks first. Head-to-head combat between Payne and Astria soon turns to something else, something soft and warm that neither one of them recognize.

When Astria finally reveals the truth behind her mysterious persona, Payne is in too deep to do anything about it.

He is now part of her, she of him.

And the results could be deadly.

Join Payne and Astria on a truly epic adventure of pirates, legends, Scotsmen, and the curse of royal blood. At the Blackchurch Guild, the premier training ground of the best warriors in the world, anything can happen… and usually does!

Numquam dedite. Never surrender.

Author's Note

What can I say about this tale?

MORE PIRATES!!

That's right—more swashbucklers. We had such great fun with those merry bands of vicious cutthroats in *The Swordsman* that we're going to have even more fun with them in this tale. And what a tale! Forget what you've ever read about pirates—I've got a couple of groups of high-seas brigands that are going to blow your socks off. And the boys from Blackchurch are right in the middle of it. It's fun already!

I'm always so excited to talk about these stories that I have to be very conscientious of not giving away the plot, or the story itself, but in this case, I will make an exception. Payne Matheson, our sexy Highlander, is our hero in this tale, and if you've read other Blackchurch novels, then you know there's kind of a running joke about Payne's mother. He's always talking about his mother. In Payne's story, how could I not introduce that legendary woman?

Speaking of legendary women, our heroine is a princess. I don't usually write about lost princesses or other incidental royalty, but in this tale, our heroine really is a princess, daughter of Sancho I of Portugal. Sancho was a real king—our princess is fictional. Sancho had many, many children—both legitimate and illegitimate—so it was simple to incorporate a fictional daughter amongst the litter of actual children. I really like this heroine because she's a tough lady—and you don't find out just *how* tough until the story progresses.

We also find out a few things about Payne, who has been a secondary character in the Blackchurch Guild series until this point. We've known him to be incredibly loyal, funny, and bold. He's also got a mouth on him, so in a sense, he has veered away from the heroes I usually write about. My very favorite hero is the strong, silent type. I just find them so endearing. What I don't normally write is a big-mouthed hero, but in this tale, I have. If you've read my de Wolfe Pack series, then you know that one of the primary secondary characters, Paris de Norville, is sort of like that. He's got a mouth on him, plus he's arrogant—i.e., an antihero. But characters like that make novels so much more enjoyable!

I like to call it The Brat Factor.

Payne has The Brat Factor.

Astria does not—but she's got something just as good. Maybe better.

In all, I think you're going to love this pairing. It's a different kind of pairing and we've got a lot of very strong secondary characters to help move the story along. Something to note— you know that when I write these books, I do a lot of research on the names of places in Medieval times. The Mediterranean Sea is mentioned in this book and even back then, it had that name associated with it. It was also called the Great Sea, and a few other things, but for ease in description, I'm referring to it by the name we know—Mediterranean. Additionally, our heroine has many titles, as a royal princess, and most of them are legitimate for someone of her birth and title, but others I've used creative license on.

Also of note here is the brief feature of gunpowder in this tale. Written formulas for it were found in the Middle East by 1240 A.D., but people who were involved in trade and piracy possibly had it earlier because of their contact with different cultures and peoples from the far east. It didn't really come to

England until the late thirteenth century, so I've taken artistic liberty with giving it to some seagoing folks in the earlier part of the century. A friend of mine with several degrees in History says *if it's not proven that it wasn't there, then maybe it was.* So—if we can't definitively prove that early twelfth-century pirates had gunpowder, then maybe they did. For my purposes, they did!

The usual pronunciation guide:

Astria: ASS-tree-uh (Not Austria, which is what it looks like—ASSS-tree-uh). It's actually a very old name!

And with that, I truly hope you enjoy Payne and Astria's story. It's a whopper of a tale!

Hugs,

PROLOGUE

Year of Our Lord 1223
The Blackchurch Guild

THE RAIN WAS merciless.

Standing at the edge of Lake Cocytus, the enormous lake that ran through the heart of the Blackchurch property, those on the shore were convinced that, at some point, a man named Noah and his giant ark would soon be appearing because the rain was truly that heavy and it had been for about a week. But this was the day scheduled for this particular exercise, so the men of Blackchurch were ready.

Rain or no rain.

The Viking was on the move.

Not a true Northman in the literal sense, although he had been one at one point in his past, but the Blackchurch trainer known as The Viking had come to the conclusion that his class of recruits was ready for their final test in the landing and conquest module, something they'd been working on for the better part of six months, so it was the job of the other Blackchurch trainers to try to prevent Kristian Heldane's class from making it not only to the shore, but to the top of the rise where a small rock shed stood.

That was the goal.

To reach that crumbling little shed.

"Kristian has some enthusiastic recruits, you know," one man said. He was enormous, with black hair and dark eyes, taller than the rest of the men around him. Tay Munro, a trainer known as The Leviathan, was the *de facto* leader of the Blackchurch instructors. "By the time they hit his class, they're almost finished with their training here. You know they're going to do everything they can in order to get to the old cottage."

Lightning lit up the sky, dancing across the dark clouds before disappearing to the west. Thunder rolled, following it. Everyone looked up, watching the sky, feeling the tension. Though this was only a test, that didn't mean it wasn't dangerous.

It meant that it was *real*.

"We're allowed to disable," another man rumbled as water ran down his face. He had a big club in one hand, one that usually held a sword. Sinclair de Reyne was known as The Swordsman and was deadly no matter what weapon he armed himself with. "We can disable and we can break bones. We just can't kill them."

"More's the pity." A thick Scots brogue entered the conversation, causing the others to grin. More lightning lit up the sky as Payne Matheson, a trainer known as The Tempest, tightened the fist-shaped leather wrappings on both hands that were covered with iron studs. When he saw the men around him smiling, he held up those studded leather gloves made specifically for fistfights. "I'm going for throats and heads with these, lads. Let me be the first line. Anyone who gets past me belongs tae ye."

As he grinned and nodded enthusiastically, a shorter, well-built man came to stand next to him, his dark gaze fixed on the turbulent lake.

"You only want to disable them, Payne, not permanently cripple them," he said in accented speech. "These men are not our enemy. They are men striving for perfection."

Payne glanced at Ming Tang. He had not been born in England, but far to the east, where he'd been raised in the Shaolin religion. It was a strict religion of great philosophy, making Ming Tang a man of many talents with a mind constantly seeking knowledge, and that curiosity was what had brought him to Blackchurch. He brought a great deal of wisdom to teach others and was wise counsel in any situation.

Even at the onset of a fistfight with an overzealous Scotsman.

"Of course they are striving for perfection," Payne said. "And they shall meet it in the trainers who have worked hard tae get them tae this point. If they are not perfect, they willna get past us."

"Are you truly going to use those iron-studded gloves on them?"

"Why wouldn't I?"

Ming Tang didn't have an immediate answer for him, but he did smile. Sort of a "you are incorrigible" smile that Payne took as a compliment.

"I would suggest you take a defensive stance rather than an offensive one," Ming Tang finally said. But he sighed heavily almost as soon as the words left his mouth. "Or am I expecting too much?"

Payne shrugged. "If they come at me, I'm ready," he said.

"Stay here with me and we shall face them together."

"I think I'd better so you will not kill someone."

Payne laughed. He clapped Ming Tang on the shoulder, meant to be a gesture of camaraderie, but he nearly threw Ming Tang off balance with the force of it. As they stood there in the driving rain, a shadow of a ship began to appear through the clouds and water.

The Viking and his trainees were approaching.

"I'm with you, Payne." Creston de Royans, a trainer known as The Avenger, came up beside him. The man had a club in his hand and he held it menacingly. "I'll help you with the onslaught. Remember that I had these recruits last year, so I am well acquainted with their tactics."

Payne looked at the big, blond knight. "I had them two years ago," he said. "I spent an entire year teaching them what I know best."

"And what's that?" Creston said drolly. "How to offend women? Or how to be obnoxious?"

Payne sneered at him. "Ye're jealous I took that dark-eyed lass from yet at the Black Cock," he said, referring to the local tavern they used as their relaxation haven. "She dinna want a blond beast, Cres. I told ye that. *She* told ye that."

Creston waved him off. "You got her drunk and told her I had already outlived six wives," he said. "No wonder she ran from me. But do not worry. I do not hold a grudge. Not much, anyway."

Payne started to laugh. "Do ye mean I have tae watch my back even now, at this moment?"

"You'll never known until it's too late."

That brought a roar of laughter from Payne. But the continued repartee was cut short when the enormous cog drew nearer to the shore. The boat was one that the Lords of Exmoor, the men who owned and operated the Blackchurch Guild, had purchased from a ship builder in London and brought out to the wilds of Devon, in pieces, and then reconstructed in the lake. It was quite large, easily holding a hundred men, but the class of recruits on it was about twenty men and one trainer. The vessel moved by rowing but also by sail, and out of Blackchurch's thousand-man army, about a hundred of them were in the hold, rowing it toward the shore where the Blackchurch trainers, all nine of them plus three assistant trainers, were waiting. Perhaps twenty men against twelve didn't seem like fair odds, but when one was dealing with the men who trained the most elite warriors in the world, the odds were fairly even.

"Spread out," Payne boomed to the men around him. "They'll come from the bow, so watch both sides of the ship."

The trainers moved into position, spreading out in layers. Payne and Ming Tang and Creston were closest to the ship while the others were strategically positioned up the hill, all the way back to the cottage where one of the assistant trainers was stationed to protect the banner that the trainees were supposed to capture. Once they had it, the exercise was up, but unfortunately, any trainees knocked to the ground and failing to get to their feet unaided would be drummed out of Blackchurch. The rules were harsh, but not without hope. Anyone who failed would have the opportunity to try again in another year. But all trainees feared that rule—if one failed at any point during the five-year training course, they were finished until the next recruit class was formed.

Therefore, this was an important moment.

As the ship went aground on the edge of the lake and men

began leaping from the bow and into knee-deep water, approaching the shore with clubs in hand, the trainers of the Blackchurch Guild braced themselves. As the wind howled and the storm surged, the moment of truth was upon them.

Chaos ensued.

☙

"IT'S LOOSE, BUT it should tighten up."

Payne had just had Ming Tang look at one of his teeth. He'd been hit so hard in the face because of the rain and the darkness that he hadn't seen the club flying at him until it was too late. Fortunately, he didn't go down, but his fury in being struck landed the man who'd hit him on his backside, knocked unconscious by the raging Scotsman. It had been enough to fail the man out of Blackchurch, a man that everyone had thought was a sure bet to finish the training, so the night of battle and cottage capturing had had some unexpected moments.

And some glorious ones.

Even now, the Blackchurch trainers were sitting in their usual alcove at the Black Cock Tavern, a rather large and well-used establishment in the village that wasn't even a mile south of the Blackchurch Guild. Some, like Payne and Creston and an assistant trainer named Axton Summerlin, were sporting some physical evidence of what had been a surprisingly brutal fight, but others were unscathed on the surface. At least, they weren't admitting the injuries that could be covered by a tunic or breeches. Everyone was gathered around the table, ale and food between them, speaking of their experience against The Viking's trainees.

Eleven had survived and captured the banner.

No one was prouder of that than The Viking himself.

"It was a difficult task, my friends," Kristian said, lifting his cup to the group. "Well done, all of you."

Cups were lifted in Kristian's direction. "Well done *you*," Tay said. "You helped get them this far, Kristian. Your teachings are not exactly simple. It is one of the more complex segments that we put our recruits through."

Kristian smiled, pleased with the acknowledgment. Very tall and very blond, as one might expect of a Northman, he was a prince of his people, something he'd left behind long ago. In that respect, however, he was actually the only royal member of the Blackchurch trainers. He wasn't conventionally handsome, but he had a strong magnetism about him, an authority and charm that drew people to him in a way other men lacked.

"I would not have a class at all were it not for most of you training them to reach this point," he said, lifting his cup to his comrades. "That is why we are the best in the world, *pojkar*. That is why we are legendary."

Pojkar. It was an affectionate term in Kristian's language, something meaning boys or lads. Soft chants of agreement to his statement could be heard around the table, a table that did, indeed, contain the most legendary and impressive trainers of warriors that the world had seen.

That was Blackchurch—legendary and impressive.

In addition to Payne, Tay, Kristian, Sinclair, Creston, and Ming Tang, there were others—Fox de Merest, a former royal knight who was known as The Protector, Cruz Mediana de Aragon, a knight from Zaragoza who trained men in covert thinking and tactics, and a glorious warrior named Aamir ibn Rashid. Known as The North Star, Aamir was from Egypt, his father was a great Egyptian warlord, and it was his task to teach men about different armies, cultures, and fighting techniques.

There was no one better at it.

The last four members of the group were the newest. They were either assistant trainers or newer full-fledged trainers, good men with a good purpose, but they hadn't quite yet earned the camaraderie that the veteran trainers had built up over the years. Bowen de Bermingham was the first, a new trainer who taught warrior etiquette and responsibilities. Assistant trainers were Axton Summerlin, Anteaus de Bourne, and Rhodes St. James, men who rotated around, working with different trainers at different times. They sat and drank, and ate, and listened because there was most definitely a hierarchy with the Blackchurch trainers and they'd not yet reached the privileged level. For them, at this time, it was *listen and learn*. Even from men who were relaxing and blowing off steam.

This was when they received the best insight into the legendary Blackchurch trainers.

"Now those eleven men go to Aamir," Tay said, indicating the Egyptian down the table. "How many recruits do you have now, Aamir?"

"Seven," Aamir said, his dark eyes glimmering with mirth. "I am the last trainer they will have. When I am finished with them, they will have completed the Blackchurch training process and can finally call themselves graduates. One of them has already had an offer from a French duc for the Albigensian Crusade. He is prepared to pay the man handsomely and it should be a prestigious post."

He was speaking of a vicious war in Southern France that had been going on for years. "It will come tae no good end," Payne said, shaking his head. "That is a feud fought by the church. No one wants tae be involved in a holy war, Amir."

"You would not go if someone offered you a good deal of

money?" Aamir asked.

Payn continued to shake his head. "I would *not*," he said. "No one wins in a holy war. It goes on and on until there are no more men left tae fight it. Look at King Richard's crusade thirty years ago. Who won? It was not the English, lads."

"The Christian armies won several battles," Aamir reminded him.

"But they failed tae capture Jerusalem," Payne pointed out. "That is why the Christian armies went in the first place, tae take Jerusalem from Saladin. Aye, I remember my history, Aamir. I know that Richard and the Christians shouldna have gone. They should have left the Levant tae the people who live in the land. There was too much death and destruction and too many fine Christian men lost."

"You speak as though it was personal, Payne," Tay spoke up, a faint smile on his lips. "War should never be taken personally."

Payne looked at him. "My da fought with Richard's army," he said. "My mother said that when he returned, he wasna the same man. It did something tae him. So, nay, I wouldna fight in a holy war, no matter how much money I was offered."

"But you would fight if Henry wanted to fight the Welsh?" Tay said.

Payne nodded firmly. "I dunna like the Welsh," he said, listening to the snorts of laughter from his friends. He looked down the table, finding one of the newer trainers. "And I dunna like the Irish, either, de Bermingham. If ye have something tae say tae me about that, do it now. Fight me if ye must."

Bowen de Bermingham knew Payne well enough to know that the man didn't mean it. Not much, anyway. Payne was vocal about disliking everyone from nearly every country and even some Scotsmen, but that was part of his brash personality. He never meant it until someone threw a punch, and then he'd grin, back down, and buy the man he insulted more drink. He was a loveable scoundrel, as Tay's wife, Athdara, so kindly put it.

A loveable scoundrel with fists of iron.

And Bowen knew it.

"I will not fight you," he said, waving his hands in surrender. "My father's father was from Ireland, but my father was born here. So was my mother. And if you must know, I find my Irish relations intolerable, too."

Payne burst out laughing. A serving wench passed him with a full pitcher and he gently grasped the girl, pulling the pitcher from her hand and pouring himself a full cup before giving it back to her so she could take it down the table. After a hard night, everyone was relaxed and jovial, and more conversations, accusations, good-natured insults, and even boasts were passed around the table. It was a regular night after a regular day of training. Everyone was looking forward to a good night's sleep.

Until St. Sebastian de Bottreaux appeared.

The heir to the Blackchurch empire was well liked by those who served him and his father. He was highly trained, just like the Blackchurch trainers were, but he tended to think more with his heart than his head. His older brother, St. Gerard, had been accidentally killed a few years earlier, so the man had stepped into an unexpected position he hadn't necessarily been trained for.

His appearance at the tavern was an unusual one. Payne saw him first and he elbowed Tay, who elbowed Fox, seated next to him. The three of them stood up to catch St. Sebastian's attention, and when they did, the entire table caught sight of what had their focus and they, too, stood up. When St. Sebastian saw them, he quickly moved through the smoky common room of the tavern and into the semiprivate alcove.

"I am very sorry to disrupt your evening of celebration," he said, looking mostly at Payne and Tay and the men around them. "Unfortunately, we've received some concerning news and my father wants all of you returned to Blackchurch. We will be sealing up the gatehouses."

Tay still had his cup of wine in his hand. "God's Bones," he muttered, puzzled. "What is so concerning that we are sealing the gatehouses?"

St. Sebastian reached onto the table and picked up Creston's cup of wine, draining it before speaking because he'd run all the way from Blackchurch. "We have just received word from Abelard," he said, referring to his father's cousin, St. Abelard de Bottreaux, the man who was in command of the more violent and scandalous arm of the de Bottreaux empire. "One of his men just arrived on a sweaty horse, having ridden all the way from Minehead."

"At night?" Tay said incredulously.

St. Sebastian nodded. "At night," he confirmed. "As you know, Abelard and his band of pirates control the coast from Minehead to Ilfracombe," he said. "Triton's Hellions are all over Bristol Channel and the southern coast of Wales."

The trainers were nodding. "We know," Tay said. "And Santiago de Fernandez and the Demons of the Sea are on the west coast of Cornwall, among other places."

St. Sebastian lifted his hand to beg patience. "They are," he said, "I am telling you what you already know, but there is a reason for that. It seems that a faction of Scottish pirates entered the Bristol Channel several days ago and tried to dock at Minehead. Abelard chased them away but he's fairly certain they simply dodged him and came ashore near Highbridge. He heard rumor that they were moving inland, down the River Parrett. Abelard got the impression that they were trying to reach Blackchurch because when they tried to come ashore at Minehead, they kept asking how to reach the Lords of Exmoor."

That brought bewilderment to the men at the table, who looked at each other in confusion.

"Are you telling us that a band of pirates is coming to attack Blackchurch?" Aamir finally said. "*Who* are they?"

St. Sebastian shook his head. "All I know is that Abelard's messenger told us," he said. "He has said they are Scottish pirates and the only Scottish pirates we know are those we do not speak of. They have terrorized the entire west coast of Scotland, England, and Wales for years, but they've never come this far south."

"But now they are," Tay said grimly.

St. Sebastian nodded, apprehension in his eyes. "Aye," he said. "It seems so."

"Medusa's Disciples."

Those softly uttered words by Tay brought consternation to a group that was already plagued by confusion. Kristian, who was their seagoing trainer, seemed particularly serious in the face of such information.

"We are safe from Triton's Hellions and the Demons of the Sea by virtue of the fact that Blackchurch is related to one through blood and to the other through marriage," he said, brow furrowed. "Because of that relationship, other pirate factions leave us alone, but do Medusa's Disciples have no such restraint?"

St. Sebastian shook his head. "It seems not," he said. "My

father is very concerned because of their leader. God, I cannot even say the name."

He shuddered, averting his gaze, but they all knew whom he was speaking of. Someone that no sane man liked to acknowledge. Tay, who had been contemplating the situation, finally dared to say it.

"Bloody Maude," he muttered. "We all know what she is capable of. We've heard the rumors."

There was some serious grunting of concern going around the table at that statement. "I met a man once who had a brush with Bloody Maude," Creston said ominously. "He said that she wears her trophies around her neck. The woman has a necklace of dead and dried male members she's put on a chain and uses it to frighten her enemies."

"It would frighten me right out of my skin," Tay said with conviction. "She cuts off men's male organs without thought. She displays them like some grotesque chain of jewels and I, for one, do not intend for my wife's greatest pleasure to become part of some macabre collection."

"And that is why we must return home," St. Sebastian said, gesturing to the door. "Come, now. We can discuss Bloody Maude as we run back to the safety of Blackchurch."

He didn't need to prod anyone. The mere threat of the brutal Scottish pirate queen and her disregard for what men held precious had them all quite ready and willing to depart, heading out into the darkness. Running out was more like it. No one wanted to stroll home leisurely with that kind of danger looming. Tay lingered behind for just a moment to warn the tavernkeep, who thought it might be a good idea to close early and lock up for the night.

But why she was coming was anyone's guess.

An evening of triumph was ending on a frightening note.

PART ONE

THE PIRATE QUEEN

CHAPTER ONE

T HIS WAS HER life now.

Captive of Bloody Maude.

Chained up to a wagon, with her wrists chafed and bleeding from being restrained and her legs bound at the ankles, it was her fault that she was in this position. She'd kicked someone in the face one too many times. She'd gouged one too many eyes. From the moment Maude and her band of pirates had captured her off the coast of the island of Formentera, her entire life had been filled with fighting. They'd managed to surprise the vessel she'd been traveling on and before she even knew what was happening, men were boarding the ship and either killing those on board or taking them prisoner.

Fortunately, she'd been taken prisoner.

Although she was beginning to question that luck.

The old wagon she was riding on lurched over the rocky road and slammed her against the bed. Grunting in pain, she tried to keep her balance, which was difficult considering how tightly restrained she was. Splinters were digging into her backside and into her arms. They'd offered to untie her when they transferred her from the ship to the stolen wagon, provided she would behave herself, but she couldn't. In this situation, it simply wasn't possible. Prisoners had a right to escape and she would try, at every opportunity, to exercise those rights.

But her resolve was wavering.

"Are ye hurt, lass?" A woman came around the side of the wagon, shouting at the driver to stop before she addressed her again. "This road is terrible, made worse at night because we canna see it well. That last hole was a big one."

The prisoner glared at her, unable to speak for the gag on her mouth, so she didn't answer. She simply looked away after a moment, which prompted the woman to remove her gag.

"There," she said. "That's better, is it not? If ye behave yerself, I'll leave it off."

The prisoner licked her dry, cracked lips. "If you were in my position, would you behave?"

The woman cocked her head thoughtfully. "More than likely not," she said. "I've told ye before that I respect the fight ye have in ye. I dunna fault ye for it. But ye've hurt three of my men and that is why I've had tae restrain ye, Princess Astria."

There it was. The damnable woman knew her name, one she'd tried to keep from her when she was first captured, but a frightened sailor was tortured into telling Bloody Maude everything about her captive.

Princess Maria Astria Julia.

Daughter of a king.

Her father had been Sancho of Portugal, a once-powerful ruler with a great army and a penchant for political games. He was gone now, but her family still held the throne. Astria had been taken to Wales, she thought, but she couldn't be certain. She'd heard some of Maude's men speaking of Wales, so she assumed that the pirates intended to hide her from her family before ransoming her. She was to be used as a prize.

She'd never been so furious in her life.

Not frightened, but furious. She knew that Bloody Maude had no intention of harming her or killing her, so she was safe. For now. But she wasn't sure how long that was going to last, and she didn't like being a captive anyway, so her attempts to escape had been frequent. Hence the chains. She was just so bloody furious that she'd come to this point in her life that all she could think of doing was lashing out, at everyone and everything. But even she knew that wasn't getting her any-where.

She had to let her brains take precedent over her anger or all was lost.

"I did not attack them," she said after a moment. "I was defending myself. But I suppose that does not matter now."

Maude leaned on the side of the wagon. "Nay, it does not," she said. Then she eyed her. "If I give ye something tae drink, ye willna spit it back at me, will ye?"

Astria shook her head. "Nay," she said, sighing heavily. "That would be foolish because then you'd never give me anything to drink again, so I will not spit it at you."

Maude motioned to someone out of Astria's line of sight and soon enough, a bladder was produced. Maude herself opened it and held it up for Astria to drink, the watered wine coursing down her parched throat. She drank until she could drink no more and Maude sealed the bladder up and handed it back to one of her men.

But she was watching Astria closely.

"Ye've been with us for five months now," she said. "Five months is a long time tae fight, lass. Are ye not tired?"

"Are you?" Astria shot back softly. "I can fight as long as I need to fight."

"As can I."

Astria sighed heavily and lifted her eyes, gazing at the woman. She was an older woman, but just how old was anyone's guess. She had two grown sons, men who served her aboard her pirate ships, so she had to have seen forty-five summers at the very least, but probably more. She had pale, luminous skin and enormous blue eyes, all of it framed by glorious auburn hair she kept tied up with bands of cloth. Several of them. It looked as if hair was erupting out of these bands all over her head, and the hair was long, falling past her elbows. She hadn't brushed it in some time and the ends of her hair had matted into tubes. For clothing, she wore breeches and boots and tunics cinched up with girdles that made her small waist smaller.

And she was barely five feet tall.

This was Bloody Maude, and had Astria not seen the woman in action, she would have never believed her to be a pirate. More than just a brigand on the high seas, but one that ruled with an iron fist.

Medusa's Disciples.

That was what this band of Scots called themselves.

And Maude was, indeed, Medusa.

"Then it seems we have a problem," Astria said after a moment. "I do not intend to remain a prisoner forever."

"And ye willna be a prisoner forever."

"Ransoming me to my father will be fruitless," Astria said pointedly. "If that is your intention, then know that he is dead. My young nephew now sits upon the throne."

Maude grinned. "Who says I'm going tae ransom ye?"

"Aren't you?"

Maude shook her head. "Lass, ye've been fighting us for five long months," she said. "Never once have we had a conversation about what I intend tae do with ye because ye've been like a wild horse ever since we found ye."

"You did not *find* me," Astria said bitterly. "You captured me."

"I did."

"And the ships that were my escort."

Maude nodded proudly. "I did, indeed," she said. "Ye fought a fine battle, but ye lost. I confess that I'm disappointed that ye've not shown much honor in yer defeat, lass."

Astria grunted at the truth, or ridiculousness, of that statement. She wasn't sure which. "How much honor would you have shown if you were *my* prisoner?" she asked. "Are you telling me that you would not fight to escape? And remember who you are, Bloody Maude. Would Bloody Maude not fight her captivity?"

Maude was smiling. "Bloody Maude would not be a captive in the first place."

Astria rolled her eyes. "Mayhap not this time," she said, irritated. "But you play a dangerous game, every moment of your life. There will come a day when you are overpowered and end up a captive. It is only a matter of time."

"But that time is not today," Maude said, amused at Astria's reaction as the woman shook her head dramatically and looked away. "Lass, I'll tell ye where ye're going and what I intend from ye if ye want tae know. But if ye dunna accept yer fate with grace, and stop fighting yer captivity, I swear that I'll tie ye limb tae limb and throw ye intae the sea. I've had my limit of yer tantrums. Do ye understand me? All of the kicking and biting in the world willna prevent what I intend for ye, so ye may as well accept it."

There was a threat in those words. Astria knew it. The pirate queen would indeed tie her limbs together and throw her into the sea, and that was not the way she wished for her life to end. She'd battled the woman for one hundred and fifty long days and nothing had come of it, so perhaps it was time to switch tactics. Perhaps it was finally time to accept that she was the prisoner of Medusa's Disciples and, over time, perhaps their guard would go down enough that she could slip away. Certainly, being combative hadn't gotten her what she wanted.

It was possible that submission was the only way.

But, God… it was difficult.

It simply wasn't in her nature to surrender.

"Then have it your way," she finally said. "Tell me what marvelous destiny I will have and how I should be grateful for it."

Maude climbed up onto the wagon bed, plopping down opposite Astria. She seemed to be staring at her quite a bit, which Astria took as a challenge. But as she studied the woman in return, it occurred to her that the gaze wasn't challenging, but more appraising. As if she were sizing her up.

And she had no idea why.

But she was about to find out.

"I have three sons," Maude said, interrupting her thoughts. "Ye've met Francis and Declan. The big lads with the red hair? Those are my boys."

It took Astria a moment to realize whom she was talking about. "The tall ones?" she said, puzzled. "The young ones?"

"Aye."

"*Those* are your sons?"

Maude nodded. "It was Francis who captured ye."

Astria wasn't thrilled to be reminded of that. "I did not realize they belonged to you," she said. "I've only heard them called the Pope and the Devil."

Maude grinned. "Pope Francis and Declan the Devil," she said. "Most of my men have names that are not their own, like the Pope and the Devil. There's also Fish, Monk, Christ, Joyosa, and The Spear. Ye've heard of them, too."

"I have," Astria said. "Strange names, all of them."

"That is true."

"But why?"

Maude shrugged. "The sea brings anonymity for a man if he wants it," she said. "If he wants tae forget who he is, or he doesna want anyone tae know where he comes from, then he becomes someone else. The sea is forgiving that way."

Astria didn't really understand. "But why should a man want to forget who he is?" she said. "Should he not be proud of it?"

"Are ye proud of everything ye've ever done?"

"Everything."

"Then I canna explain it tae ye."

Astria shrugged. "I suppose," she said. "And you? Is Maude your real name?"

Maude grinned. "Ye'll never know, love."

Astria had to admit that there was some humor in that, and she smiled weakly. "Fair enough," she said. "But what does the talk of names have to do with your intentions for me?"

Maude's smile faded. "It's not the talk of names, but talk of my sons," she said. "I have three but only the two youngest serve me. My husband died last year and my eldest son is now the Earl of Lismore."

Astria found it difficult to conceal her shock. "You are a

countess?"

Maude barely nodded, as if not wanting to acknowledge such a thing. "Difficult tae believe, is it not?" she said. "My Bowie was a powerful man, from a long line of powerful Highlanders, but his mother was descended from the princes of the Isles. Northmen, ye know. Fair and lovely, she was. My Bowie took after her, I think. He dinna have the temper of the Highlanders but was cunning like the Northmen."

She was speaking rather lovingly of her husband, which surprised Astria. "Did he not sail with you?"

Maude shook her head. "Nay," she said with resignation, as if she'd accepted such a thing long ago. "Nay, he dinna have a taste for the sea."

"But you did?"

Maude nodded. "My father had one offspring—me," she said. "He was a great seaman, Irish by birth, and he inherited Medusa's Disciples from his own father. Red Shane Connacht was my father and my lineage goes back three hundred years, lass. Three hundred years of the family way. When my da passed, I took the helm. And here I am."

"Here you are," Astria confirmed. "And now you have three sons to carry on your family business."

But Maude shook her head. "Only two," she said. "When I give this up, Declan will take the helm because I know my eldest willna. He's the earl and will fulfill his destiny as such. That is where ye come in."

"Me?" Astria said, puzzled. "Why me?"

"Because ye're going tae be his wife."

So much for surrender.

The fight, for Astria, resumed in earnest.

CHAPTER TWO

Blackchurch Guild

"**T**HEY'RE COMING IN from the east, my lord," Creston said. "Our scouts have spotted them coming on foot and on horseback. They should be here within the hour."

The message was grim. In the keep of Exmoor Castle, the rather large tower in the center of the Blackchurch compound, Creston and Cruz were giving their report. The pair, along with several recruits, had been out scouting the countryside for signs of Medusa's Disciples and found them on a small road heading west from the village of Bampton. That was only a scant hour from Exebridge and, consequently, Blackchurch.

They were situated in the large solar belonging to St. Denis de Bottreaux, the lord and master of the Blackchurch operations. The Earl of Exmoor, St. Denis had inherited the role and title from his father, who had inherited it from his. The list of de Bottreaux men went back to the days of the Duke of Normandy, when a de Bottreaux ancestor was granted the title and the lands in Exmoor for his service at the Battle of Hastings.

In fact, there were two brothers, both of them young and ambitious, both of them dedicated to William of Normandy. St.

Giles de Bottreaux was the older of the two, his younger brother being St. Lyon, and it was St. Giles who distinguished himself on land while St. Lyon remained shipboard and devastated any hope of Edward the Confessor receiving any help from the sea. No reinforcements for the battle, no assistance of any kind thanks to St. Lyon, but it was St. Giles who had received the earldom. St. Lyon received several ships in gratitude for his service, hence the birth of Triton's Hellions. St. Giles went on to form the Blackchurch Guild, a guild that was now on edge because of the most recent report.

Bloody Maude really *was* approaching.

"How many men?" St. Denis asked. A short but powerful man, he had a head of white hair and a razor-sharp intellect. "More importantly, what power do they have if they've left their ships behind? That is their preferred fighting medium."

Creston nodded. "I realize that, my lord," he said. "But we saw at least six wagons with cannons, being pulled by teams of oxen that they have undoubtedly stolen. As for men, I would say no more than two hundred."

St. Denis seemed startled by that answer. "*Two* hundred?" he repeated. "They intend to take Blackchurch with only two hundred men? We will destroy them with our numbers alone."

Creston didn't seem convinced. He looked at Cruz, the Aragon knight known as The Conquistador, who almost seemed amused by St. Denis' arrogance.

"We are speaking of Bloody Maude, my lord," Cruz said. "She only needs two hundred men because if they get inside our walls, they will methodically destroy every Blackchurch man they come up against. Do not think you can simply throw men at them and they will be subdued. This is not an ordinary army."

St. Denis was back to being somewhat concerned. "Then what would you suggest?" he said. "I am not afraid of her, but I do not want her injuring or maiming our soldiers. Or us."

As Creston and Cruz shrugged, Aamir spoke up. "Ask her what she wants," he said simply. "We have no known conflict with Medusa's Disciples, so what could she possibly want from us?"

"Who knows?" St. Denis said. "It could be real or imagined. Those who scavenge the seas do not need a reason to pillage."

"That is the point," Aamir said. "Pillaging Blackchurch would be suicide. Unless God himself comes to earth with two hundred angels to destroy Blackchurch, I would not worry. But, clearly, Bloody Maude wants something if she is coming here."

All of the Blackchurch trainers were listening to the conversation, Payne included. He was back against a wall, leaning against the stone with his big arms folded across his chest. He could see the concern and puzzlement and, quite frankly, the fear. No one wanted their manhood taken as a trophy of war, but it was more than that. Bloody Maude had a hell of a reputation as a fearsome fighter and a merciless foe.

And she was coming for Blackchurch.

Payne couldn't believe it had come to this. He'd spent many happy years at Blackchurch concealing a family secret that most men couldn't have concealed for that long. But he'd done it ably. He hadn't exactly lied, but he hadn't exactly been forthcoming, either. Not that a man's past really mattered at Blackchurch because as long as he performed flawlessly, a man was judged on his own merits. But now... now, something was happening that Payne had never anticipated, and he had to come clean or risk much when those close to him discovered the truth.

The moment for him to be completely transparent had come.

But, God, he was dreading it.

"I dunna believe it is as bad as all that," he finally said, watching all eyes turn to him. "I wouldna worry so much."

"How would you know, Payne?" Tay asked curiously from his seat near St. Denis.

How would you know?

He'd been asked a direct question. He had to answer honestly or forever risk mistrust. As Payne came away from the wall, he sighed heavily. His big shoulders slumped. He had been looking at his feet but, gradually, his gaze came up to meet St. Denis' confused expression.

"I've been with ye nine years, m'laird," he said in a low, steady voice. "Nine years of proving I'm one of the best. Would ye say that's a fair statement?"

St. Denis didn't hesitate. "You are one of our very best trainers," he said. "We would be lost without you. But… oh, God, Payne… do not tell me that you plan to sacrifice yourself somehow in order to protect us."

Payne snorted, but it was without humor. "Nay, nothing so noble," he said. "But I was trying tae make a point. My father is the Earl of Lismore. We have bloodlines that go back tae the Northmen, tae kings of distant shores, but also back tae Calgacus, king of the Caledonians, who tangled with the Roman overlords. I'm a direct descendant of that foolish bastard who took on the Roman army. Therefore, I've got a pedigree that I'm not sure ye, or anyone, knew about. I know I act like an irreverent fool sometimes, but that fool has breeding."

By the time he was finished, most of the men in the room were grinning. Even St. Denis was sitting a little taller.

"I knew your father was an earl, but I did not know the rest of it," he said. "Your bloodlines are impressive, Payne. But what does that have to do with Bloody Maude's approach?"

Payne took another deep breath. "Because I must I tell ye something I've not told anyone."

"And what is that?"

Payne scratched at his ear hesitantly. "Ye know I've spoken of my mother," he said. "We've been making jokes about her for years now. She's become something of a legend at Blackchurch. I tell ye that she's eight feet tall, as strong as an ox, and can swing an axe better than any man. I know some of ye have doubted she was real, but I assure ye, she is."

"I will ask again—what does that have to do with Bloody Maude?"

"That's my mother."

A collective gasp went up in the chamber. More than one jaw dropped. Payne felt as if he'd just bared his soul, quite literally, by ripping open his chest and showing the entire room of men he greatly admired of the rather scandalous secret he'd kept concealed. He couldn't help but feel some anxiety as he looked to Tay and Sinclair and Fox, perhaps his closest friends in the group.

All he could see was their shock.

"Your *mother* is Bloody Maude?" Tay finally managed to say. "God's Bones, Payne… We've spent years joking about your mother. Years and years. I've jested about writing to her and telling her what a terrible son she has raised."

Payne nodded, hanging his head. "I know."

"Honestly, I did not believe your mother was real!"

"She's very real."

As Tay reeled with the news, Fox spoke up. "You told me

once that your mother could best the finest knights," he said incredulously. "I thought you were jesting."

Payne shook his head at his black-haired friend. "I was not jesting," he said. "The reality is that my mother *can* best the finest knight."

More hisses of surprise went around the chamber as the news sank in deeper. Creston and Cruz were over in the corner, shaking their heads and whispering, something that made Payne feel ashamed. Men he loved and trusted were whispering about him. He couldn't feel good about that.

Sinclair, who was probably closer to him than anyone, stepped forward, moving around Tay and Fox, heading for him as he stood there, alone and vulnerable. Sinclair's expression wasn't full of condemnation, but rather curiosity.

"I must admit that I did not see this as a possibility," Sinclair said. "Christ, Payne, you become seasick if there is too much water in your bath, yet you spent an entire year at sea, to pay my debt, no less. All the while, you had the blood of a pirate in your veins. And you never spoke of it, not ever."

Payne looked at him, shaking his head. "Nay, I dinna," he said softly. "There was no need."

"Did Santiago know?"

"Nay," Payne said. "He considers Bloody Maude an enemy. And I like the man. I dinna want him tae consider me an enemy, also, so please dunna tell him."

Sinclair understood. It was true that he'd married Santiago de Fernandez's cousin and was therefore part of Santiago's pirate family, so he understood more than anyone what it meant to be linked to someone with an unsavory reputation. He was truly at a loss with this stunning information.

"But why not?" he wanted to know. "Payne, surely you

know we would not judge you for such a thing. Why keep such a secret?"

"Sinclair," St. Denis snapped softly. "Quiet. I want to speak with Payne."

As Sinclair backed off, Payne took a deep breath for courage, facing St. Denis as the man stood up from his chair and came toward him.

"Now you will tell me everything," St. Denis said when their eyes met. "No more withholding important information. I believe that every man is entitled to his secrets, but not when those secrets threaten Blackchurch. Do you understand me?"

Payne nodded. "Aye, m'laird."

"Tell me about your mother," St. Denis said. "*Why* is she coming here?"

Payne shook his head. "I do not know and that is the truth," he said. "I've not seen my mother in about ten years, well before I came tae Blackchurch. Since we are speaking of truths, my truth is that I was raised by my father. I am his heir and he dinna want me tae go tae sea with my mother, who had inherited Medusa's Disciples from her father. It is her legacy. She took my younger brothers with her while I remained with my da. I trained as a knight in Northern England and served the Scottish king until I made the decision tae come tae Blackchurch. Ye know I came here only tae be a Blackchurch-trained warrior, but somehow, I ended up being a teacher instead. It is the best thing I've ever done and I'd like tae keep doing it."

There was a plea there. St. Denis could see that. In fact, he could see a great many things in Payne's expression that he'd never seen before. The man wasn't the serious type unless he was teaching or killing because most of the time, he conveyed someone who was passionate about life, jovial, extremely loyal, and sometimes even foolish. In great contrast to that character, he could also do mathematics in his head almost instantly, could recall the smallest detail from five years ago, and had a head for money and finances that most men didn't. Aye, he was a paradox, but never in his wildest dreams could St. Denis have imagined that Payne was the son of one of the most feared pirates in the western seas. There was depth to the Highlander that not even he knew.

Perhaps that made him see the man a little differently now.

"No one says you will not continue in your current position," St. Denis said, backing down a little. "Your loss would be massively felt here at Blackchurch, so I have no intention of releasing you. But I want to know why Bloody Maude is coming here, Payne. Surely you can understand that."

Payne nodded, feeling a good deal of relief in St. Denis' statement. He visibly relaxed, trying not to let the plethora of emotions overwhelm him.

"I do, m'laird," he said. "But given that I've not seen her in ten years, I'm curious as well. Would ye like me tae ride out and meet her before she arrives? Mayhap I can discover what this is all about."

It wasn't a bad idea. St. Denis leapt at the suggestion. "I would agree to that," he said quickly. "Creston, what road is she on?"

Creston came forward. "The old bishop's road from the east," he said, pointing. "I would like to ride with Payne, my lord."

"And me," Cruz said quickly.

Men began stepping forward, quickly volunteering—Sinclair, Fox, Tay, Aamir, Ming Tang, Kristian, and Bowen. Every trainer in the chamber. They were all demanding to ride escort, and St. Denis raised his hand to silence them.

"I know you are deeply loyal to one another, but since this is the first time Payne has seen his mother in years, he would probably like to go alone," he said, looking at Payne. "Do you?"

Payne nodded, but he was looking at his friends. "Ye know I'd kill or die for ye, but Lord Exmoor is right," he said. "I should go alone. I dunna know why she's coming, so we should be vigilant. Creston, Cruz, I'll take ye with me, since ye've already scouted the area. Ye know it. But stay out of sight. Dunna let her see ye."

Creston and Cruz were pleased that they would be accompanying him, already heading to the door so they could get to the stables and claim their horses. As they quickly filtered out, Payne turned to the collection of friends behind him.

"She willna hurt me," he said quietly. "But not knowing why she's come, I canna guarantee yer safety. My mother and I have shared a complicated relationship, as ye can imagine. The last time I saw her, she told me that I was dead tae her because I wouldna go tae sea. And that's, mayhap, why I dinna tell ye about her. I never thought I'd see her, or hear from her, again. But here she is—and I will admit that I'm curious."

Tay forced a smile, though he was clearly disappointed he hadn't made the cut to play escort. "Understandable," he said. "No need to explain. We shall await your return."

Payne nodded, smiling weakly as his friends departed the chamber, one after the other. When the room was finally empty of everyone other than Payne, St. Denis, and St. Sebastian, Payne turned to the Earl of Exmoor.

"They willna stay here," he muttered. "Ye know they'll find a way tae follow me."

St. Denis sighed in resignation. "I know," he said. "I cannot stop them. They're running for the stables as we speak. But do make sure your mother does not try to cut off vital body parts, will you?"

Payne chuckled. "First, I must ensure she doesna try tae do it tae me."

"Are you concerned?"

Payne shook his head. "As I said, I'm curious," he said. Then his eyes took on a distant cast. "I wish ye'd known my mother when I was young. She wasna a pirate back then. Just a woman. We were never apart, she and I. Even when she gave birth tae my younger brothers, my memories of her are of always holding her hand. She was kind and loving. Not the woman men fear today."

"What happened?" St. Sebastian spoke up. Usually, he stayed out of the conversations that his father had with the trainers, mostly because most of his life he had suffered a speech impediment that he'd only recently mastered. A stutter that seemed to fade with age, so he was more confident these days. "When did she become this… this pirate?"

"When her father died," Payne said softly. "She was his only child, and one did not disobey Shane Kilkenny. He taught her what his father had taught him because the pirate legacy in her family runs deep. Shane wanted her tae marry well and my mother had an enormous dowry, one that attracted my father. But Shane wanted something as well—the Isle of Coll. He demanded it as part of the marriage contract, and my grandfather, who was the Earl of Lismore at the time, gave it tae him. The island is where the pirate fleet anchors when they are not at Lismore."

"So your mother is Irish?" St. Sebastian asked.

"She is," Payne said softly. "But my father bleeds the Highlands. It is the blood in his veins and the song in his heart. Old Shane, and then my mother, moved their operations tae Scotland and England and Wales because it was more lucrative than simply raiding the Irish coast. Instead, they raid their enemies."

St. Sebastian shrugged. "That is what I would do," he said. "The Irish are too poor."

Payne eyed him a moment before breaking down into soft laughter. "I would expect nothing less from ye," he said. "Ye'll always see things from a business view."

"And that is fortunate for the continuation of Blackchurch," St. Denis said, his focus on Payne. "But this place might suffer if Bloody Maude has murder on her mind, for whatever reason, so go now. Meet her on the road and discover her intentions. And do not let your fellow trainers come to harm at your mother's hand."

Payne shook his head. "I will not," he said. "And I'll do my best tae keep her away from Blackchurch."

"I am depending on you."

Payne knew that. He'd never been so acutely aware of anything in his life. His mother was coming, his friends were on edge, and he wasn't quite sure how he felt about any of it. But one thing was for certain.

He was going to get to the bottom of this.

His only fear was what, exactly, he would find at that bottom.

God help him.

CHAPTER THREE

THE BLASTED WOMAN had actually knocked her out.
Hit her in the head!

Astria knew that because when she opened her eyes, she was watching the sky and trees pass by overhead and the last thing she remembered was Maude saying something about a marriage to her eldest son. There was a fight.

Then… nothing.

"Are ye calm so that we might continue our discussion?"

It was Maude, standing somewhere behind her. Astria tried to lift her head, but the pain was too much.

"You broke my skull," she groaned, hand flying to her head. "You did not have to do that."

"Aye, I did," Maude said frankly. "Lass, ye need tae understand something. Ye canna escape. Ye have nowhere tae go. All of the fighting in the world will not force me tae release ye, so it would be better for all of us if ye cooperate. Do ye understand?"

Astria did, but she was stubborn. Too stubborn to admit defeat. Still, the sensible part of her had something to say about this, given the fact that she'd received a fairly serious blow to the head. She couldn't take another one, so it would be to her benefit to behave herself at this time.

But, God, she hated the mere thought of it.

Surrender wasn't in her nature.

"I understand," she muttered, eyes closed against her throbbing head. "But I cannot marry your son."

"Why not?"

"Because I am already married."

Maude came around the side of the wagon bed where she could look Astria in the eye. "I'll give ye praise for a good effort," she said, her eyes twinkling. "I happen tae know ye're not."

Astria's eyes flew open, her brow furrowing. "How would you know?"

"Because when we boarded yer ship, that lovely vessel I plucked ye from, the captain begged me tae show mercy because ye were a new widow," she said. "He said that yer husband was Armand de San Miguel, Duc de Tarragona, a very old man who died last year. Now, if ye're truly mourning him, then I'll give ye time tae do that, but not forever. One way or the other, ye'll marry my eldest."

"If he doesna want her, I'll take her."

The words came from someone standing off to Astria's left. Maude looked at the man speaking but Astria couldn't manage to move her head in that direction because she was still in too much pain. She watched Maude's impatient expression as the woman focused on the man who'd made the offer.

"She's not meant for ye, Declan," she said, but she motioned him to stand next to her at the rear of the wagon. "But come over here so I can introduce ye. My lady, this is my middle son, Declan. I know ye've seen him around, so it's time ye made his acquaintance. Declan, this is Lady de Tarragona. She's not tae be trifled with."

Astria's gaze fell on the big, handsome man who bore a faint resemblance to his mother. He had brown hair instead of her vibrant red and eyes of the darkest brown that were fixed on Astria with interest. But she clearly had no interest in him, or anyone else, as she struggled to push herself into a sitting position.

"I am *not* Lady de Tarragona," she said angrily. "I am Maria Astria Julia, Princesa Real, Princesa of Beira, Duchess of Braganza, Duchess of Barcelos, Countess of Faria, Countess of Neiva, and, by marriage, Duchess of Tarragona. I am my father's youngest daughter and aunt to the current king, who is, even now, surely gathering a fleet of ships to save me. When he does find me, I will make sure to tell him how horribly I have been treated and what barbarians you are. You are on borrowed time, all of you, so make yourself right with God because soon, you shall meet him."

She was shouting by the time she was finished, and there was a moment of stunned silence before the entire group standing around the wagon burst into laughter. Astria looked around in shock as the pirates practically screamed with the hilarity of what she'd just said. Maude was actually wiping tears from her eyes. Still laughing, she patted Astria affectionately on the foot and turned to the men around her, lifting her hand.

"Move forward," she commanded. "We must make Black-church by the time darkness falls. I dunna wish tae be late."

The men moved swiftly to do her bidding, but they were all in a good mood, still chuckling at Astria's expense. Declan, however, remained at the rear of the wagon, a grin on his lips as he watched Astria fume.

"Dunna take it so hard, lass," he said. "Ye made a good

effort but ye lost. The sooner ye accept that, the better for ye, because we can keep laughing at ye from sunrise tae sunset. And we will if ye keep being ridiculous."

Astria didn't think she had been ridiculous. In fact, she was gravely insulted over the laughter because no one had ever laughed at her, or her titles, or anything she'd ever said. When she spoke, men jumped. At least, that was the norm until now.

Now, they simply laughed.

It was a rude awakening.

"Leave me alone," she said, turning her head away from him.

But Declan didn't leave. In fact, he grabbed a man that was just walking by, pulling him to the end of the wagon bed.

"This is my brother, Francis," he said. "They call him the Pope because he prays all the damn time. He willna shut his mouth with all of that praying. And I'm known as Declan the Devil, though ye wouldna think that by looking at me. I dunna look like a devil, do I?"

Astria refused to answer. She was hurt and angry and didn't like Declan's subtle attempt to charm her.

"I told you to leave me alone," she said. "I meant it."

Declan turned to Francis. "She's trying tae seduce me," he said. "I can hear it in her tone."

Astria looked at him sharply, red-faced. "I am *not*," she said. "You are the last man I would want to seduce."

Declan was still looking at his brother. "See what I mean?" he said. "She likes me."

Francis shook his head. "Ye're delusional," he said before his attention shifted to Astria. "M'lady, can I bring ye something tae make ye more comfortable? A blanket, mayhap?"

Astria wouldn't look at him, either, although she'd seen him around over the past month. Francis was very tall, blond, and rather thin compared to his brother, who was big and muscular. He'd never spoken directly to her before, however, and nor had Declan, which told her that Maude must have ordered them to stay away from her.

The only person she'd had any real contact with was, in fact, Maude.

It was possible that Maude simply wanted to control the situation and therefore didn't want any of her men talking to the prisoner. But it was equally possible that she was trying to protect Astria somehow. These were pirates, after all, and there was no telling what ideas they would get into their heads about a restrained female prisoner. They might even try to steal her away from Maude. Whatever the case, Maude was most definitely watching out for her.

"Nay," she said after a moment. "I do not need anything except my freedom."

Francis shook his head. "I canna give ye that," he said. "But I can bring ye something tae make ye more comfortable if ye wish."

"Stop trifling with her," Declan warned. "I told ye that she's sweet on me, so stop trying tae turn her head."

Francis, thinking his brother was ridiculous, rolled his eyes and walked away. The wagon Astria was riding in began to lurch forward, moving slowly along that horrifically bumpy road. It didn't do Astria's head any good as she struggled to sit up and keep her balance, all the while avoiding Declan's grinning expression. Since his mother had finally introduced them, he'd decided that it was perfectly acceptable for him to flirt with the captive.

Astria wanted to punch him in the nose.

Keeping her head turned, she kept her focus on the surrounding countryside and not Declan's smug face. So Maude wanted her for marriage, did she? That didn't seem like something a pirate would do. Marriages of convenience or for political gain were made by lords and kings, not by pirate queens. But it seemed that the further and further they traveled into this barbaric country, the more her fate was being sealed.

But Astria knew something they didn't know.

A little secret she'd been hiding.

It was true that she'd been married at a young age to a very old duke in a political marriage of her father's doing. Quite honestly, it hadn't been a marriage, more simply a relationship between a young woman and an old man. She had been sixteen years of age when she married the Duc de Tarragona, a man who had been a political ally of her grandfather and a very powerful man indeed. He had one son and had wanted more children but the truth was that beyond the wedding night, which was the embarrassing and uncomfortable situation, he'd never touched her. There had been a slight possibility that the wedding night might have produced a pregnancy, but when her menses returned shortly thereafter, they knew there was no chance of a child and the duke didn't seem interested in trying again.

Even though Astria had known her responsibilities going into that marriage, she'd been very glad when the duke decided that there would be no more intimacy between them. Given his performance on their wedding night, she wasn't surprised—and, quite frankly, she was relieved. After that, he had treated her like a daughter. He was very generous, and he'd made sure that she always had the best of everything, but there was nothing more than polite interest on his part.

His only son, however, was another story.

Asteria knew something that Maude, in all of her seeming wisdom, did not know. She was quite certain that if the woman did know, she would have said something. What Maude didn't seem to realize was that the Duc de Tarragona ruled the Balearic Sea. His family had made their money in shipping, but somewhere in that legitimate business, something more sinister rose.

Something dark.

Truthfully, Astria wasn't even sure her own father had known about the dealings of the San Miguel family, but she couldn't imagine that he didn't. Her father, Sancho, seemed to know everything about everyone. As king, that was his right. But the reality that Astria discovered once she married into the family was murky, indeed. That was why Maude had found her on one of the ships that were bound for the Tarragona port.

But she didn't capture all of the ships.

Maude had made a mistake when she attacked and confiscated the ships that were under Astria's control. She hadn't swept the area for every Tarragona ship, meaning one of them had been missed. The ship that hadn't been captured was captained by none other than the new Duc de Tarragona, Arnaldo de Fernandez y de San Miguel. Astria's stepson, her husband's only son. Given that Maude had captured two of the Tarragona vessels, the *Pontus* and the *Thalassa*, the third one—the *Brizo*—was fully capable of pursuing, and Astria would stake her life on the fact that Arnaldo was doing just that.

Pursuing.

But that wasn't a good thing, either.

All part of that little secret she'd been hiding.

Astria was lost in thought when she began to notice that

men were scurrying to the front of the escort. Francis came rushing back as men were rushing forward, and he ordered some of them to bring the cannons forward. The wagon Astria was riding in lurched to a halt and she sat up a little taller, trying to get a look at what had everyone so agitated. It didn't take long for her to overhear the men around her, speaking in rumbling tones.

Rider.

A rider was approaching.

CHAPTER FOUR

W AS THIS SUCH a good idea? Payne still didn't know.
But he was about to find out.

Less than an hour out of Blackchurch, he came across a small army heading in his direction. He'd come into a clearing and, as the road carved through the green landscape into the distance, could see a collection of men and wagons about a half-mile away. He didn't usually make it over to this area, east of Blackchurch, and as he loped along the road astride his blonde beast with the black mane, he found himself looking at the heavy thicket of trees and smelling the wet grass in the meadows. Everything was lush, dense with forest, and he knew that outlaws tended to populate this area. But the only outlaw he was concerned with was a certain female pirate, and as he drew closer to the group in the distance, he could see that they had come to a halt.

Payne was alone at this point because the moment they'd spied the small gang of men in the distance, Cruz and Creston had ducked into the trees that surrounded the road. However, now Payne was in a clearing, with the trees off to the north and to the south, somewhat far away. He wouldn't have immediate assistance if he needed it. However, that was probably for the better. He didn't want his friends in the proverbial line of fire and could see that the group in the distance were on the defensive. They'd even started bringing wagons that contained cannons forward.

That was when Payne moved swiftly.

He wanted to get close before they could line up those cannons. It was perhaps a bit silly to produce cannons at the sight of a lone rider, but he had to respect them for being unwilling to take any chances. He moved so fast that they didn't have time to line anything up, but he could see a couple of the men producing crossbows. Not wanting to be pierced by a bolt, he quickly dismounted and used his horse as a shield.

"I mean ye no harm!" he bellowed. "Stow yer weapons!"

"Not likely, little man!" someone yelled in return. "What's yer business?"

Payne was peering around the breast of his horse. "I've come tae discover *yer* business," he said. "Tell me who ye are and what ye want."

There was a pause. "That's brave talk from a lone man," the same voice called out to him. "I dunna see much tae back up those words."

"They're in the trees."

"I dunna believe ye, little man."

"Test me and find out."

Payne could see the men looking around, into the trees. His threat was enough to delay them. But more than that, he was focused on the man he'd just had the conversation with.

That voice.

He hadn't seen his brothers in several years, but he knew the voice. That smug voice that could only come from one person—that little toad of a bairn he'd most happily beaten down when they were children, a sibling he'd shared a most contentious relationship with. But at this moment, he didn't remember the anger and resentment. He only remembered the love. When he realized that, he found himself fighting off a grin.

"Ah," the voice said. "'Tis a challenge ye give me. I like challenges."

"Ye dinna when ye were a wee lad with a runny nose," Payne said. "Ye ran from challenges then. And ye ran from me, ye little coward."

There was another pause, longer than the first one. "And just who are ye?"

"Can ye honestly say ye dunna recognize yer own brother?"

In the collection of men, a united grunt of suspicion went up. But amongst the sound, there was a shriek.

"Payne?" It was Maude. "Payne Matheson, is that ye?"

Payne came from around the horse. "Aye," he said, standing tall and proud in the middle of the road and facing what was to come. "Have ye come tae kill me, Maudie? The last time we spoke, ye told me that I was dead tae ye. Have ye come tae finish the job?"

Maudie. That was what he'd always called his mother, what his brothers had called her as well. Maude burst out from behind some men, her hair like flame, her pale face pinched with shock. For a moment, she simply stood there and stared at her eldest son as Declan and Francis came to stand with her. Francis was smiling from ear to ear, but Declan didn't seem entirely happy about it.

Suspicious was more like it.

"Of course I've not come tae kill ye," Maude finally said, misty-eyed. "It's been a long time, lad. Have ye been well?"

Payne had to admit that he had a lump in his throat at the sight of his mother. As much as he'd joked about her over the years, mostly at her expense, the sight of her took him back to the days when he was her shadow, following her around everywhere. He'd described that to St. Denis, but it was never so strong in is memory as it was at this moment.

My mother.

"I have," he said after a moment. "How did ye know where tae find me?"

"Yer father," Maude said, taking a few steps toward him. "He told me ye'd gone tae Blackchurch. Ye never returned from it."

Payne shrugged. "I've made a life here," he said. "I've found a place where I belong, where I'm respected. The men I serve with are like my brothers."

"Ye're happy?"

"I am."

Maude sighed, perhaps in relief. Her expression suggested that it did her heart good to see that Payne was well and thriving. Before she could say anything more, however, Declan came forward.

"Ye've got tae go home," he said, pointing northward. "Da died during the winter of a poison in his chest. Ye're the new earl, Payne. Ye must go home."

That was shocking news, brutally delivered, and Payne's eyes widened. "Da… he's d-dead?" he stammered.

"I said he was," Declan said. "But ye never went home tae visit him over the years, so what do ye care?"

"Shut yer lips, Declan." Maude finally found her tongue, slapping Declan on the side of the face as she passed by him on her way toward Payne. Her focus was on her eldest. "I'd hoped tae tell ye in a gentler way. I know ye loved yer da, and he loved ye."

Payne felt as if he'd been kicked in the gut. The initial shock of the news was settling in to a deep and abiding grief as he watched his mother come closer. "I did," he said, sounding lost. "I loved him. I told him that every time I sent him a missive. I tried tae do it frequently, telling him about my life at Blackchurch and apologizing for not having the time tae return home. I should have, but my duties keep me so busy that… Christ, even as I say that, it sounds like a horrible excuse."

Maude came to within a couple of feet of him and came to a halt, holding up her hand in a soothing gesture. "He knew ye loved him, Payne," she said. "He knew ye were doing important work at Blackchurch. He dinna fault ye for it."

Payne was on the verge of tears as he eyed his mother. "How would ye know that?" he said. "Ye're at sea most of the time."

Maude nodded. "I am," she said. "But I've been home more than ye have in the past ten years. Think what ye will about my marriage tae yer father, but we loved each other in our own way. He knew what I had tae do. Who I had tae be."

Payne had to swallow hard and avert his gaze. He simply couldn't look at his mother, fearful he was about to break down for all to see. So he focused on his feet, on the ground in front of him, hands on his hips as he struggled to regain his composure.

But he couldn't quite manage it.

"The last time I saw ye, ye told me I was dead tae ye," he said, trying not to weep. "Now, ye come tae tell me that Da is dead and I'm the new earl, with no mention of the way ye and I left things when we last spoke. I've gone the past ten years thinking ye hated me."

Maude sighed heavily. "I shouldna have said such things tae ye," she said. "I was angry ye weren't willing tae follow me tae sea and I let that get the better of me. I'm sorry, Payne. Truly. I dinna mean any of it."

She may have been apologetic, but Payne realized that he wasn't in a forgiving mood. The hurt he'd felt those years ago, something he thought he'd managed to overcome, was threatening to come forth again, like a scar that had been reopened.

A wound that never went away.

"And ye never thought tae tell me?" he said with some agitation. "Ye wait until now?"

Maude could see how upset he was. Not that she hadn't been expecting it, but it was taking courage to face it. "The years have been very busy for me," she said. "Keeping yer grandfather's legacy alive. So much depends on me, Payne. I wish I could tell ye all of it."

His head came up, angrily. "*What* depends on ye?" he demanded. "What about a son ye disowned? Am I not more important than the ships ye command or the people ye rob?"

Maude was starting to struggle. "Look behind me," she said. "All of those men depend on me tae make them money. Most of them have families. Did ye ever stop tae think why I continued yer grandfather's legacy? It was because an entire world revolves around Medusa's Disciples, and I have a moral obligation—"

He cut her off loudly. "A *moral* obligation?"

"Aye, a moral obligation tae continue yer grandfather's profession so these men can send money home tae their wives and children," Maude nearly shouted at him. "Dunna judge me, Payne Matheson. Ye did it ten years ago and that's why I told ye that ye were dead tae me. Ye have no right tae judge me when ye serve at Blackchurch and train men tae kill and sack and conduct all manner of underhanded warfare. Dunna pretend tae be so noble because yer hands are as dirty as mine, only in a different way. If ye canna see that, then ye're lying tae yerself. And I dinna raise a fool!"

Payne was eyeing his mother stiffly. He didn't like anything she'd said, but the problem was that she was right. Well, mostly. Blackchurch's reputation for training the very best warriors in the world also meant they knew how to do all manner of underhanded warfare. Whatever it took to win. Some people thought Blackchurch was without honor because of it.

And Maude knew it.

Payne postured a little, tightening his jaw, his features contorting with rage, but he didn't snap back at her. She was glaring at him with those pale blue eyes that had the ability to drill holes through a man. He'd feared those eyes when he'd been a child. Truth be told, he probably feared them now as well. He was about to say so when he caught a flash of a body from the corner of his right eye and instinct told him to duck.

It was a good thing he did.

Declan had thrown a wild punch at his head.

The momentum of the swing, and the miss, carried Declan a few feet away. He nearly lost his balance, but he recovered quickly, whirling around to face Payne, who had assumed a defensive stance.

"She's come all the way tae lay an earldom in yer lap and all ye do is fight with her," Declan said angrily. "I'll not let ye treat her that way."

For Payne it felt like old times, facing off against Declan again. There were sixteen months between them, close enough that they couldn't remember life without one another, but also close enough that Declan resented Payne for having been born first. It had always been that way, and the old dynamic hadn't changed over the years and was probably going to get worse now that Payne had inherited the Lismore earldom.

"Shut yer yap, Declan," Payne said, an enormous balled fist ready to launch at his brother's head. "This isna yer business, so stay out of it."

"I willna!"

Maude put herself between the pair. "Declan, enough," she said. "Go back tae the wagon and bring the lass. But keep her tied up because she'll try tae escape if ye let her, so carry her. I want yer brother tae see what I've brought him."

Declan was furious. "And ye give him a princess?" he said, incredulous. "Can ye not see what an ungrateful whelp he is?"

"I can see what a jealous one ye are," Maude said steadily, pointing an imperious finger in the direction of the wagons. "Do as I say. Fetch the lass."

Declan went, but he was deeply unhappy about it. He glared at Payne as he walked past him and Payne didn't lower his balled fist. He was taller than Declan, and more powerful, but Declan was nothing to be trifled with. He made a hell of a pirate.

The man was a killer.

As he watched Declan walk away, he caught sight of his youngest brother. Francis was far less confrontational and, in fact, was quite congenial, which made for an odd situation given the profession he was in. When their eyes met, Francis grinned and headed toward Payne, giving Declan a wide berth. When he came within range of Payne, he launched himself at the man, hugging him happily. The reaction of Payne's two brothers to his appearance could not have been more different.

"Payne," Francis said, squeezing the breath from him. "Declan may not be glad tae see ye, but I am. I've missed ye."

Payne hugged the man tightly. "Ye are a pain in my backside and every time I see ye, I want tae take a stick tae ye, but I love ye madly," he said, releasing Francis and clutching the man's face between his two hands. "Thank God ye're alive and well."

Francis was beaming. "That is what life on the sea does tae a man," he said. "I'm bronze like a statue and twice as strong."

Payne chuckled, mostly because Francis had never been terribly strong, but he was, indeed, bronzed by the sun and the elements. He patted his brother on the cheek and dropped his hands.

"Are ye happy, at least?" he asked.

Francis nodded. "Verily," he said. "Are ye?"

"More than I deserve."

Francis' smile faded. "I would congratulate ye on being the new earl, but I dunna think this is a happy occasion for ye," he said. "But dunna be troubled. Da dinna die a painful death. God was merciful and he was at peace. He spoke of ye, Payne. He told us tae tell ye that he was proud of ye."

Payne's joyful expression morphed into something sorrowful. "I wish I'd known he was ill," he said. "I would have gone home. I would have rushed all the way."

Francis shook his head. "It took him quickly," he said. "We happened tae be at Achanduin when he became ill. In three days, he was gone."

Achanduin. The great castle of Payne's branch of the Matheson clan. There was a second castle on Lismore Island called Coeffin, plus a port that shielded Maude's multitude of ships from the weather and other hostile seagoers. Payne was born at Achanduin. Even the mere mention of it brought a sense of longing.

"I'm very sad tae know that," he said. "But I suppose it was a blessing if it was swift. I wouldna want the man tae suffer."

"He dinna," Francis said, but something behind his pale eyes hardened and his voice dropped to a whisper. "But much has happened since his death, Payne. Beware of Declan. He wants what ye have for himself."

Payne didn't react to the warning, but he also wasn't surprised. Not in the least. "The man has always been ambitious," he muttered. "'Tis nothing new."

Francis shook his head. "It is different now," he said. "He will take the helm of Medusa's Disciples when Maudie is no more, but it may be sooner than ye think."

"What do ye mean?"

Francis glanced at their mother, whose focus was on the wagon where Declan was. "I mean he pretends tae be protective of her," he mumbled. "But I think he plots."

"To harm her?"

Francis nodded but would say no more. Even so, he'd said enough. That put Payne on his guard against the brother who had always envied him. Always competed with him. But Payne felt as if no time had passed since the last time he saw his brothers, because nothing had changed. Declan was still dangerous and resentful and Francis was still the weak one, the brother who couldn't compete against his older, more powerful brothers.

It certainly gave Payne something to think about.

Movement caught his attention, however, and he turned to see Declan carrying a small body over his left shoulder. That had Payne's curiosity more than anything, and Declan hauled the figure over to Maude and plopped it down at his mother's feet.

Payne heard a grunt as the body hit the ground.

"Ye dunna have tae be so rough, Declan," Maude scolded, pulling the person into a sitting position. "Next time, I'll send Francis tae do my bidding and ye can sit in the wagon and sulk."

Declan was unapologetic. He folded his big arms across his chest, his focus on Payne.

"Just want a new earl needs," he said. "A princess for a wife. Ye'll have royal children, Payne. Does that not thrill ye?"

Payne was quite confused. He was also quite irritated at his brother. He went over to his mother as she helped the figure on the ground. He was about to ask her what Declan was talking about until he got a look at the face of the person his brother had manhandled.

A bolt of shock ran through him.

It was a woman. Not just any woman, but a beautiful woman with a sweetly oval face, very dirty blonde hair, and eyes with the longest lashes he'd ever seen. She wasn't looking up, however, so he couldn't see the color of her eyes, but he could see everything else about her.

She was exquisite.

"Who is this?" he finally demanded.

Maude pulled the young woman to her feet. "This is Maria Astria Julia, Princesa Real, Princesa of Beira, Duchess of Braganza, Duchess of Barcelos, Countess of Faria, Countess of Neiva," she said. "She's the only daughter of Sancho, King of Portugal, and she is my prisoner. Ye'll marry her today, Payne, and she'll become the mother of the next Earl of Lismore. She's a magnificent prize, dunna ye think?"

Payne's mouth was hanging open in shock. "A *princess*?" he repeated. "Ye've brought me a Portuguese princess?"

Maude was quite proud. "It's not been easy," she said. "This lovely lass is quite violent. She likes tae fight and she'll bite ye if given the chance, so watch yerself. Dunna treat her lightly."

Payne was appalled. He could see how tightly the woman was bound and she was absolutely filthy, like an animal. While he had no reason to doubt his mother as to the validity of her claims, he simply couldn't believe that he was looking at royalty.

"How did she come intae yer possession?" he asked.

Maude was standing rather proudly next to the forlorn figure. "We've expanded our territory," she said. "The Aragon and Portuguese pirates have been roaming the coastlines of England and Scotland for years, so we decided tae head for the Iberian coast. We even ventured intae the great sea that the Romans used tae call Mare Magnum. We'd found success along the coastline of Castille when we came across Her Grace, Princess Maria Astria Julia, and took two of her ships. She happened tae be on one of them."

"So ye kept her."

"Why wouldn't I?"

"Did ye intend tae ransom her?"

Maude nodded. "I did until yer father died," she said. "Then I had a better use for her."

Payne looked at her, frowning. "How long have ye had her?"

"Five months."

Payne's eyebrows shot up. "Ye've had her—like this—for five months?"

Maude nodded. "Once we captured her and her ships, we took them back tae Lismore," she said. "That took us almost two months as it was. We were there for about a month when yer da fell ill."

Payne's gaze lingered on his mother for a moment before he returned his focus to the beaten, dirty, weary captive. "Did Da know about her?"

"He's the one who suggested her for yer bride."

A thought occurred to Payne as he put the pieces of the puzzle together. "Is *that* why ye were coming tae Blackchurch?" he said. "To bring her tae me?"

"Aye, lad. And tae make sure ye married her."

So there it was, all wrapped up in a neat package for him to digest. But all he could manage to feel was disgust for the way this small woman had been treated. He could see the widening divide between his mother and brothers and himself simply in the way they lived their lives. While a male captive, treated horrifically, would have been perfectly acceptable, it was not acceptable to treat a woman the same way. Perhaps Blackchurch was without honor to some, but Payne wasn't. He was a trained knight, had taken an oath, and part of that oath was protecting the weak, which all knights took to mean women and children.

He just didn't like what he was seeing.

But arguing with his mother or even Declan about it wasn't going to get him anywhere. He had to be careful how he handled this because, beneath it all, he was dealing with one of the most feared pirates that had ever sailed the seas. Even if she *was* his mother. But there was one thing he was going to do whether or not she liked it.

"We'll discuss marriage later," he said, sounding irritated. "But ye've come this far, so continue tae Blackchurch, but take lodgings in the village. Dunna come tae the fortress or ye'll be met with a thousand-man army. They know ye're coming, so stay clear for now. That's why they sent me out tae discover yer intentions."

Maude wasn't surprised by the order to stay clear of Blackchurch. "Now ye know."

"Now, I do," Payne said. But then he reached out and grabbed the captive by the arm, pulling her toward him. "But this is going tae end. Ye'll not treat a woman like this in my presence and I dunna care who she is or what she's done. I'll not stand for it."

Maude stood back as Payne untied the heavy rope that was binding Astria's arms together behind her back. "Careful, lad," she warned. "I told ye that she bites."

Payne was on the last loop. "She probably bites because ye treat her like an animal," he said. "No good can come from frightening a delicate woman tae death."

Maude didn't say a word. She didn't have to. Before she could reply, Astria's freed right hand came up and flew straight into Payne's face. A small fist met with his left eye with as much force as the young woman could muster.

Maude laughed so hard she thought she might choke.

CHAPTER FIVE

T HEY'D BEEN WATCHING from the shadows.

Creston was to the north and Cruz was to the south, or so Creston thought. He was watching Payne speak to a small, flame-haired woman so intently that he was caught off guard when Cruz joined him. In his surprise, he nearly took the man's head off. As Creston settled down, Cruz grinned and made sure the man tucked away the dagger that had nearly come flying at his head.

"Be at ease, *amigo*," he said, patting Creston on the shoulder. "I am not your enemy, but I fear we have company in these trees."

Creston nodded. "I know," he said. "I saw the men from that escort flee into the trees to the north, but they've not made it over this far yet."

"But they will."

"And when they do, we will be ready for them."

Cruz was watching Payne in the distance. "These are ruthless killers," he said. "Truthfully, I am still having difficulty believing that Payne is the son of Bloody Maude. It seems impossible."

Creston shrugged. "We all have parents," he said. "And our parents must be something in life—sinner or saint, we cannot choose."

"Are you trying to tell me that your father is something terrible?"

Creston looked at him, grinning. "My father is a great man," he said. "And my mother is a woman of noble birth. I have no surprises with my lineage like Payne has."

"Nor do I."

"Speaking of surprises, where are our colleagues?"

Cruz looked over his shoulder. "To the west," he said casually. "They've been very good at concealing themselves, but they are moving forward to get a better look."

"Shall we go and meet them?"

"No need. They will be here soon."

As soon as Cruz got the words out of his mouth, a branch snapped behind them. Cruz ducked back into the foliage and whispered loudly.

"You'd better show yourselves before Creston draws his sword," he said. "No need to hide any longer. You may as well see what we are seeing."

The first one to come out of hiding was Ming Tang. He moved like the wind, darting up to the front where Creston was watching from behind a tree. His movements brought Amir, Tay, Sinclair, Fox, and Kristian out of their hiding places. As they began to move forward, Tay paused by Cruz.

"How long have you known we were here?" he asked.

Cruz snorted. "Since we left Blackchurch."

Tay rolled his eyes, chuckling, but moved forward with great stealth. They all did. Creston found himself surrounded by his friends and comrades, all of them watching Payne in the distance as one of the men suddenly threw a punch at him, which he deftly ducked.

"Who's that?" Fox said. "Sin, do you know who that is?"

Since Sinclair was closer to Payne than anyone, they assumed he knew more about the people in Payne's life, and their relationships, but Sinclair had no idea. He shook his head slowly.

"I cannot tell you," he said. "I know he has younger brothers. We all heard him tell St. Denis. Is it possible that is one of his brothers?"

No one had an answer, but Tay grunted softly. "I would be willing to bet that the woman with the red hair is his mother," he said. "I've never seen Bloody Maude in the flesh, but that small woman with hair like liquid flame could be no one else."

"It has to be," Kristian said from his position on his belly, watching everything from the clearance under a bush. "And all of those wagons—I can see a cannon in one of them."

"There are more, I am sure," Tay said. Then he paused, straining to catch a glimpse of what was happening. "Look—the man who threw the punch is leaving. What now, I wonder?"

No one replied. They were too busy watching another man run at Payne and hug him happily. It seemed like a joyful reunion of sorts.

"That must be another brother," Sinclair said. "Payne mentioned that he has two."

"Mayhap one tried to hit him and the other is hugging him?" Tay said. "Seems like a true family to me."

The few that heard his comment grinned. "Is that how you and your brother greet one another?" Sinclair asked. "Either throwing punches or hugging?"

Tay smiled faintly. "My brother is not the violent kind," he said, referring to the disabled brother they were all aware of. "Sometimes I wish he could hit me. I would welcome it."

Sinclair looked at him. "You know I did not mean to make light of your brother's situation."

Tay held up a hand to indicate he was not offended. "Of course not," he said. "But I would be happy to dodge a blow."

"Do you think Payne is happy to dodge a blow?" Fox asked.

He was closer to the action than anyone, as he had moved up to almost the very edge of the trees. Fox was the one known as The Protector, and his instincts for protection and defense were second to none. In this case, it was protecting and defending the men in the trees, and his senses were on high alert.

"Nay, I do not think he was pleased," Sinclair answered him, his focus returning to Payne in the distance. "But he is clearly happy to see the other man."

Cruz suddenly ducked away, heading off toward the north and losing himself in the bramble. Given that several men had broken off from the army in the distance and disappeared into a collection of trees connected to the ones the Blackchurch trainers found themselves in, it was prudent not to be caught off guard should those men come any closer. Cruz was going to ensure that didn't happen. The rest of the group continued to watch, finding great interest when the man who had tried to strike Payne returned with a bundle over his shoulder.

"Look," Creston said. "He's brought something—"

"A body," Sinclair said, interrupting. "A woman?"

They could all see the long, matted blonde hair and the fact that the woman was trussed up with ropes. Payne was working to release them, clearly in discussion with the red-haired woman at the same time. Perhaps even scolding her, from his body language. But they all saw quite clearly when the newly freed captive threw a fist into Payne's face.

A collective gasp went up from the group.

Payne's head snapped back but he didn't fall. Not even close. He didn't even put a hand to his face where she'd struck him. As the red-haired woman laughed uproariously, Payne grabbed the captive by the arm and dragged her over to one of the wagons. Propping his buttocks on the back edge of the wagon, he threw the captive over his lap, then forced her head and shoulders down with one big arm while his free hand spanked her within an inch of her life.

It was all the Blackchurch men could do not to burst out in loud laughter.

The pirates, in fact, did laugh loudly. They *howled* with laughter. Everyone seemed to be having a grand time out of Payne spanking their captive, but he kept going until the flame-haired woman told him to stop. She actually grabbed his hand. He stopped, but he also stood up and let the captive fall to the ground, where she promptly jumped to her feet and attacked him with her fists. All Payne did was push her away so that she fell on the ground. But she got up and did it again. And again. Finally, Payne took the rope he'd cut off her, and the next time she charged him, he wrapped her up in it and tossed her into the back of one of the wagons.

At that point, the woman with the red hair was motioning her group to move forward, so the Blackchurch trainers scattered, returning to their horses and heading back to Blackchurch at top speed. Truthfully, everything they'd witnessed had been… strange. Strange and volatile. And that was the report that went to St. Denis about an hour before the group led by the red-haired woman, and Payne, reached the village of Exebridge, a mile from Blackchurch.

Bloody Maude and Medusa's Disciples had finally arrived.

And Blackchurch was ready.

CHAPTER SIX

"Now," Payne said slowly and deliberately, "tell me about this lass. I want tae know everything."

They were in the private alcove at the Black Cock, the one used by the Blackchurch trainers when they were relaxing after a hard day's work. But this time, the room contained Maude, Declan, Francis, and a few of Maude's trusted men, old sea dogs with names like Fish, Monk, Joyosa, and Turpis. Those were not their real names, of course, but as Maude had once explained to Astria, men at sea tended to go by nicknames for ease of identification and also, perhaps, for the protection of their families. They had all served with Maude's father, so they were old and seasoned and had the look of death about them. Especially Turpis—his name meant *foul* in Latin, and the man was, indeed, foul. Missing teeth and a penchant for skinning the flesh off his living victims were part of his aura.

Dark.

The owner of the Black Cock, a man named Hobbes, was keeping his serving wenches away from the alcove for that very reason. He was serving the pirates himself, along with his wife, who could probably best any one of those men at the table.

Hobbes and Margit were quite a pair, but they were friends of the Blackchurch trainers and always treated them well. In turn, the Blackchurch trainers protected the tavern. Given that it was their favorite place in the village—even if it were the *only* place—they weren't about to leave Hobbes and Margit without any defenders.

In fact, it was Hobbes and Margit whom Payne had consulted with when Medusa's Disciples arrived in the village. Given their vocation, they were used to simply taking whatever they wished for food and comfort, but Payne told Maude he would make sure that her men had food and a place to set up an encampment provided they did not raid the village. Even though the pirates had plundered every village and town they'd passed through the moment they came ashore, Maude knew this was one such village that was off-limits. The Blackchurch Guild was about a mile away and had far more men than Maude did, so she was forced to agree to Payne's terms or face the consequences.

Difficult as it was for someone unused to compromise.

Therefore, under Hobbes' guidance, the pirates were able to set up an encampment behind the Black Cock, under some trees and next to a stream. Hobbes also agreed to help feed them in exchange for their taking a hands-off approach to any patrons coming in or out of the establishment. The past hour had seen Maude and Declan and Francis settling the men down for the night, but Maude and her sons required sleeping rooms in the tavern, which they were given. Payne kept vigilant of everything going on, mediating when he had to, knowing that St. Denis didn't want Maude here, but she'd come with a purpose.

It was a complicated situation.

Now, the sun had gone down and they were sitting in the alcove with Maude's men stuffing themselves on boiled mutton. Declan and Francis were also eating as if they'd never seen food before. Only Payne and Maude weren't eating, but they were most definitely drinking. It was decent ale that Margit made herself, but she used fermented apples in it that could get a man drunk quite quickly. Therefore, Payne was pacing himself.

But he had questions.

"What more can I tell ye about the lass?" Maude said. "I told ye everything already. My lads and I have been branching out in other waters. The Three Magi were east of Valencia when we came across the princess and her ships. We captured everything. Now, I have two more Tarragona ships. Nice ones, too."

The Three Magi was what Maude called her three largest ships. They were named the *Mother Mary*, the *Caspar*, and the *Balthazar*, which absolutely inflamed the Catholic Church, but they'd been called that for decades and Maude saw no reason to change anything. In fact, she took fiendish delight in the furious responses from the bishops in Scotland and Ireland every time the ships flying Medusa's Disciples banners made port. Payne didn't care about the names of the ships, or the fury of the church, but he was concerned for the woman they'd dumped in the cold house outside.

That was his focus.

"What was she doing on those ships?" he asked. "Who do they belong tae?"

Maude shrugged. "They are her husband's ships," she said. "Or *were* his ships."

Payne looked at her in surprise. "She's *married*?" he said. "And ye brought her tae me as a bride?"

"She's widowed."

"Did *ye* kill the husband?"

Maude frowned. "Nay," she said. "Not even tae bring ye a royal bride. She's been widowed for some time."

He understood. "And ye dunna know where she was going or where she was coming from?"

Maude took another drink of her ale. "The captain of one of the ships, the one that confessed the lady's identity, said they were coming from Palma," he said. "The lady's dead husband seemed tae be a merchant. There was a good deal of merchandise in the ships we took."

"And ye think she was carrying on in her husband's stead?"

"Possibly."

That made sense to Payne. Women were often known to take up their husband's professions when they died. But that understanding gave way to something that was far more pressing in his mind.

"And she is truly a Portuguese princess?" he said, sounding rather incredulous. "What about her father?"

"What about him?" Maude said before taking another drink of that powerful ale. "I dunna know anything about him other than he's dead. Her nephew is the king now. But I dunna even think she is close tae her family."

"Why would ye say that?"

"Because she doesna seem like the kind," Maude said, eyeing him. "There's no compassion in that one, lad. No heart. She's the Duchess of Tarragona, married tae the duke, but he's been dead a year. No children from the marriage, from what I was told. But her loss is yer gain. Now, she can marry ye and bear ye children. Ye canna do any better than a Portuguese princess."

That was true, but the reality was that Payne was still over-whelmed by the whole thing. It seemed fantastic to him, still. "And Da truly knew about this?"

Maude nodded. "There are plenty of witnesses I can pro-duce for ye if ye dunna believe me," she said. Reaching across the table, she put her hand over his. "I know the news today wasna good. About yer da, I mean. But he's gone, ye're the new earl, and ye must marry. I've brought ye the best bride I could find, Payne. Dunna insult me by refusing her."

She meant it and Payne knew that. She didn't see her cap-tive the way he did. She simply saw the princess as a gift, a prize, and nothing more.

"I'm not refusing her," he said. "But ye were right when ye said the news about Da wasna good. I've lost my father, gained an earldom, and have a bride given tae me all on the same day. Ye must let me get used tae the idea of it all."

"What's so hard about it?" Declan said from down the table. He, too, had been drinking the strong ale, and it was going to his head. "When did ye become such a weakling, Payne? Ye have everything within yer grasp, but ye ask Maudie questions like she's lying tae ye or is trying tae trick ye. What's wrong with ye?"

Payne wasn't in any mood for his brother. Further words might see them taking more swings at each other, and he had promised Hobbes that he would keep the peace. But he didn't like Declan calling him weak.

"Being the greedy and ambitious sort, ye wouldna under-stand," he said in a steely voice. "All ye see are possessions and money because that's what life at sea has done tae ye. Ye have gold where yer heart is and daggers where yer brain should be. Ye've forgotten how decent people behave, Declan. Push me too far and ye'll see just how weak I am."

Declan's expression tightened. "Now ye threaten me?"

"I'm simply telling ye how it's going tae be if ye keep up yer hostility," Payne said. "I've not wronged ye, but ye act as if I have. I be happy tae wrong ye with hardly any effort if ye persist."

Maude put up a hand to stop the momentum of their conversation. "Easy, lads," she said. "No family fights tonight, if ye will. I have all of my lads with me and I'd like tae enjoy it a little, please."

Payne didn't feel like being a family at that moment. He had a lot to think about and didn't want to spend the evening posturing threateningly against his brother.

That meant he had to get out of there.

Rising from the table, he headed out of the alcove and into the common room of the tavern because he knew that Creston and Cruz were still around, somewhere. He hadn't seen them since his initial contact with Maude, but he knew they wouldn't have returned to Blackchurch without information for St. Denis. An entire fortress was on alert because of Bloody Maude's approach, so he knew Creston and Cruz must still be around. A quick perusal of the common room showed only a few people he didn't know, so he stepped outside the front entrance and walked out into the street.

"Looking for someone?"

The voice came from the shadows, but Payne wasn't alarmed. He recognized it.

"I thought ye'd still be here," he said, watching Creston come out of the darkness. "Where is Cruz?"

"Here," Cruz said, coming out from the alley next to the Black Cock. "Are you in one piece still, *amigo*?"

Payne smiled humorlessly. "Still," he said. "I will remain here tonight, but I need ye tae return tae St. Denis and relay a message."

Both Creston and Cruz nodded. "Of course," Creston said. "That woman with the red hair—that is truly Bloody Maude?"

"It is," Payne said. "Ye can tell Lord Exmoor that my mother dinna come tae Blackchurch tae cause trouble. She came tae give me news."

"What news?" Creston asked.

Payne sighed faintly, not particularly keen to repeat what he'd been told, but there was no way to avoid it. "That my father died," he said quietly. "That was what she came tae tell me. I'm now the Earl of Lismore."

Creston and Cruz seemed to stand up straighter at the news. "Truly?" Creston said, amazed. "You're an earl?"

"That's what she tells me."

He didn't seem thrilled about it. Both Creston and Cruz could sense it. "I am sorry about your father," Creston said. "Of course that was not easy news to hear."

Payne shook his head. "Nay, it was not," he said. "I loved my father. He let me do what I needed tae do in life. He never made me feel guilty that it took me away from him even though I was his heir. He was a good man."

"You have my sympathy," Cruz said, grasping Payne's arm in a show of support. "We'll relay the news to Exmoor."

Payne simply nodded and the pair turned away, preparing to head back to Blackchurch, but Payne stopped them.

"There is more," he said, thinking about everything he'd been told or see over the past few hours. He finally shook his head. "Maudie brought me a bride."

Cruz and Creston looked at him in shock. "A bride?"

Creston repeated. Then he looked even more surprised, as if a thought had just occurred to him. "The woman that hit you in the face! Was it her?"

Payne looked at him. "Ye saw that?"

"We all saw it," Creston said. "You know that Cruz and I were not the only ones hiding in the trees. Our Blackchurch brethren would not stay behind and joined us in our vigil. We were all watching when the woman hit you in the face."

Payne put a hand to his left eye, which was starting to bruise a little. "As my da would say, she crowned me with a glorious fist," he said, fighting off a grin. "Aye, that was the woman. Ye'll not believe who she is."

"Who?"

"Princess Maria Astria Julia, daughter of Sancho of Portugal," Payne said with some irony. "A genuine princess, lads. Maudie captured the ships she was traveling in, and at first she thought tae ransom her back tae her father, but when my da died, she thought she'd be a better wife for the new earl. A royal bride for the Earl of Lismore."

Creston and Cruz were sincerely shocked. "God's Bones," Creston said. "A princess? Here?"

Payne nodded. "That will bring an entirely new host of problems tae Blackchurch," he said. "Ye know we remain neutral in all things, and we canna let the King of Portugal think we've sided with pirates or are holding a political prisoner. But I dunna want ye tae tell Exmoor this. It should come from me."

Creston held up his hands in surrender. That was a bit of information he would gladly keep to himself and let someone else take the responsibility for.

"We'll simply tell him that Bloody Maude came to tell you

about your father," he said. "We'll tell him that Medusa's Disciples are no threat."

Payne nodded. "Tell him that, but I canna vouch for the pirates who have set up camp in the woods behind the Black Cock," he said. "Ye may want tae keep Blackchurch locked up while they're here tae avoid any… misunderstandings."

"Agreed," Creston said. He knew what the man meant—pirates would always be pirates, on land or at sea, and they didn't want any of them wandering into the Blackchurch compound uninvited. "We'll go now."

"Tell him not tae worry."

Creston wasn't so sure that was the truth, but he didn't contradict Payne. He simply nodded. "Shall we return on the morrow?" he asked.

Payne shook his head. "Nay," he said. "I'll come back as soon as I can, but for now, I want tae spend a little time with my mother and brothers. I've not seen them in years."

It was completely understandable. Creston and Cruz waved a farewell as they turned for their horses, tethered behind the livery across the street. Payne watched them go, thinking that he really didn't want to return to the alcove where Declan was. At least, not at the moment.

There was someone even more combative than his brother that he wanted to see.

He only hoped he would survive their second encounter.

C3

Maybe fighting back really *was* futile.

Astria was no better off than she had been when Bloody Maude first captured her. She'd been kept in ropes or in locked chambers the entire time, her freedom stripped along with her dignity. Upon meeting the man she was to marry, she'd turned him against her as well by throwing her fist into his eye.

He'd tried to be kind at first. His words were chivalrous and his intentions seemed honorable. But she was so frightened, so angry, that she immediately tried to fight him. Even when she charged at him after he'd spanked her, all he'd done was push her to the ground. He never hurt her or struck her. Other than the spanking, which she had to admit she rightfully deserved, he'd not lifted a hand against her.

She'd gotten a good look at him. He was a very big man, tall and muscular, with a crown of light brown hair with a hint of red to it, and perhaps the most handsome face she'd ever seen. Shockingly so. He also had enormous hands, which she had gotten a taste of when he had spanked her. But Maude had called him off, as the woman had strangely been both her captor and her protector for the past several months, and Astria's bindings had been returned before the escort resumed their forward momentum.

And now she found herself in a quaint little village.

She still didn't know where she was, but the collection of cottages and businesses she found herself in seemed rather bucolic and quiet. It was surrounded by dense forests and the roads seemed to be perpetually muddy, but she got quite a sense of peace from it. Peace that was so rare in her life. The sense of it was almost like a shout in the dark, startling and eye-opening.

There was great tranquility here, far from stormy seas.

Someone had taken her to an outbuilding behind a tavern with the name *Black Cock* carved above the door. The outbuilding contained foodstuffs—cheese, butter, and earthenware containers with things like pickled onions and fruit. She could smell it. It was an outbuilding made of stone, and very cold, as it was meant to preserve things. Astria ended up on the floor, leaning against a cold wall and pondering what had happened since the day she'd been captured. Dirty, hungry, and scared, she was at the bottom.

This was what her life had come to.

Astria had spent months being tied up, tossed around, confined, and laughed at. Oddly enough, she'd never been starved or beaten, except when she'd initiated violence, so in that sense, her captivity hadn't been horrific. But it had been wearing. Everything about it was wearing on her—spiritually, mentally, and physically. She refused to eat half of the time and could see how bony her wrists had become. She hadn't seen her reflection, *truly* seen it, since she was captured, so she could only imagine what she looked like.

An animal.

The reality of that was heartbreaking to her. Astria had always been someone who took pride in her appearance. Her hair had always been neatly styled, and, against the physic's wishes, she liked to bathe frequently because she didn't like the smell of body odor. Everyone had it, of course, and it was considered quite normal, but she'd never been fond of the smell, most especially on her.

She couldn't remember when she last took a bath.

It was difficult not to feel sorry for herself. Five months of captivity meant five months of struggling to survive. Everything in her world now was a struggle simply to breathe, but she knew that she would continue to live like this if she didn't stop behaving like a wildcat. If she wanted a bath and food and at least a comb, then it was probably time that she stop her wild battles and realize the gravity of her situation. An uncooperative prisoner might eventually find herself dropped over the side of the ship, hands bound, so she could sink to a watery grave. She'd heard someone threaten her with that once.

But a cooperative prisoner would live to fight another day.

The problem was that surrender was so contrary to her nature.

As she sat there, shivering, it occurred to her that there was food just a few feet away and she was starving. Literally starving. She couldn't remember when she'd eaten last. They had her arms bound with rope, but it wasn't particularly tight because Bloody Maude didn't like it when it was cutting off her circulation, so the result was rope that was barely binding her.

It was rope that was easy to get off.

She had become good at that, too, over the months. There had been a few opportunities for her to shrug off her bindings, but Maude and her men had never been the wiser about it. Therefore, she shifted on her bottom and bent her legs up against her chest, trying to get her arms underneath her bottom so they were in front of her and not behind her. She had to work at it a few times before she was able to bring her arms forward. Once they were in front of her, it was simply a matter of sliding out of the ropes.

Free of her confinement, she quickly stood up and went to the shelves that contained the food. The first thing she came across was a half a wheel of white cheese and she immediately tore off a hunk of it, shoving it in her mouth. But there were many other things in this cold storage, and she began pulling the cloth off bowls. She found fruit that she put in her mouth after she finished swallowing the cheese, and on another shelf, she found part of a meat pie.

With so much to choose from, she just started grabbing things. When her hands were full, she sat down on the ground and began to stuff her face. It didn't even occur to her that she was eating like an animal, and a starving one at that, because she was so hungry that nothing else seemed to matter. Manners didn't matter. Decorum or etiquette didn't matter. All that mattered at that moment was getting that cheese and fruit and meat pie into her belly.

She'd never tasted anything so delicious.

Once she'd managed to devour everything, she stood up to go in for another round. On the far end of the shelves, there seemed to be some kind of bread or cake of some kind. It was sweet and had oats in it as well as raisins, and she shoveled that into her mouth. There was something else behind it that was covered in a cloth, and when she took the cloth off, she could see that it was some kind of a honey cake because she touched it and her fingers came away sticky. Thrilled, she grabbed the entire thing and begin eating it like a barbarian. No forks, no knives, just her hands and teeth to make short work of the honey cake. She had a mouthful of it when the door to the cold storage abruptly opened.

The big man she'd slugged in the eye was standing there.

Astria wasn't sure what to do at that point. Her mouth was full and she knew if she didn't chew, she would probably choke, so she resumed chewing at a slower pace, but set the rest of the cake down and balled her fists, preparing for a fight.

Here we go again.

But the big man threw his hands up.

"Easy, lass," he said calmly. "I've not come for a brawl."

Astria was feeling nervous and cornered. "What do you want?"

"Tae talk tae ye."

"Why?"

She was as edgy as a caged cat. He paused a moment, his gaze lingering on her, before pointing to the shelf in front of her. "Finish yer food," he said evenly. "I've not come tae harm ye. I just want tae talk."

That only seemed to make her more defensive. "What about?"

He could see that he hadn't eased her, so he lowered his hands and stood as far away from her as he could without actually leaving the outbuilding. "Yer grace, I need ye tae understand something," he said. "I'm not a pirate. I'm not part of the crew who captured ye. I'm not yer enemy, so if we canna be friendly, then let's at least be civil. Or have ye forgotten how?"

Astria swallowed the bite in her mouth, staring at him with enormous blue eyes. *Had* she forgotten how to be civil? That was a damn good question. But more than that, he addressed her formally and properly. She'd almost forgotten her station in life.

Your grace.

Hearing that come out of his mouth seemed to remind her of who, and what, she was.

A reminder of just how far she'd fallen.

"Sweet Mary," she murmured, sinking back against the wall. "I've not heard that in months."

She had a sweet, soft voice, gently accented. "Heard what?" he asked.

She looked at him. "You addressed me properly," she said. "I'd almost forgotten."

He could see how bewildered she was. "I will always address ye with respect," he said. "Even if ye weren't a princess or a duchess, I'd still address ye as a proper lady. I'm not like the others, yer grace. I told ye that and I meant it."

Astria's gaze had been distant, perhaps even misty-eyed, but she looked at him and studied him for a moment. "The pirate queen," she finally said. "Who is she to you?"

"My mother."

Astria's expression softened with realization. "You must be the eldest."

"Aye," he said. "Ye heard what she intends tae do with ye."

Astria nodded, almost wearily. "I am to be your bride."

Payne nodded back, studying her face and trying to gauge how long her calm mood was going to hold. He saw the ropes on the floor, meaning she had clearly removed him. Was she planning on escaping? God, he hoped not. He really didn't want another battle with her. He was hoping calm conversation might ease her a bit, at least enough so that she wouldn't react violently to him again.

He proceeded carefully.

"To be honest, I'm as surprised as ye are," he said. "I've not seen my mother in years, and when I do, she has come tae tell me that my father is dead and I've inherited the earldom. And ye're evidently part of that bargain."

Astria was listening to him with surprising calm. "So I was told," she said. "In fact, when your mother first told me, I tried to fight her."

"How did that end for ye?"

"Not well, I'm afraid."

Payne smiled faintly. "Nay, I dunna imagine it would have," he said. "Maudie gets what she wants. And she wants us tae wed."

Astria sighed heavily. "It seems so."

That was all she had to say about it, which was surprising.

In fact, it was the first time Payne didn't see abject rage in her expression or manner. She seemed exhausted more than anything, but he was glad to see that. He could use it to his advantage. Hoping to build some kind of rapport with her, Payne got an idea.

Perhaps sympathy would get him somewhere.

"It seems as if ye've had a rough time of it since Bloody Maude captured ye," he said. "I think that's a fair assessment."

Astria snorted softly. "Fair, aye," she said. "But I've given as good as I got. I'll not let those filthy Scots get the better of me."

He grinned. "Am I included in that?"

She arched a brow. "I do not know," she said. "Are you?"

"I'm Scots," he said. "Maude is my mother."

"But you said that you are not a pirate."

He shook his head. "I am not."

"What are you?"

"A highly skilled knight," he said. "I'm also a trainer at the Blackchurch Guild."

"What is the Blackchurch Guild?"

"An advanced school for warriors," he said. "We train some of the most elite fighters in the world."

"Where is Blackchurch?"

"Devon."

"Is that where I am?"

"Do ye not know where ye are?"

She shook her head. "I do not," she admitted. "They would never tell me, and after we left Scotland, I lost track. I thought we might be in Wales."

Now he was starting to understand why the woman was so belligerent. Kept in the dark about her whereabouts, treated like a criminal… He couldn't honestly say he wouldn't have reacted in the same fashion. As much as he felt some sympathy for her, that was usually something he kept well hidden. Payne's dark secret was that he tended to be quite empathetic when it came to women in particular, and it was something he wasn't proud of. He considered it a weakness, but at this moment, he couldn't help but feel empathy for Astria's plight.

"Ye're in Devon, yer grace," he said. "Ye came by way of the Bristol Channel, I'm guessing. Now that ye know where ye are, may I offer tae help ye?"

"What *kind* of help?"

He gestured at her. "Ye look as if ye could use a bath," he said. "I could find ye some clean clothing, I think. If ye swear tae me ye'll not try tae escape, I can arrange for yer comfort."

The suggestion seemed to perk her up a little. "A bath?" she said.

"Aye."

She thought on that, but not for long. Soon enough, she was nodding quickly. "Aye," she said. "I would like that."

"I'll not tie ye back up if ye promise not tae run."

"I promise."

"I'll even find a comfortable bed for ye."

Astria nodded so much that Payne was certain her head was going to bob right off her neck. It was the most enthusiasm, and even joy, that he'd seen since he first met her. He was fairly certain it was genuine, but he couldn't be sure. He extended a hand to her, encouraging her to come with him, but this was the moment of truth. Either she was willing to trust him or she wasn't. This was the instance that would define if he could trust her in return.

Truly trust her.

As she hesitantly came toward him, he gently grasped her

arm and lowered his voice.

"If ye are lying tae me in any way, then know this," he muttered. "I'll never trust ye again. Ye'll lose the only ally ye have in this entire situation, so dunna be stupid. Dunna give me a reason tae regret this moment."

She looked at him sharply as if wanting to snap at him, but the words died on her tongue. He wasn't threatening her. He was simply stating a fact.

Something told Astria not to test him.

Perhaps just this once, she wouldn't.

With his iron grip on her arm, she allowed him to lead her out into the cool, damp night.

CHAPTER SEVEN

S HE DIDN'T EVEN protest his staying in the chamber.

Payne felt as if he had to guard against Astria slipping from the window or otherwise trying to escape, so he planted himself by the entry of the rented chamber at the Black Cock and, facing the door, listened to the lady splash about in her bath behind him, assisted by Margit.

Given the fact that Margit had three daughters, she knew a little something about baths and women in general. When Payne brought Astria in from the cold house, Margit had been in the kitchens and had seen them enter. Payne had asked for a bath and soap and any spare clothing Margit might have. Fortunately, she was the right person to ask, because in little time, a copper tub, round and with high sides, had been brought into the only chamber they had left. It was a tiny chamber, with a little bed, and an even smaller window for ventilation, but it was suitable.

The bath went in and so did the lady.

Stripped of her filthy clothing by Margit, Astria plunged into the hot water and gladly so. This was the first moment in five months that she'd felt human, and she wasn't going to risk it with an escape attempt. Margit had soap that smelled of lavender and rosemary, and she proceeded to scrub Astria from head to toe, but not before she tried to chase Payne out of the chamber. It wasn't proper for him to be there, but Payne wouldn't budge. The lady was a prisoner and that was all there was to it.

He wasn't leaving.

More scrubbing and rinsing went on. All he could hear was the splashing and Astria's occasional grunting when Margit scrubbed too hard. More servants moved in and out of the chamber, serving wenches that Payne recognized, and they brought things like flat ale for hair washing and towels and combs.

As Margit worked, Astria ate whatever the woman put in front of her. Bread and butter, a stew of beef and carrots, and other things. Crumbs fell in the bathwater, but Astria didn't care. She was feeling clean and normal again, not hunted and persecuted, and such a simple thing as a bath did wonders for her state of mind.

Even if it wasn't exactly a private experience.

Perhaps it was odd that a princess royal bathe with a man who was not her husband in the chamber, but it was no odder than the course her entire life had taken since that fateful day Bloody Maude came into her life. Many things were odd these days. Astria didn't recognize who she'd become, that was the truth, and the bath had done more than wash away the dirt. It had washed away the cobwebs in her mind, cobwebs of unrealistic expectations of her captivity.

There were a few things she was going to have to face.

She was still thinking of those things when Margit finished rinsing the dirt off her and pulled her out of the bath. Then she went to work drying her vigorously with a big towel. Meanwhile, the only clean garment Margit had come up with was a simple shift and light woolen garment her daughters had outgrown. Astria was thin from months of stress and bad nutrition, so the shift and undyed garment with long sleeves and a square neck went on easily. Margit cinched up the ties on the side, trying to make the dress fit, but Astria was just too skinny. Once she finished with the dress and began drying the woman's hair with the towel, she glanced at Payne, sitting back by the door.

"This lass needs to be fed, Payne," she said as if it were a dire situation. "I don't know what her circumstances are, or why she's here, but I am telling you that she needs food, and lots of it, or she is going to become very ill. If you don't want to see such a thing happen, then you must take better care of her."

In the chair, Payne sighed heavily. "May I turn around now?"

Margit finished toweling her hair and pulled Astria into the nearest chair. "Aye," she said, taking out a wooden comb. "Are you hearing me? This young woman needs good food and rest. She's like bones with skin. And she has bruising over her body. That's not like you lads at Blackchurch to thrash a woman."

"That is because we dinna," Payne said as he turned his chair around to face the chamber. "She came with the pirates and…"

His voice trailed off when he got a good look at Astria. Margit had been combing her damp hair, but when the woman moved aside, Payne saw what Princess Maria Astria Julia truly looked like. Without the filthy clothing, the dirt covering her face and hair, and a hostile expression on her face, it was as if the sun had just emerged from behind the clouds.

She was breathtaking.

Her hair was a shiny blonde color—he could see it in the weak light of the hearth and the tapers. It was straight and heavy, but it glittered like gold. The oval face was still there, but it was clean now, displaying a well-shaped nose, glorious blue eyes, and those long, long lashes. Her mouth was clean, revealing full lips that were quite beautiful.

She was wearing something Margit had brought for her, a colorless dress that was simple in construction, but even Payne could see that it was too big for her. Her collarbone was quite prominent, as was her jawline. She had all the signs of a woman who hadn't eaten much as of late, and that realization created a spark of anger in him. Anger with Astria for being belligerent and violent, anger with his mother for starving the woman because of it.

It was no wonder Astria was behaving like an animal.

"Pirates," Margit scoffed in disgust. "No wonder she is the way she is. Payne, can you keep her here for a few days? Away from them? I'll feed her all she can eat if you do."

Payne nodded. "I can keep her here as long as needed," he said. "Ye're kind, Margit. I'll not forget it."

Margit was vigorously combing the blond hair that was drying in the heat from the fire. "Poor lass," she said. "To have been treated so unkindly. Payne, there should be a serving wench right outside the door. Send her for more food and drink."

Payne stood up and stuck his head out of the chamber, calling to the nearest wench, who happened to be over in the common room, in his line of sight. He waved her over and gave her instructions, and she headed off to the kitchens. Payne returned to the chamber, quietly shutting the door.

"I'll see what I can find for her to sleep in," Margit said, now braiding Astria's slightly damp hair. "My youngest married a rich merchant, you know. He bought her all new things when they married, so I still have her old clothing here. I'll see if I can find more serviceable things for the lady."

"She's a princess, Margit," Payne said quietly, his gaze lingering on Astria. "She's not any lady, but a princess. She's royalty. And we'll treat her with all due respect."

Margit turned to him, surprised, before looking at the head of the woman whose hair she was plaiting. "I see," she said, bewilderment in her tone. "A proper princess will have anything I can provide for her, then."

She tied off the two long blonde braids she'd made before reaching down to pick up the damp towels from the floor. Hustling over to the door, she disappeared for a moment before returning with two servants, who emptied the tepid bathwater before hauling the tub out of the chamber. That left Payne alone with Astria, who had, so far, not moved a muscle. She simply sat by the hearth where Margit had put her, staring into the flames. Even when the food came and it was put on a small table for her, she seemed to be moving stiffly, as if she were in a daze.

All the while, Payne simply watched her.

Truth be told, he was trying to determine if this was a ruse. This was the same lady who'd nearly put his eye out earlier, all flame and fire, but now she was almost catatonic. There was plenty of food on the table, and even though she'd eaten twice earlier that he knew of, she still took big bites of it, finally stabbing one of the pork sausages with a dull knife and holding it up to her mouth. Seeing the woman as she was now was day and night from what he'd known of here earlier. She appeared every inch a princess, beautiful and meant to be worshipped.

But he had a lot of questions.

"Did the pirates not feed ye, yer grace?" he asked.

She slowed her chewing. "Not much."

"Why not?"

She shrugged, taking another big bite. "You would have to ask them," she said. "I simply wasn't provided with food very often."

"So they starved ye."

She swallowed the bite in her mouth and looked at him. "As much as I hate the very sight of the woman who is your mother, I am not going to speak out against her to you, her son," she said. "I do not know you. I do not know what you will use against me, and my treatment, poor as it has been, could become worse. Therefore, do not ask me further questions about my time as the captive of Bloody Maude. Whatever has happened is between only us. I will keep it there."

There was a seed of honor in that statement. In fact, it was one of the core beliefs taught at Blackchurch. When there was a personal conflict, it was solved only between those it involved. To complain to others, to seek intervention for something that was the individual's responsibility, was considered a sign of weakness. Frankly, Payne was surprised to hear that she felt that way, but in doing so, he could see that she was a woman of honor. Small as it was, it impressed him.

"I know ye dunna know me," he said, "but I assure ye, I am a knight of the highest order. Honor and responsibility tae myself and tae my brethren are paramount. But I will be honest when I tell ye that I see before me a situation that is much larger than a woman being taken captive. I see an entire country being pulled intae a situation that could be quite volatile, and unfortunately, I'm being pulled intae it as well."

"How does this involve you?"

"Because my mother is demanding we wed," he said. "Ye know this."

She did. After a moment, she took another bite of the sausage. "And you intend to do as she wishes, I assume," she said, chewing.

"As I told ye, Bloody Maude gets what she wants," he said. "If I dunna, she will make me wish that I did. She's not tae be trifled with, yer grace."

Astria swallowed the bite in her mouth. "I know," she said. "I've tried. You see where it has gotten me."

No self-pity in the statement, simply fact, but there was no hint that she was not going to put up a fight when it came to marriage, and he tried not to be offended by it.

"She could ransom ye back tae yer family," he said. "Mayhap ye'd rather she do that than marry me."

Astria started chuckling, a sound without humor. She swallowed the bite in her mouth, but the laughter didn't stop. She continued with it as if Payne had just said something quite funny, finally grasping the cup of ale that came with the meal and drinking deeply.

Then she chuckled some more.

"My family," she said with irony. "My nephew, also named Sancho, has ascended the throne. I told your mother that my nephew, the current king, is probably sending a fleet of ships after me, but that is not the case. No one is coming for me and no one will pay a ransom, which means that if I do not marry you, the pirate queen will probably ransom me to the highest bidder. A genuine princess for the price of a prize mare."

She sounded bitter, and he didn't blame her. It was a hell of a predicament. "I do not have much faith in the life ye would lead if someone purchased ye," he said. "It could be far worse than what ye've known here."

She shrugged and took another drink of the ale, the one with the fermented apples. "Why should you even think about it?" she said. "I am nothing to you. We do not know one another. What happens to me should be of no matter."

He scratched his neck thoughtfully. "That is not exactly true," he said. "Maudie gave ye tae me. Ye, therefore, belong tae me. I suppose I could sell ye tae the highest bidder and use the money tae buy another fine stallion."

She stopped drinking and glared at him. "Do as you must," she said. "What is the price of a woman's life, after all?"

"Can I ask ye a question?"

She snorted, rolling her eyes. "Ask."

"I'm assuming ye were bound because ye've tried tae escape," he said. "Is that true?"

Astria regarded him a moment. "I have not been a willing captive."

"Where did ye intend tae go if ye escaped?"

"Back to Tarragona, I suppose."

"What is there for ye?"

"My home," she said, though her manner was softening at the turn of subject. "I lived there for ten years."

"And yer children?"

"I have no children."

He nodded. "I see," he said. "So ye're simply returning tae the place where ye live."

"Aye."

He averted his gaze, clearly thinking about something. He almost looked as if he disbelieved her. "Yer grace, forgive me if this is a blunt question, but people usually dunna fight so hard tae escape simply tae return tae the place where they live, especially if there are no children," he said. "Do ye have a lover waiting for ye?"

She sighed. "Sometimes I wish I did," she said. "But there is no lover. There is no one. I am alone."

It was his turn to smile without humor. "A lass as beautiful as ye?" he said. "I find that hard tae believe."

"Do you think I am lying, then?"

"Nay," he said. "I just find it hard tae believe that every man in yer village is not pining away for a lock of yer hair."

She frowned. "Do things like that happen in England?"

He grinned. "I wouldna know," he said. "I've never done it before and I've never had any lass follow me around enough tae care, but I've heard that such things happen. It might be nice if someone thought enough of me tae beg for a snip of my hair."

She peered at him as if he were suggesting something ridiculous, but the smile on his face was infectious.

He had the most marvelous smile.

"Do you think so?" she asked.

He shrugged. "I dunna know," he said. "No one ever has."

"If they did, would you give it to them?"

He ran his fingers through his softly mussed hair. "And ruin my comely locks?" he scoffed. "I wouldna do it no matter how much they begged."

Astria was fighting off a smile. "Then why did you say it might be nice if they did?"

"Because I could boast about it. Why do ye think?"

That made her laugh. Just the way he said it actually made her laugh. Astria wasn't sure she'd smiled in the entire time she'd been in captivity, but there was something liberating about it. A conversation with this big, arrogant Scotsman had done something to her soul. The fear, the rage she'd felt for all of those months, was somehow eased by his manner and by the food and bath. Everything that he had been responsible for.

She was starting to feel human again.

But her defenses weren't down entirely.

"I am sorry to say that I'll not give you anything to boast about," she said. "Mayhap one of the serving wenches will."

He grunted unhappily, waving a hand in the general direction of the common room. "That lot?" he said. "Nice lasses, all of them, but not women I'd boast about."

"You have my sympathy, then."

He snorted, his eyes twinkling at her in the firelight. "Can I tell ye something?"

"What is it?"

"I like ye better when ye're not throwing a fist intae my eye."

"And I like you better when you're not spanking me."

"Oh, lass," he said, shaking his head in disapproval. "Ye deserved it."

"Did I?"

He pointed to his left eye and the bruising around it. "Do ye think women are going tae follow me around now after what ye've done?" he said, feigning outrage. "Ye've marred my face."

Astria couldn't help the grin now. There was no chance of stifling it. "I've given you character."

His eyebrows flew up. "Is that what ye call it?" he said. "I thought ye called it a bruise."

"If anyone asks, tell them you were fighting against twenty men and barely made it out alive."

He grinned again. "I will," he said. "Because I surely wouldna tell them the truth."

Astria had to look away, struggling against a smile. "Poor man."

"Are ye sorry ye did it?"

"Should I be?"

He chuckled, shaking his head at her. "Ye're a stubborn one, lass."

Before Astria could reply, Margit appeared. The door swung open and she stepped in with an armful of clothing. She was also carrying a small, well-worn satchel and a few other things, and she bustled over to the bed and dropped it all.

"There," she said, brushing stray locks of hair out of her face. "I went through my daughter's trunk and I believe the lady can use all of this."

Payne was on his feet, surveying the haul. "What did ye bring?"

Margit began going through it. "Two shifts," she said, holding up the white, woolen garments. "These are good ones, too. I paid good money for them in Exeter. And there are three surcoats that are serviceable. Probably too big for her, still, but that cannot be helped at the moment. There are also two pairs of shoes and two pairs of hose. I've also pulled out ribbons and another comb and a few other things she might find useful."

By this time, Astria was on her feet too, looking at everything with interest. Timidly, she fingered one of the shifts.

"Very fine," she said. "Are you certain you want to give these to me? You should sell them."

Margit looked at her. "Do you have any money?"

"I do," Payne said, digging for the purse on his belt. "I'll pay ye for them, Margit."

But Margit waved him off. "Not to worry," she said. "I'm

just glad they'll be getting some use. I think I have a few more things for her. Do you want to look at them?"

Payne shrugged. "Mayhap tomorrow," he said. Then he pulled the woman over near the door to try to have a private conversation with her. "I must go about some business, but I canna leave the lady unattended. Would ye be willing tae sit with her while I'm gone?"

Margit appeared confused. "Sit with her?" she repeated. "Why?"

"Because I fear she'll try tae escape if she's not watched."

Margit's brow furrowed as her gaze moved to the lady over near the bed. "She's not well, Payne," she said seriously. "She may try to escape, but I doubt she'll go very far."

"I'd rather not take the chance. Please?"

Margit nodded. "As you wish," she said. Then she moved away from the door and back toward Astria. "Let's get these things back into the bag and get you into bed. The best thing for you is a little sleep."

She was indicating the shifts and items on the bed. The satchel was on the floor at the foot of the bed and she picked that up, collecting the garments one at a time to roll up and put into the satchel. Astria didn't make a move to help her. She simply watched her do it. It wasn't that she was being rude, but rather that she'd never really done that kind of thing for herself before. She'd never packed a satchel. Others had done it for her. So she watched Margit as the woman carefully rolled all of the clothing she'd brought her and packed it away neatly. The other small things went in after, and the satchel was sealed up and put on the floor.

That was when Payne silently excused himself.

Astria was well aware when he left the chamber, but she

didn't react to his departure. She simply sat in the chair, watching Margit pull back the coverlet on the bed. It wasn't a big bed, or even well appointed, but the truth was that it was better than anything she'd slept on whilst in captivity. It was soft for the most part, a mattress stuffed with dried grass, so it had far more give than the ground or slats of a wagon or a boat deck, and far more comfort.

In she went.

She was asleep the moment her head hit the pillow.

CHAPTER EIGHT

Blackchurch Guild
Exmoor's Keep

"AND NOW YE know," Payne said. "Bloody Maude has no intention of sacking Blackchurch. She came purely with news for me."

St. Denis and St. Sebastian, roused from their beds, were sitting in St. Denis' solar and listening to what was, by all accounts, good news. There was good news in the sense that Bloody Maude and her band of marauding pirates had no intention of making war upon Blackchurch, but it was also sad news for Payne. His mother had come to tell him that his father had passed away and he was now the Earl of Lismore, which put him as the highest-ranking noble among the trainers at Blackchurch. Not only that, he was now socially on the same level as St. Denis himself.

The news had been a revelation, indeed.

"Cruz and Creston essentially told us the same thing," St. Denis said. "That relieved my mind, of course, but please allow me to extend my condolences on the passing of your father, Payne. Losing a father is never an easy thing."

Payne shook his head. "Nay, it is not," he said. "Although I'd not seen my father in years, we were still close. I loved and admired him. Big Bowie Matheson was a great man, much respected by his clan. I will miss him."

"What will you do?" St. Sebastian asked quietly. "You are an earl now, Payne. That means you have an earldom to manage. Will you go home?"

Payne shook his head. "Not right away," he said. "I may ask for time tae return home and settle things there, but I have no intention of returning tae stay at this time."

"But being an earl means you have responsibilities, Payne," St. Denis said. "Of course, I do not want to lose you, but you have lands and people to administer. Who will do it if you do not?"

Payne looked at him. "My father has a former priest who served as his majordomo for years," he said. "The man goes by Old Bones and, tae be perfectly honest, I dunna know his real name. My father affectionately called him Obie and I'm sure he's still there, still in charge. He was loyal tae my father and therefore loyal tae me, but I would still like tae return tae ensure that loyalty is still strong. My family has ruled over our lands for more than two hundred years. I willna be the link that breaks our legacy by abandoning it."

He seemed resolute in what he needed to do, so St. Denis didn't argue with him, but as a man who ruled an earldom, he knew there was more to it than simply leaving the management of it to others. Perhaps they would discuss that in the days to come, but not today. Today was a day to allow Payne the time he needed to mourn the loss of his father.

"Take what time you need, then," St. Denis said. "If you wish to leave right away for Scotland, I will understand."

Payne shrugged. "Not immediately," he said. "But I thank ye for yer generosity. I must still deal with a few things before I go."

"Like what?"

There was the question. It was a perfect opening for Payne to tell St. Denis something he'd been wrestling with. He wasn't quite sure how to tell him what else Bloody Maude had brought to the steps of Blackchurch, but here was his opportunity.

He took a deep breath.

"There's something more ye should know," he said. "Part of Bloody Maude's visit tae me was tae tell me of my father, but the other part was tae bring me something."

St. Sebastian was curious. "What did she bring you?"

"A bride."

That brought a measure of surprise from both St. Denis and St. Sebastian, but the expression on Payne's face suggested it wasn't welcome.

"Are congratulations in order?" St. Sebastian said. "It does not seem so from your expression. I sense there may be something amiss with this bride."

Payne nodded. "Ye could say that," he said. "The truth is this... Ye both know what Bloody Maude is. Ye know what she does. Five months ago, she attacked a pair of ships off the coast of Palma. The bride was on those ships. Her name is Maria Astria Julia, Princesa Real, Princesa of Beira, Duchess of Braganza, Duchess of Barcelos, Countess of Faria, Countess of Neiva, and by marriage, Duchess of Tarragona. Her father was Sancho of Portugal and her nephew now sits upon the throne, and my mother is determined that I, as the new Earl of Lismore, should marry her. And what Bloody Maude wants, Bloody Maude gets."

By the time he was finished, St. Denis was looking at him in horror. St. Sebastian seemed shocked.

"A Portuguese princess?" St. Denis finally said, aghast. "Bloody Maude has brought you a royal captive to wed?"

"She has."

St. Denis nearly stammered his next few words. "You… you cannot do it, Payne," he said. "Do you know what will happen if you do?"

"Of course I know," Payne said quietly. "But this is a bigger problem than ye know. If I dunna marry her, the fact that I am disobeying my mother notwithstanding, then the princess' future is in doubt. My mother could, and would, sell her tae the highest bidder. Do ye know how poorly the Portuguese would react tae that?"

"That is none of our concern," St. Denis said, waving his hands around. "She is not our responsibility. Payne, if you marry her, then I cannot have you continue as a trainer. I cannot risk the Portuguese turning their anger on us when we are sworn to remain neutral in all things."

St. Sebastian started to protest, but Payne held up a hand to silence him. "I have thought of that," he said patiently. "Trust me when I tell ye that I understand the implications. So many implications. But there can also be an outcome that makes the Portuguese royal family in Blackchurch's debt."

"What's that?"

Payne was as serious as anyone had ever seen him. "I marry her and we send word tae the Portuguese royal family that we saved her from Medusa's Disciples," he said. "I would even send her back tae her family if they wanted, but she would remain my wife. That is the price for saving her. The royal family will simply have tae accept that. Moreover, it would make Blackchurch linked, by marriage, to the Portuguese royal house, which elevates our social standing. It will legitimize Black-church in a way none of yer predecessors have been able tae do."

To his surprise, St. Denis didn't discount him outright. He started to, but thought better of it, mostly because what Payne was saying made sense. It *would* give Blackchurch a legitimacy that they'd never had before. St. Sebastian was looking at his father rather anxiously as the man mulled everything over.

"He's right," he insisted quietly. "To have one of our train-ers married to a princess royal would create social standing for us where none has existed before. It could work to our advantage, Papa."

St. Denis grunted as if his brain hurt as he tried to see all sides of the situation. There was so very much to contemplate. Wearily, he went to sit in his chair.

"Send for Amir," he said. "And Ming Tang. I want them to hear this."

With a hopeful glance at Payne, St. Sebastian went to find a servant to send for the men whom St. Denis put a great deal of trust in. Amir's father was an Egyptian warlord with twenty thousand men at his disposal and a good deal of clout in the politics of the land, and St. Denis had learned to depend on Amir's advice over the years. He had a way of seeing the larger picture, whereas Ming Tang was always in sync with the moral implications. Not only were the men trainers, but some of the best advisors in the land.

Payne knew this and was grateful that St. Denis was at least considering the proposal. He hadn't really thought of the Blackchurch Savior suggestion until he'd come into the chamber. Now, he could see a way to please his mother, his liege, and still keep his position at Blackchurch. The truth was that he very much wanted to please his mother, especially after their angry parting ten years ago. He didn't want a repeat of that because there may not be forgiveness a second time. It wasn't that he didn't have the courage to stand up to her—it was more that she was his mother and he respected her. She was a pirate because she'd chosen to accept the legacy of her father, which had taken great courage.

Payne didn't want to disappoint a woman with that much courage.

But part of it was his giving in to his weakness again. *Empathy.* He had empathy for Astria when he shouldn't, but he couldn't help it. He was certain that she didn't care about him in the least, or what became of him, so he wasn't sure why he had any concern for her.

But he did.

He hoped that wasn't going to betray him in the end.

"I've sent for them, Papa," St. Sebastian said as he came back into the solar. "They'll be here soon."

And with that, they waited.

Payne sat down in the nearest chair, leaning his head back against the wall. It was quiet in the chamber but for the gentle snapping of the hearth, and Payne closed his eyes, simply to rest, while they waited. But he must have fallen asleep, because the next thing he heard was Amir's voice. St. Denis was repeating everything Payne had said, including his solution, and asking for Amir and Ming Tang's advice.

Amir was the first to speak.

"Chances are that the Portuguese royal house already knows that one of their own has been taken captive," he said. "It has been five months, you've said?"

St. Denis nodded. "That is what I have been told."

Amir rubbed his eyes wearily. He'd been awoken from a dead sleep by his lord's summons, only to be facing an unexpected crisis. "In five months, word should have reached them," he said. "At the very least, they are probably looking for her. If we were to send word that we rescued her from her captor, it would indeed put us in their debt and emphasize our neutral position in all matters."

"But Payne is right," Ming Tang said, looking at Amir. "If he marries her, it secures her safety. It also introduces Blackchurch into something it has never had before—a shadow of nobility. That commands respect."

Amir considered that. "Blackchurch has respect in military circles," he said. "Blackchurch-trained warriors are the most sought after in the world."

"True," Ming Tang said, "but there has always been the long-standing belief that Blackchurch is ruthless and no better than the pirates associated with it. Given that St. Abelard is attached to Blackchurch, it is something that cannot be escaped."

"And you feel a marriage to a captured princess somehow legitimizes Blackchurch?"

"If Payne marries her to save her from being auctioned, it does," Ming Tang said. "It gives us an added dimension we are not known for—compassion."

"For forcing a captive into marriage?"

"For saving a captive from a terrible fate."

There were two sides to the argument, which really wasn't an argument as much as it was simply a discussion. Payne was fully awake by this time, listening to Amir and Ming Tang, trying to see the situation from all sides. But no matter what was said, he'd already decided what he was going to do.

No amount of discussion was going to change that.

"I realize this is a difficult situation," he interjected. "I realize there is no simple answer. But the reality is this—if I dunna marry the lass, there is no knowing what my mother will do. She could sell her or keep her for the men's comfort. Is that the fate ye wish for her?"

"But your mother is a woman," Ming Tang said quietly. "Surely she would not consign the captive to a fate such as that."

"A whore tae the men?" Payne said plainly. "Above all, she must keep her men happy. Their contentment outweighs the life of a single woman. It has nothing tae do with her personal feelings and everything tae do with her business—a business of piracy—and in order tae ensure she has pirates who willna stage a mutiny, she'll do what she needs tae do in order tae keep them happy. Even give them a royal whore."

Ming Tang sighed sharply at that horrific prospect, looking at St. Denis. "And Blackchurch would be responsible," he said to the man. "We have an opportunity to save her now. Will you truly not do what is right simply because you do not want Blackchurch involved?"

The chamber fell silent. Everyone was looking at St. Denis, including Payne, waiting for the man to make a decision one way or the other. He was a man of principles, so of course he didn't want to be responsible for a woman being used for sexual relief for a gang of bloodthirsty pirates. But he also didn't want problems with the entire country of Portugal.

"The question is whether or not the Portuguese believe we have saved her from such a fate," he said. "If she marries Payne…"

"If she marries me, I'll take her home if she wants tae go,"

Payne said. "I'll speak tae the king myself and tell him what happened. I will face their praise or condemnation personally, and if it is condemnation, I'll assure them that Blackchurch had no part in my decision. But if it is praise…"

"If it is praise, you will ensure that Blackchurch takes some of the credit."

"I will."

It seemed like a satisfying solution. All eyes turned to St. Denis, who was still contemplating everything. He had more opinions now, from men he trusted, but it only seemed to make a final decision more difficult. Since Blackchurch had historically remained neutral in any given conflict, having one of their trainers marry a captive princess didn't exactly put them in the middle of a conflict. There *was* no conflict other than the fact that the woman was a captive of a pirate.

In that respect, their neutrality wasn't in danger.

With a heavy sigh, he looked at Payne.

"Do what you need to do," he said. "But keep me apprised of every move you make. I must know what has happened and what is going to happen. I want Blackchurch to come out of this in a heroic manner. Is that clear?"

Payne nodded. "Aye, m'laird."

St. Denis unexpectedly grinned. "You do not have to address me as such," he said. "We are of equal ranks now, you and I."

"Not as long as I am a trainer, m'laird," Payne said, a glimmer in his eye. "I will always be sworn tae ye."

St. Denis chuckled. "Mayhap it is for the best," he said. "A castle cannot have two kings."

"Ye're the only king of Blackchurch, m'laird."

St. Denis acknowledged the show of respect with a nod.

"Go, now," he said. "Make sure Bloody Maude does not do something with this princess that we would all regret."

Payne stood up and headed for the door. When it shut softly behind him, Amir looked at St. Denis.

"If this situation is not handled with the utmost care, it will erupt in our faces and we will be trying to mitigate it for years to come," he said. "It could damage the chances of our graduates finding lucrative positions."

St. Denis shook his head. "It will not," he said confidently. "We are still the premier training guild for warriors in the world. No one will remember a Portuguese princess who was abducted by the mother of one of our trainers because no one will ever know of the relationship between Payne and Bloody Maude. I suggest that is something we never speak of. Not even to each other where it can be overheard. Agreed?"

Amir and Ming Tang nodded, as did St. Sebastian. With the subject matter at hand settled, Amir and Ming Tang headed back to bed.

If they could even fall back asleep.

The night was cold, with a half-moon hanging in the sky, unnaturally bright. The stars above were brilliant as well, presiding over the darkened landscape, filling the heads of the sleeping with dreams.

"Payne is now an earl," Amir said quietly as they left Exmoor's keep and began to walk back to their homes beneath that brilliant sky. "Our big, brave, sometimes irreverent, and always entertaining Scotsman is true nobility now."

Ming Tang smiled faintly. "He will be an excellent lord."

"You think so?"

"And you do not?"

Amir nodded. "I do," he said quickly. "He is suited to it, but he must learn to keep his emotions in check. I could see it in his expression that he is concerned for this princess."

Ming Tang nodded too. "As could I," he said. "Payne feels that he is hobbled by the fact that he feels deeply, especially when it comes to women, but I do not think that is the case. I think it gives him great capacity for understanding."

"Some men do not want to understand. They only want to fulfill their wishes."

"Payne is not like that."

"Nay," Amir said slowly, "he is not. He has the ability to make the right decision more than most, but he needs to trust himself. He has always been in the position of follower more than a leader, so he must trust himself as a leader now. The knight must become the earl… and in command of his destiny."

Ming Tang thought on the big Scotsman who always projected a devil-may-care attitude, as if he didn't take life very seriously at times.

But he was going to have to take it seriously now.

"Time will tell," he said quietly.

Time would, indeed.

CHAPTER NINE

MAYBE THIS WAS right.

Maybe it was wrong.

He simply wasn't sure.

Payne had presented such a strong case to St. Denis that he felt as if his path was set for him now. He couldn't question it or back out of it. He'd told St. Denis that Blackchurch would be heroic for saving the princess that had been snatched away by pirates, the leader of whom was his own mother.

Was it possible he was trying to save her, too?

Like a child who didn't understand the consequences of actions—Payne felt as if that was his mother. Maude had grown up with a pirate father, an outlaw of the sea, but she hadn't gone to sea until after he died. She was carrying on her father's legacy the best way she knew how. After ten years of it, she'd figured it out. She did as she pleased, and that included abducting a Portuguese princess. Perhaps in saving that princess, Payne was somehow trying to make it so the Portuguese wouldn't go after Bloody Maude for revenge. God knew, they had the ships for it. Everyone knew that the Portuguese armada was formidable.

And here he was, trying to save everyone.

His mother.

The princess.

Even Blackchurch.

There were about two more hours until morning when he headed back to the Black Cock. Mostly, he wanted to see his mother, but he'd also left Margit guarding Astria, and there was no telling how that would go if Astria became belligerent. Margit would be the type to hit her over the head with a piece of wood, and Astria would be the type to punch the woman in the eye, so the more he thought about it, the more he thought he'd better check on that pair first.

He was starting to question why he'd left them so long to begin with.

It was a short walk from Blackchurch to the Black Cock, and he picked up the pace on the road, traveling beneath the bright half-moon in full confidence of his safety. There were no outlaws anywhere near Blackchurch for several reasons, but the most predominant was that any outlaws would have to be completely daft to inhabit the woods close to a world-class training guild. The second most important reason was that St. Denis ordered periodic sweeps of the woods surrounding Blackchurch simply to make sure no one had set up shop, so the truth was that the entire area surrounding Blackchurch, including the village, was completely safe. Probably more so now with a pirate encampment on the outskirts.

Unless the pirates decided to ravage the countryside.

But Payne couldn't worry about that now. He picked up the pace, and by the time he reached the Black Cock, it was locked up for the night and he had to rouse Hobbes to let him in. Unhappy that he'd been pulled out of his bed, Hobbes admitted him to the tavern and Payne headed to the small chamber near the kitchens where he'd left Astria. The door wasn't locked, so he was able to very quietly open the panel, sticking his head into the dim room to see that it was completely quiet.

A low fire burned in the hearth, giving off a comforting glow. Payne heard soft snoring, and looked off to his left to see Margit in a chair, head back and snoring away. As his eyes grew accustomed to the light, he peered over at the bed, seeing the coverlet bunched up. He thought it was bunched up over Astria's sleeping body, but it took him a moment to realize there was no body at all.

The bed was empty.

He bolted.

Cʒ

SHE SHOULD HAVE run.

Could have run.

But hadn't.

After slithering out of the window in the rented room, which was made easy because Margit was snoring like an old bull, Astria rushed into the livery yard with glee. It was the first true freedom she'd had since Bloody Maude and her pirate horde had confiscated her vessels, so there was almost a euphoric sense of delight at the fact that she was no longer a captive.

Truly free.

But she made it just past the stable before she came to a halt.

There was an encampment behind the tavern, full of the same pirates who had abducted her, so she couldn't run in that direction. She could, however, go left or right or to the front of the tavern. She had all the space in the world to run and escape her captors.

But she couldn't seem to do it.

Why?

In God's name, why couldn't she do it? Why wasn't she running? Perhaps it had something to do with the fact that she was in a country she didn't know. She was in an area she didn't know. She didn't even know where the nearest village was, and that would mean running through woods and lands that were possibly teeming with outlaws, and she'd be worse off than she was now if they captured her. She didn't want to jump out of the frying pan into the fire. That was her caution talking.

But there was also something else.

Ye'll lose the only ally ye have in this entire situation, so dunna be stupid.

Words that Payne had spoken to her. The only person she'd met during the course of her godforsaken captivity who had actually been kind to her. That big, handsome Scotsman had her second-guessing her desire to escape and here she was, trying to rationalize *why* she wasn't taking this obvious chance.

Was it really because she didn't want to disappoint a man she didn't even know?

Or was it something else?

Astria had no idea.

There was an upended stump next to the livery and she plopped down on it, watching the bonfire in the distance. It began to occur to her that because Payne had shown her such respect, she simply wasn't willing to throw it all away. She wasn't willing to shame the only person who had been willing to protect and defend her. He's started that from the moment they'd met, so it wasn't a matter of his protecting a princess. He hadn't even known she was one at first. Or had he? She couldn't remember. But she did remember one thing.

His kindness.

She'd never met anyone who had shown her such kindness.

Not even her husband. He'd been pleasant, but it was out of duty. And then there was her stepson…

Arnaldo.

She was certain he was looking for her, but even that certainty was damaged by doubt. Arnaldo was her husband's sole heir, and even when she had been married to his father, the man had tried to seduce. her. He'd been annoying and aggressive. She'd had to slap him on more than one occasion because he'd been too forward with her. There had been no respect there, no kindness. When her husband finally died, Arnaldo was responsible for it. She had proof of it. But before she'd been able to prove it, his attitude toward her changed completely and he'd taken to sea.

They's become rivals.

Arnaldo, the new Duc de Tarragona, didn't want the dowager duchess involved in the family business. Oh, that family business that seemed to be so respectable, so legitimate. Her husband and his father before him had made their money with a fleet of merchant ships, but the truth was so much different than that.

El dios del mar.

The Sea God.

That was what her husband had been referred to, and his father before him. The merchant fleet was legitimate. The pirate business was not. The House of San Miguel had made a good deal of money in shipping, from all over the Mediterranean, but that was only part of their empire. The other part was the fleet of pirate ships that roamed the coasts, sacking towns and burning those who resisted. Stealing from those who had paid them for shipments. They knew where all of the big and valuable shipments were going, and once their merchant ships delivered them, the pirates would come in behind them and clean up. Her husband had let her in on that little secret after they were wed. He ran the legitimate shipping business while Arnaldo headed the pirate venture as *El dios del mar*.

Only he wanted it all.

And Astria had tried to take from him.

Astria hadn't only wanted the merchant business. She'd wanted the pirate business too, because when she'd married Armand, the merchant business was close to floundering. His marriage to a royal bride had breathed new life into the merchant business because everyone wanted to do business with the man who had married a princess.

Then came the pirate business.

Astria wasn't stupid. She understood economics because that was the one thing her father had done for her—he'd wanted his children to understand the economics of a country. She had applied those principles to the shipping business and then to the pirate business, which Arnaldo completely resented. He and his father had a terrible argument about it, and Arnaldo was exiled for a couple of years because of it. That was when Astria took over the pirate business and grew it. But Arnaldo eventually came back, killed his father, and inherited everything.

But Astria wasn't willing to readily give up that which she had built.

Even if it technically wasn't hers.

That was the situation when Maude overtook the two vessels Astria had been in command of. They weren't her ships, but

Arnaldo's, because Astria had stolen them from Palma and was quite sure Arnaldo wanted them back. *That* was the dark little secret that she knew and Maude didn't—Arnaldo wasn't coming to rescue his stepmother. He was coming for his ships. Astria was quite sure that he would thank Maude for capturing her.

He wouldn't care at all about the fate of his stepmother.

So… if she escaped, where would she run to?

She literally had nowhere to go. But if she married a certain Scottish earl who would protect her, from Arnaldo mostly, perhaps this is the best that she could hope for. So why had she been trying to escape so badly from Maude for five straight months? Because she didn't want to be turned over to Arnaldo when he caught up to them.

And that was the truth.

"Ye dinna run."

The voice came from the darkness behind her. Astria wasn't startled by it. Somehow, she thought he might find her, eventually, because he seemed like the attentive type. Slowly, she turned to look at him, noticing that he seemed out of breath.

"You were running after me," she observed.

He shook his head. "Not at all," he said. "I knew I would find ye out here."

"Then you must always breathe hard when you are calmly walking into a livery yard."

"I do, in fact."

"Why?"

"Because I find it exhilarating."

Astria had to fight off a laugh at the man trying to pretend he wasn't breathless because he had been preparing to chase her down. She turned away, returning her focus to the pirate encampment in the distance.

"Shall I tell you what just happened?" she said.

"With what?"

"You."

"I told ye nothing happened."

She shook her head. "I think you went to the chamber you left me in and when you saw that I was gone, you thought I'd escaped," she said. "You came running out here to find a horse to go in pursuit."

He snorted. "That shows how much ye dunna know."

Astria shrugged. "That is probably true," she said. "I do not know half as much as I probably think I know. But one thing is for certain."

"What is that?"

She was still looking at the pirates, still focused on the distant fires. "If I had wanted to escape, I could have," she said. "I would have been long gone by now. But I did not go. I could not."

He didn't say anything for a moment. "Why not?" he finally asked.

Astria tried to think of a clever reply, but she couldn't. She wasn't even sure why she'd told him she couldn't leave, but she had. Of course he wondered why. Now, she had to explain herself. Fed, bathed, and somewhat rested, she was feeling much more like herself, and she knew what a precarious position she was in. With every second that passed, it weighed on her more and more. And perhaps Payne's declaration of being her ally was weighing on her most of all.

She wondered if he really meant it.

"Because you told me that your trust was only given once,"

she said. "You have been, more than anyone I've met since the start of my captivity, the kindest person I've come into contact with. Even after I struck you, you still showed kindness when you did not have to. I could not run because I knew that if you caught me, it would mean the end for me. No more kindness, no more baths or food. Your mother once threatened to bind my arms and legs and throw me overboard. If she were to do it, there would be no one left to save me."

Payne considered that for a moment. Then he moved forward, finding another stump to sit on. Out in the livery yard, there were plenty of them by the wood pile.

"And ye want me tae save you from my mother?" he asked.

She looked at him. "You've no reason to," she said honestly. "I have not been very gracious to you, but I want to thank you for the bath and the food and the clothing. I very much appreciate it."

"Ye're welcome."

"What happens now?"

He shrugged, glancing off toward the pirate encampment because there was some shouting going on as men sat around a great bonfire and drank.

"I am not entirely certain," he said. "My mother wishes for us tae marry, but I dunna know if she's made plans beyond that."

She watched his profile, the moonlight giving him a ghostly appearance. "I cannot imagine that you want a wife," she said. "If you did, you would already have one at your age."

He frowned and looked at her. "Just how old do ye think I am?"

"Old enough."

He frowned a split second longer before breaking into a

grin. "There's not been time tae take a wife," he said. "Being a Blackchurch trainer keeps me very busy and keeps me rooted tae Devon."

"If you take me for a wife as your mother wishes, then what?" she said. "You are now the Earl of Lismore. Will you take me back to Scotland with you?"

He shook his head. "'Tis too soon tae speak of that," he said. Then he eyed her. "But I told ye once that ye belonged tae me. Ye seem tae have accepted that."

"And you said you might auction me off and buy a prize stallion."

"I lied."

She did let a smile break through, then, however small. "I am relieved."

He chuckled. "I thought ye might be," he said. "There's nothing like an uncertain future tae make everything seem grim."

"That is true."

A silence settled between them, but it wasn't uncomfortable. Simply a silence in the cold night air as the distant sounds of drunken men wafted upon the breeze. Payne listened for a few moments, wondering if those drunk pirates were going to stick to their encampment or wander through the village, but his thoughts soon returned to Astria.

He had a few things on his mind.

"I asked ye once where ye would go if ye escaped," he said. "Ye told me back tae Tarragona. After we marry, do ye want me tae return ye home? Or back tae Lisbon instead?"

She looked at him. "I've not lived in Lisbon for many years," she said. "I was born at Sintra Palace, but it belongs to my nephew now."

"Then ye would return tae Tarragona?"

"You would not take me with you back to Lismore, to Achanduin Castle?"

"Ye've been there?"

She nodded. "Remember that your mother took me back to Lismore Island for quite some time after she first abducted me," she said. "I met your father, in fact. You look like him."

Payne smiled. "I know," he said. "My da was a dear man. I miss him."

Something in her expression changed. "You speak well of him."

"Of course I do," he said. "Do ye not speak well of yer own father?"

Astria shrugged. "I hardly knew him," she said. "I was the youngest of nine children. My father was focused on his heir, or my mother, or his mistresses, or his bastards. He did not have time for a young girl who was studious and would rather write poetry or paint pictures of flowers than tell witty stories for the nobles or sing most beautifully. Moreover, my mother died in childbirth with me. I do not think my father could bear to look at me. A worthless girl, he once called me. He loved my mother and clearly blamed me for her death."

Payne was listening seriously. "I am sorry," he said quietly. "It's not right that he should do that."

"Right or wrong, that is the way I grew up," she said. "I did not have a sister nor a brother who treated me with any regard except Afonso. He did, a little, more than anyone else, but that stopped once he became king."

It sounded like a lonely childhood to Payne. "What about friends or cousins?" he asked. "Surely ye had family and friends around ye."

She shook her head. "Not really," she said. "As a princess, I lived a rather isolated life. I was barely fourteen years of age when I was betrothed to Armand and sixteen years when I married him. I told you that he was more of a father figure. He already had a son, but he wanted more. I never bore a child and he told everyone I was barren, but the truth is that he only touched me once, on our wedding night, and never again after that."

"Yet ye accepted the blame of a childless marriage," Payne said. "That was courageous of ye."

She averted her gaze. "There was nothing else I could do," she said. "I cannot honestly say I've ever had a close friend or relative, or anyone else who cared about my welfare."

"That is a difficult way tae live."

"It is simply the way of things."

"And then a pirate queen abducted ye and ye found yerself in England."

She smiled weakly. "That is true," she said. "And having a conversation with a man I do not know, but one who has shown me more regard in the few hours we've been acquainted than almost anyone in my life. That is why I could not run. That would show ingratitude for what you've done, and I do not wish to be ungrateful."

He matched her smile. "Thank ye for not destroying my trust in ye," he said. "I suspected that ye're a woman of honor, and I see that I was right."

Her smile vanished. "Is that what you think?" she said. "That I am honorable?"

"Ye just proved it by not running away when ye had the chance."

Astria stared at him. Really stared at him. For the first time in her life, she was building some sort of a relationship with someone she didn't even know. *Really* building one. That was the strangest thing about it, because she'd known plenty of people in her life. But, as she had told him, she'd never really, truly had a friend or someone she could count on. The fact that he had called her honorable made her feel sick to her stomach because she wasn't honorable. She knew that.

She couldn't let the man think she was something other than what she was.

"May I ask you something?" she finally said.

He nodded. "Go ahead."

She took a deep breath. "If I asked you to swear upon your oath as a knight not to tell your mother something, would you do it?"

He grew serious. He didn't reply right away, but he sat forward, elbows resting on his knees, rubbing his hands together in thought. He seemed pensive. Finally, his head came up and his eyes met hers.

"If I'm not betraying my family by swearing, I would," he said quietly. "If I'm not betraying my Blackchurch brethren or anything I believe in, I would. Keep that in mind before ye ask me tae swear, but know I willna swear anything unless ye tell me first. Only then can I make that determination."

For the first time, she saw the steely knight in him. The intensity of his gaze, the tightness of his jaw, and his body language told her everything she needed to know. He was so unlike anyone she'd ever met before, and that both intrigued and intimidated her. She'd come this far, however, with her question to him and couldn't back out. If she did, he would know she had a big secret she'd been hiding. And even if she told him and he decided to tell his mother, she couldn't imagine that things would get worse.

But she knew the situation *would* change.

"Very well," she said, trying to be brave. "I will tell you. If you choose to tell your mother, so be it. But if you choose to keep it to yourself, know that you will have my undying trust and loyalty."

"Is it that important tae ye?"

"It is."

"Then speak."

Astria took a deep breath. "I'll start with another question," she said. "What do you know of the different pirate factions who sail the known seas?"

He shook his head faintly. "A little, I suppose," he said. "I know Medusa's Disciples are mostly Scotland and Northern Ireland and Wales, but my mother told me that she captured ye off the coast of Valencia, so apparently now she's over in the Great Sea."

"What else do you know?"

"I know Triton's Hellions because they are linked tae Blackchurch," he said. "I also know the Demons of the Sea because I spent a year with them, serving on board one of their ships."

Her eyes widened. "*You* are a pirate?"

He shook his head. "Nay," he said flatly. "I only did it tae pay off a debt and nothing more. But I also know of the Irish faction, Kraken's Horde."

"Have you ever heard of Titans of the Deep?"

He cocked his head in thought. "I think I heard them mentioned, once," he said. "French pirates, I think. Or from lands further east."

"They are Aragon," she said. "Have you heard of *El dios del mar*?"

"Who is that?"

"The Sea God."

The light of recognition came to his face. "Aye, I've heard that name," he said. "Why do ye ask?"

"Because your mother did not overtake a merchant ship when she took me captive," Astria said quietly. "I had just stolen two ships from my stepson, who had stolen them from me last year right after my husband died. The ducs of Tarragona made their money in merchant shipping, but they also had another line of work—piracy. I only found that out when I married into the family."

Payne was listening intently. "I see," he said. "But… but *ye* stole ships?"

"I did."

"I dunna understand."

She sighed softly, finding it difficult to tell him what she must. "I was The Sea God until my husband died."

Payne's face didn't change expression but he suddenly sat up, staring at her, clearly in disbelief. "What's this?" he demanded. "*Ye* were The Sea God?"

She nodded. "My husband was old when I married him," she said. "It was usual in the San Miguel family that the father should manage the merchant business and the son would become The Sea God, only my husband did not wish to relinquish anything to his son because the man is very greedy and he is very ruthless. Therefore, I assumed the business in my husband's stead and spent nine years keeping it away from Arnaldo, but when his father died, by his hand no less, and he legally became the duc, most of the pirates became loyal to him as my husband's heir. It was tradition. But some continued to serve me because they do not like Arnaldo, and it has been a battle for a solid year for the control of the San Miguel empire."

Payne was shocked. Genuinely shocked. "God's Bones," he muttered. "He killed his father?"

"He did," she said. "I had the proof, but Arnaldo escaped to sea before justice could be served. I was in the process of taking away what he'd killed his father for when Maude found me."

Payne lifted his eyebrows at the dark tale. "Then I suppose it makes sense that ye've fought so hard against captivity," he said. "The punch ye threw intae my eye was well aimed. I would venture tae say ye've had tae do it before."

Astria nodded. "Aye," she said honestly. "But I am not telling you this to boast. I am telling you this because the two ships your mother took from me belong to Arnaldo and he is going to want them back. It is my belief that he is following Medusa's Disciples even now. How many ships does your mother have?"

Payne had to think. "I know of three for certain," he said. "Ships she calls The Three Magi. There are more at Lismore, but I dunna know how many. Why?"

Astria sighed sharply. "Because The Sea God and his Titans of the Deep have thirteen," she said. "They are all heavily armed. If he brings all of them, he will easily destroy your mother and her fleet, and her along with it."

His expression cooled as the reason for her confession became clear. "And ye dinna want me tae tell her this?"

Astria struggled through her answer. "I do not want her to know that I was The Sea God," she said. "The truth is that I should want Arnaldo to destroy your mother and her ships for what she's done to me. But you have saved her, my lord. Your kindness to me has prompted me to show kindness in return. If you can think of a way of warning her without telling her the information came from me, that would be best. Arnaldo is a killer and he will not hesitate to murder her if he can."

She had lain an enormous burden on him with the revelation. Payne pondered the situation without a rather serious expression on his face as Astria sat there and looked at the ground. She was having a difficult time looking him in the eye. He watched her lowered head, wondering if this was some kind of plot to betray him or his mother.

That was his professional training talking.

Part of what he taught at Blackchurch was a class that assessed an enemy by reading body language, the tone of the voice, where the eyes were focused, and other things. That was part of what he did best—read people.

And he was reading her at the moment.

The most important thing that stuck with him was what she had said about withholding the information from Maude—if she hadn't said a word about it and her stepson showed up to obliterate Medusa's Disciples, then that would have been a betrayal. He would have judged her quite harshly for not warning Maude of what she had gotten herself in to. But, instead, she had told him so he could warn his mother. If anything, she seemed embarrassed to tell him, but he knew why she did it. It kept going back to the same thing.

If ye are lying tae me in any way, I'll never trust ye again.

Instead of lying, she had confessed.

He had no reason not to believe her.

"So ye've been battling with yer husband's killer over the San Miguel empire," he said. "And ye think the man has followed ye."

She nodded. "I know he has," she said. "He was chasing us when Maude intercepted me. He must have seen what happened and turned away to fight another day, but I know Arnaldo. He is clever and he will not give up."

"If that is true, then why did he not find ye when Maudie docked at Lismore Island?" he said. "He could have caught up tae her."

Astria shook her head. "There must be hundreds of Scottish islands," she said. "He would have to check every one of them and it would certainly take him longer than a few months, which is as long as we were at Lismore. Or mayhap he ran into trouble or did not make it to Scotland. I do not know. But I do know that he will track Bloody Maude to the ends of the earth, and she had better be ready to fight him if she wants to keep those ships. Mayhap you should help her."

He snorted softly. "My mother doesna need my help."

"She will with this."

A noise from the direction of the tavern caught their attention, and they turned to see Maude emerging from the rear of the establishment, followed by Declan and Francis and a couple of other hardened men. Astria immediately tensed up, but Payne remained calm.

"Have ye come tae join us?" he asked, speaking loudly so they could hear him. "We were watching the falling stars."

Maude glanced up as she approached them. "'Tis a bit cold tae be stargazing," she said. "Tell me what ye're truly doing out here, and no lies. Did the lass try tae run?"

Payne looked at Astria, seeing the stress on her face. "Surprisingly not," he said. "It seems that she canna sleep well, being watched the way she is. We came out here tae breathe in the night air."

Maude let her gaze linger on her son, trying to determine if he was, indeed, lying, but he seemed sincere enough. Her focus shifted to Astria.

"Is that so?" she said. "Well, I'm not surprised. Ye're constantly ready for a fight, so I suppose it must be difficult tae be in a nervous state all the time."

Astria had no idea how this conversation was going to go. She'd just had a rather electric chat with Payne, and he was in possession of some critical information, including the truth that she was actually part of her own pirate faction. She wondered how Maude would react to having captured another pirate queen. Or pirate princess, as it were. Everything was dependent on Payne. Would he betray her?

Would he keep her secret?

Apprehensively, she wondered.

"I find the night peaceful," she said. "Your pirate brethren seem to be enjoying themselves."

Maude looked off to the north, where her men and wagons with cannons were situated in a clearing. "They'll do this all night," she said. "Payne, ye should tell the tavernkeep tae lock his doors. And ye should send word around tae the rest of the villagers tae lock their doors. My men aren't used tae being told they canna have what they want, so the village must take precautions."

Payne looked at her. "They're yer men, Maudie," he said. "If ye command them not tae raid the village, they'll have tae listen."

Maude's gaze was on the fires in the distance. "Ye'd think so," she muttered, but she wouldn't elaborate. Her attention returned to her eldest. "Is there a church in the village?"

Payne nodded. "St. James the Apostle."

"Do they do daily mass?"

"They do," Payne said. "Ye'll hear the bells before dawn,

bells that Blackchurch donated tae them, no less."

Maude turned toward the village. "Then let us make our way tae the church for the Lauds mass."

"Why?"

"Because ye have a wife tae take."

There it was again. The entire reason for Maude's presence at Blackchurch. Payne looked at Astria to see what her reaction was, but all she did was look at him with a neutral expression. She wasn't running. She wasn't crying. Silent resignation was more like it.

There was no use fighting it.

"Will ye walk tae the church without trying tae run away, or do I need tae carry ye?" he asked her.

Astria stood up from the stump she'd been sitting on, smoothing the simple peasant dress she was wearing. "I will walk."

"Good lass," Maude said in approval. "I knew we'd get on well, eventually. Things aren't so bad, are they? My Payne is a good lad. He'll make a good husband."

Astria didn't know what to say to that. It wasn't like she could refuse. She also didn't want to seem agreeable about it, either, because she truly wasn't, but so many things would fall into place once she married the Earl of Lismore, not the least of which was the fact that, as her husband, he would be obligated to protect her from Arnaldo. For the woman who had lived her entire life alone, with few friends or family, the idea of marrying a man who could actually protect her was the greatest lure of all. Perhaps with time he'd even help her wage war on Arnaldo and take control of the Titans of the Deep. She'd be The Sea God once again and they'd have their own seaborne empire.

Whatever the case, she no longer thought marriage was a

terrible idea.

Maria Astria Julia lost something of herself that night, though she wouldn't realize it until much later.

Loneliness.

She was no longer alone.

CHAPTER TEN

Port of Rousse
Guernsey

"SHE TOOK MY goddamn ships and I want them back!"

The nearly shouted statement came from a young man with a good build, a handsome face, and dark, sultry eyes. He was gathered with a collection of men that seemed to run from the well dressed to the positively slovenly, all of them collected outside a seaside tavern in the small port town of Rousse. Overhead, the gulls cried and a sea breeze blew steadily inland, smelling of salt and surf. In front of a sea-bleached tavern called L'egout, which loosely translated to "sewer," the man with the dark eyes seemed to be bellowing at some men across the table.

It was the meeting of two rather volatile groups.

"I understand the situation," said a man who went by the unlikely name of Crusty Appleton. "We've received the message you sent around to other ports. You are looking for Bloody Maude and Medusa's Disciples."

"I am," the dark-eyed man said, slapping his open palm on the table. "She captured two of my ships and also captured my stepmother, who stole the ships from me in the first place. I do not understand these women, thinking they can rule in a man's world. There can only be one Sea God, and that is me!"

He slapped the table again, furious and insulted. Crusty had spent the past twenty minutes speaking to the young and passionate Duc de Tarragona, Arnaldo San Miguel, a man who insisted on being called *your grace*, but the truth was that he was a pirate just like the rest of them. Crusty and his men were from Kraken's Horde, a faction of pirates out of Dublin who mostly controlled the Irish Sea when the Spanish weren't trying to take their territory or the English weren't trying to steal their ships.

It was a delicate dance in the hotly contested sea between England, Wales, and Ireland.

The Irish, however, were more apt to deal with fellow factions. They knew the value of alliance and in doing favors for those who were usually the enemy. That was the reason they had sent word to The Sea God, who had been off the coast of Le Havre, because rather than chase Bloody Maude around, he'd simply put out word that he was willing to pay a reward for information leading to her whereabouts.

And the Irish knew a little something about Bloody Maude.

The old bitch was perpetual thorn in their side.

"Here's a little something you should know," Crusty said as one of his men put a cup of cheap ale in front of him. "Bloody Maude's father was Red Shane Connacht, who was my mother's uncle. Maudie comes home to Ireland now and again, though she's not been in a while. We've seen her in Scotland, but I heard from a Spanish merchant ship recently that they saw her in Bristol Bay."

Arnaldo looked at him in surprise. "Bristol Bay?" he repeated. "What is she doing in Bristol Bay?"

"That'll cost you."

Sighing sharply, Arnaldo threw the man a small purse with gold coins, which Crusty handed off to his men to count. "Tell me," Arnaldo demanded. "Why is she in Bristol Bay?"

Crusty waited until someone counted all the coins and gave him a nod. This was, after all, a business, Satisfied, he continued.

"She had a run-in with Triton's Hellions," he said. "You know that they rule Bristol Bay. No one gets in or out without them knowing. And no one wants to go up against St. Abelard de Bottreaux. Not even Bloody Maude. But she's looking for something, I'm told."

Arnaldo was more confused than he had been since the conversation started. "What is she looking for?" he asked. "The woman has my bloody ships—*that's* what I'm looking for. Did she take my ships into Bristol Bay?"

Crusty shook his head. "This, I cannot tell you," he said. "But the Spaniard told me that she was seen going inland. Her ships are moored in Combwich."

"Where's that?"

"If you travel the south side of the Bristol Channel, you come to a sea town called Burnham," Crusty said. "The mouth of the River Parrett is there. If you travel down the river a mile or two, you'll come to Combwich."

Arnaldo could picture that in his mind a little. He wasn't hugely familiar with the Bristol Channel, so he mostly had to take the Irishman's word for it.

"But why?" he asked. "Why would she do that?"

"Who knows?" Crusty said. "But if they are your ships, then now is the time to go and get them. If she's moored them inland and has traveled somewhere into England, those ships will be lightly guarded. She's probably paid some men to watch them, or left men on board to watch them, but they'd be no match for The Sea God."

Arnaldo's mind was whirling with the possibilities. "I could get them back," he said, excited for the first time since the conversation started. "But it seems incredible to me that they are in Bristol Bay. I followed Bloody Maude's trail to Scotland, but I lost her in those damnable islands to the north. I tried to look for her along the coast of Wales, but the Welsh hate pirates more than the English do. No one would give me information on her, not even for a price."

"Then you are fortunate I will," Crusty said, mirth in his expression. "Also, if it matters to you, the same Spaniard told me that Maude has a prisoner with her that she may ransom. A woman."

Arnaldo stiffened. "And she took the woman inland?"

"I would not know, but it is possible that is where her buyer is," Crusty said. "You might find out if you find her moored vessels."

That didn't seem to please Arnaldo. "Damnable woman," he muttered. "I want my ships back, but I also want her."

"Who?"

"The woman who stole my ships."

"Is that not who we are speaking of?"

Arnaldo shook his head. "Nay," he said. "My father's wife took them from me first. Bloody Maude happened to capture both her and the ships."

"And you want your father's wife returned along with the ships?"

Arnaldo nodded firmly. "Indeed, I do," he said, his dark eyes taking on a dangerous gleam. "I have something particularly interesting planned for the dowager duchess."

Crusty wasn't sure what it was, but he knew it wasn't good. Arnaldo clearly had a vendetta against his stepmother. Family feuds were always the most brutal because blood and emotion were involved, so he didn't ask further questions.

It wasn't his business, anyway.

"My suggestion would be that you go to Bristol Bay, to the River Parrett, and gain access to Combwich," he said. "I've told you all I know. But a word of caution—if you do go, beware of Triton's Hellions. Their home port is close to the mouth of the River Parrett. You do not want to tangle with St. Abelard de Bottreaux, nor do you want to tangle with Santiago and his Sea Demons. They have been known to moor at Fremington, which is along the western Devon coast."

Arnaldo was listening carefully. "Then how do you suggest I get to the River Parrett and not cross their paths?"

"Do you have maps?"

"Of course."

"Bring me a map of England and I'll show you."

Arnaldo sent one of his men on the run back to the *Brizo* and Crusty did, indeed, show him how to get to the mouth of the River Parrett by staying clear of Santiago de Fernandez and St. Abelard de Bottreaux, but it cost Arnaldo another sack of gold coins. For what Astria had cost him so far, he was going to take it out of her hide and then some.

The *Brizo* set sail before dawn.

CHAPTER ELEVEN

T HEY WERE MARRIED.

Walking back to the Black Cock after having just been married at the door leading into St. James' church, Astria could hardly believe they'd done it. They'd actually done it.

She had a husband.

Again.

By the time they reached the Black Cock, Maude and her men headed to the pirate encampment, and that included Payne's brothers. Astria was glad to see them go, or at least Declan, because he had made the entire ceremony awkward. From the moment they'd headed over to St. James' church, Declan had kept up a running commentary on how he felt about the entire situation. The marriage was stupid, in his opinion, and they would have done better had they ransomed their prize. They could have shared the money. That was the general gist of his complaint, and he had made it directly to Maude, who basically ignored him.

That only made him turn his chatter toward the group as a whole.

He spoke to his younger brother about his concerns, which

weren't concerns as much as they were insults toward his oldest brother. When Francis didn't respond, Declan turned to the two other men who had come with them, pirates who had served their grandfather, and whispered his complaints to them. Maude and Payne and Francis could hear the whispers until Maude finally turned around and told Declan to shut his mouth or she would stitch it shut. Given the fact that Maude had done things like that during the course of her pirate career, Declan took the threat seriously. At the very least, he did shut his mouth.

But that set the tone for the mass. It wasn't so much a mass as it was simply a blessing, made at the entry to the small stone Church of St. James, but it was enough for a marriage. The truth was that hardly anyone showed up to mass at St. James as it was, being a remote location, so the priest was more than happy to perform the blessing.

At least it gave the man something to do.

But it all seemed so informal and abrupt to Asteria, whose first marriage had been a gigantic affair. There had been a big mass followed by three days of feasting. It was during the feast that Astria's stepson had first made advances toward her, hoping to seduce his father's young bride, but that was the first of many rejections. Austria had a complicated relationship with Arnaldo, something that continued to this day.

She tried not to think about it.

On the street outside the Black Cock, it was just the two of them now, facing one another after the group departed. Payne smiled weakly when their eyes met.

"I suppose we've got a day of duty ahead of us," he said.

She knew what he meant. The last time she'd done something like that had been on her previous wedding night, so it was a struggle for her to not feel embarrassed or apprehensive.

"I suppose so," she said. "Where will we go?"

He glanced northward, where Blackchurch was located. "I have my own domicile at Blackchurch," he said. "There is a small village where the trainers and their families live and I have a cottage there, but I'm afraid it's not fit for female habitation."

"What does that mean?"

"It means pigs would be comfortable there. Not a lady."

She fought off a grin. "That is where we'll be living, is it not?" she said. "At least for now?"

He nodded. "Aye," he said. "But I'll have tae have someone clean it so that it's fit for a woman. I dunna think ye want tae go there."

"If I am going to live there, then mayhap I should clean it," she said. "I can do it with help. Do you have servants at Blackchurch?"

Payne nodded. "We do," he said. "But we can just as easily clean the cottage later. We can retreat tae yer rented room for now."

She looked at the Black Cock, the wattle-and-daub walls, the vines growing up over the western side of it. It had a rather charming appearance, one she hadn't noticed when she first arrived. That had been a turbulent moment, but not surprisingly, she was seeing things a little differently today.

"It is simply a little room with a little bed," she said. "If we are going to live at your cottage, then why not simply go there?"

"Ye dunna mind?"

"If you find someone to help me clean it, then I do not."

A smile crept over his lips. "As ye wish, m'lady," he said. "Let me get yer things and we'll go tae Blackchurch."

They headed back into the tavern, where they were met by a common room that was just starting to awaken at this hour. There was a good deal of stretching and yawning and farting going on as patrons who'd spent the night in the common room began to rise for the day. Astria's rented chamber was toward the back, so Payne headed into the corridor, entering the room where Margit was still sleeping. The woman hadn't moved a muscle. Payne glanced at Astria, both of them grinning at the sight, before Payne reached out to gently shake Margit awake.

It took the old woman a moment to come around, and when she did, she looked at the pair in surprise. Payne explained that everything was well and that he was only there to collect the possessions that Margit had packed for Astria. Margit lurched to her feet, still yawning, to make sure that Astria knew exactly what was in the small satchel. She pulled out the shifts, the comb, and even shoes. Since the shoes Astria was wearing were rather worn after all of the wear and tear she had brought down on them on her journey over the past five months, she took them off and replaced them with a pair of well-made slippers that had belonged to Margit's daughter. The shoes were a little big, but they would do.

Astria was very grateful.

Payne explained to Margit that they had been married an hour earlier and were returning to live at Blackchurch, something that seemed to please Margit immensely. Marriage always pleased a woman with many daughters, even if this particular daughter wasn't hers. Payne collected the satchel and, with Astria in tow, headed into the common room once again. Margit was right behind them, however, and she insisted they take food with them for their morning meal. Into a woven basket, she put bread that had been baked that morning, stewed fruit, a large chunk of white cheese, pickled onions, and turnips. It was a veritable feast, and Payne was very grateful. He even kissed Margit on the cheek, which both thrilled and embarrassed her.

He and Astria headed off to Blackchurch.

Since Astria had never been to Blackchurch, she wasn't sure what to expect of this nearly mythical place. There was a large main road that led through the village and continued northward, and that was the road they found themselves on. It was lined by heavy trees and, at this time in the morning, the birds were very active. Birdsong rang throughout the air as they walked along the road on this cold but clear morning.

It occurred to Astria that this was the first morning in five months that she hadn't woken up as a captive. So much of the past five months had been full of discomfort and uncertainty and even fear, so as she walked along the road this morning, she felt a good deal of relief.

Relief that her circumstances had become marginally better.

Only time would tell if that sentiment was her permanent one.

The cause of that freedom, of course, was the very big man walking next to her. Payne seemed rather quiet this morning, perhaps for the same reason she was, and that was the fact that they suddenly found themselves married to strangers. What did one say to someone they hardly knew, yet were going to be spending the rest of their life with? Astria remembered from her first marriage that there hadn't been a lot of conversation. Armand liked to speak to his friends and advisors, but not to his wife. Truthfully, it wasn't that they'd had a lot in common or could speak on a great many subjects—although Astria had been quite educated and could therefore converse on many things—but simply the fact that Armand had no real desire to speak to a woman who was young enough to be his granddaughter. That had made their wedding night uncomfortable and awkward.

She rather hoped this wedding night wasn't going to be the same.

The difference, in this case, was the fact that she was marrying a man of the appropriate age and, in fact, found him quite handsome. She was attracted to him, which was a strange sensation because she'd never really had an attraction to anyone in her life. All the time growing up, she had been kept well away from the opposite sex, and until she married her husband, she'd hardly had any interaction with a man outside of members of her own family. That was usual in royal households, but the fact that she found herself married to a stranger who was incredibly handsome had her heart racing. That was the truth of it. Her heart had been racing all morning and she simply thought it was apprehension at the marriage itself.

Now, she realized it was for something else.

That was going to make this day… interesting.

"How long have you lived at Blackchurch?" she asked, breaking the silence between them.

He smiled at her. "Ten years," he said. "Ever since I came here."

"Why did you come?"

He shrugged, glancing down the road as the gatehouse of Blackchurch came into view. "I had an excellent formal education, trained by some of the best in England," he said. "My da wanted that for me, so I was formally trained at Berwick Castle. That's in the north of England, one of those castles that seems tae change hands frequently between the Scots and the

English. In any case, that is where I received my education and earned something of a reputation for myself."

"What *kind* of a reputation?"

"As a skilled warrior, of course," he said, grinning at the way she'd asked that question, as if he'd meant something unsavory. "William the Lion was the King of Scotland at that time, and once my training was complete, I went tae serve the king as a gift from my father."

Astria was listening with interest. "Your father gifted you to his king?"

Payne nodded. "Exactly," he said. "A new, highly trained knight who was also a Highlander was happily accepted in the Scottish court, and I enjoyed my time there. I learned a great deal about people and politics and how the world works. But I wanted more."

"More training?"

"Mayhap," he said, shrugging as the gatehouse loomed closer. "More training, more responsibility. I wanted tae be part of something important."

"And being part of the king's entourage was not important enough?"

"Nay," he said, shaking his head. "I was simply a knight amongst many, men who had served William for many years. I was just one of the group, nothing special. Because I'm big, and powerful, sometimes I felt as if I was just for presentation. So it looked as if the king had big men around him."

Given that Astria grew up in a royal court, she understood the mentality. "How did you find Blackchurch, then?"

He grinned. "Every fighting man knows about Blackchurch," he said. "I decided it was time for me tae become a better warrior. More skilled, with better techniques. So I came and I trained here. I made it through every class they had. In the end, Lord Exmoor offered me a position because they'd just lost the man who taught enemy assessment. Given the time I'd spent in William's court, I was perfect for it."

She looked up at him as they walked. "And that's what you do?" she said. "Teach men how to size up their enemy?"

He nodded. "That is what I do," he said. "I also work with some of the other classes, like hand-tae-hand combat. I also work in the swordsmanship class."

"And you enjoy this?"

"I love it."

They were nearing the gatehouse now. Blackchurch had an enormous perimeter wall around it, one that was nearly three miles if one walked all the way around. It was built from gray granite quarried in Cornwall, a pale gray the color of storm clouds. The wall itself was about fifteen feet high, and this height was consistent around the perimeter. There were only two ways in and out of Blackchurch, with the main gate being the first access point, and then another, smaller gatehouse on the eastern side. Both gatehouses were manned by fifty men at any given time and Blackchurch itself had an army of about a thousand men. Though they were never pulled into any conflicts because of their consistent neutral position, the fact remained that sometimes they did need the might of an army. Out in the wilds of Devon, anything could happen.

As Payne and Astria drew closer, they could see the activity in the two-storied gatehouse. It was morning now and men were going about their rounds as the main gatehouse remained open so business could be conducted with both the kitchens and the castle. Right in the center of Blackchurch was Exmoor Castle, mostly a large, cylindrical keep and a small hall. It used to have its own wall many years ago, but over the years the wall wasn't maintained and, in fact, was dismantled by the current Lord of Exmoor's grandfather. Those stones had gone on to build a stable off to the east, and it was a very big stable. There were actually four different buildings that comprise the stables, which in addition to horses housed cows and goats and several families of cats.

Blackchurch, as a whole, was an enormous operation.

Astria could see that as they drew closer to the open gatehouse. There was no moat and no drawbridge, but the gates that secured the entry were made of iron that was as thick as her torso, welded to an oak door that was about as tall as the walls were. In addition to the reinforced iron gates, there was a portcullis also made of iron. On the whole, Blackchurch was extremely well fortified—and for good reason. It was an enormous empire with precise operations going on at any given time in training classes. Once Austria passed through the gatehouse and got a look at the interior, she could see just how vast Blackchurch was.

"This is *all* Blackchurch?" she said incredulously. "All of it?"

Payne came to a stop, pointing toward a green, sloping expanse of grass and rock that was nearest to them. "All of it," he said. "See that field?"

She could see it, in the near distance. "Aye."

"That is the field of dregs," Payne said, looking at her. "Dregs are the newest recruits and the class they face is a test of stamina and strength. If they dunna pass it, then they're sent home. Once they pass the initial class, they're called recruits, and if a recruit fails a class at any time over his five-year training course here, he's sent home."

The sun was just coming over the eastern horizon and

Astria shielded her eyes from the blinding rays. "Because you do not train men who fail," she said softly.

He shook his head. "Nay," he said. "We dunna train women who fail, either."

"You train women as well?"

"We do."

"*Women* warriors?"

"We train anyone if they pass the initial tests," Payne said. "If ye passed The Leviathan's stamina test, we'd even train ye."

He meant her, personally. There was mirth in his eyes as he spoke. Still shielding her eyes from the sun, Astria looked up at him. "Who is The Leviathan?"

"Tay Munro," Payne said. "He oversees the first class that dregs are part of. If ye can master his class, ye can master anything."

"Why do they call him The Leviathan?"

Payne started to walk again, following a small road away from the gatehouse, heading north. "Because the man is the size of one," he said. "Every trainer at Blackchurch has a moniker, something that defines him. Something that speaks of who he is and what he does."

"Do you have one?"

"I do."

"What is it?"

He winked at her. "The Tempest."

A smile played on her lips. "I'm afraid to ask why they call you that."

He grinned. "Because when I fight, I am a storm," he said. "In battle, I am a violent wind, blowing down all in my path. I am the rain that blinds an enemy, the lightning that destroys him. I am all those things when it comes tae warfare, and

Tempest was the name given tae me by my brethren."

She was still smiling at him. "You must be fearsome, indeed."

He simply nodded because that was a given. He was fearsome, dedicated, and fearless. But not wanting to talk about himself and extoll his battle virtues to the woman he'd just married, because he was sure there were other virtues she might be more interested in, he pointed ahead.

"See the gathering of cottages down there?" he said.

Astria could see what he was indicating—it looked like the main avenue of any village. The road was lined with small cottages, some two-storied, all of them with wattle-and-daub construction. There had to be more than a dozen of them on each side of the road, all of them neatly kept, and then further down the road seemed to be a village center of sorts. She could see even more cottages down there.

"I do," she said. "It looks like a town."

"It is," Payne said. "Or, at least, it used tae be. When one of Lord Exmoor's ancestors expanded Exmoor Castle tae include surrounding lands, he paid the people of the village for their homes and housed his men there. We all have cottages in the village."

She glanced at him. "And you have a filthy cottage that you do not want me to see."

He fought off a smirk. "I am not a maid," he said defensively. "I dunna clean homes."

"Nor do I," she said. "But I will supervise people who do. That is what *I* was trained for."

The comment made him look at her, perhaps hesitantly. "I dunna live grandly," he said. "In fact, no one at Blackchurch does."

"What does that mean?"

"It means I dunna have servants. We do for ourselves."

She eyed him suspiciously. "You are trying to tell me something, aren't you?"

He snorted at the humorous way she said it. "I am trying tae tell ye that I may be able tae find ye a servant or two tae help clean, but that willna be a permanent arrangement," he said. "Ye'll have tae learn tae do for yerself."

She seemed unconcerned. "There are always people willing to work for hire," she said. "I can go back to the Black Cock and hire some of the women there. Five or six should do."

"How big do ye think my cottage is?"

She shrugged. "I would not know," she said. "Is that too few? Do we need more?"

He grunted. "We dunna even need that," he said wryly. "Lass, I dunna know if ye can comprehend our situation, so I'll be plain. I live in a little cottage with four chambers—two upstairs, two downstairs. I've got a kitchen and a hearth for cooking, a table, a bed, and little else. It's not a grand palace, so ye dunna need a servant. Ye'll have tae do for yerself."

Astria didn't reply right away. She was contemplating what he was telling her. The man was an earl, but a new earl, and he evidently lived like a pauper. What he was explaining to her was foreign in concept.

"I grew up in a palace," she said. "When I married Armand, I went to live in *his* fine palace with an army of servants at my disposal. I do not mean to sound stupid, but I have never cooked a meal in my life. I know recipes and how to manage kitchens and stores, but there were servants who were trained as cooks and I supervised them. I might burn the house down if I try to prepare a meal."

He knew she came from nobility and wasn't accustomed to menial tasks or chores, so he took some pity on her. "I can probably find ye a servant tae help with daily tasks," he said. "And some of the trainers have wives who would be happy tae teach ye what they know. Would ye be willing tae learn?"

"Do you expect me to be a beer wife?"

He chuckled. "Nay, but I expect ye tae understand I live simply," he said. "That means ye'll have tae learn how tae manage a home yerself."

"I've never lived simply in my life."

"Ye lived pretty simply as a captive over the past few months."

"That's different," she said. "That is survival."

"True," he said. "But what if I told ye that it would mean something tae me if ye were tae try tae make a nice home for the two of us? I've never had one, ye know. I always thought my wife would make a nice, warm home for me."

She shrugged. "I can try," she said. "I cannot promise I'll be any good at it, but I will try."

"I'm sure ye'll be perfect."

Astria wasn't used to praise or anyone having confidence in her. It made her feel uncomfortable, but also giddy. She couldn't remember ever having been commended in her life— not by her nurse or tutor or even her parents. No one ever had.

But Payne had and he didn't even know her.

They entered the collection of cottages, noting the children playing up ahead on the grassy area that comprised the village center. There was a well there, protected with an iron cage from nosy children or clumsy people. Some young boys were running around and watching them were two women, one with a baby in her arms. As Payne and Astria drew closer, two of the little boys spied Payne and ran at him.

There was a lot of screaming going on as they crashed into the man's legs. Payne groaned loudly, making sure to hand the satchel over to Astria before he plunged to his knees. That only seemed to feed the boys' bloodlust, because they began jumping on him, trying to knock him over.

He went down in a heap.

Gleefully, the children climbed on him, thrilled that they had managed to bring down a grown man. There were two other children playing about, and when they saw Payne lying on the ground, they joined the fun. Payne soon had four boys crawling over him and he lay there, stone-still, until one hit him in the nose.

After that, he was forced to sit up.

"You'd do better to remain down, Payne," one of the women said as she walked over with the other lady. "You know they'll try to choke you now."

As predicted, one of the lads threw his arms around Payne's neck and squeezed. Payne had to move the arms so they wouldn't hit his Adam's apple.

"Ye're raising a pack of wild animals, both of ye," he said. "These ruffians are going tae burn Blackchurch down someday and ye'll be blamed for it."

The women snickered. "I'll only be blamed for two of them," a tall, beautiful woman with dark hair said. "The other two are de Merest children. Gigi and Fox can take credit for their own bad parenting."

"And I only have the baby," the shorter woman with a lovely face and accented speech added. "I will ensure my son does not grow up like a wild animal."

Payne grinned. "'Tis probably true," he said. "Sinclair is an elegant man. Yer son will reflect his father."

"And Tay is not elegant?" the tall woman said, cocking a dark eyebrow. "Be careful of your answer, Payne. Unless you wish to provoke me."

Payne grabbed the nearest boy, who happened to be a son of Fox de Merest. "Tay Munro is a beast of a man, but I'd not have him any other way," he said. "Now, if ye wish tae strike me, go ahead, but ye'll have tae go through my human shield first."

He held the boy out at arm's length in between him and the tall woman, who broke down into soft giggles. That prompted Payne to set the boy on his feet and stand up, but as he did so, he noticed that the women were now focusing on Astria, who was gazing at them somewhat nervously. Dislodging the lad from around his neck, he lifted an arm in Astria's direction.

"I'm sure ye're wondering who this lovely lass is," he said. "Ye'll not believe me when I tell ye."

The women were looking at Astria openly now. "Who, Payne?" the one with the baby in her arms asked.

"My wife."

That brought gasps of shock. "*Wife?*" the same woman said. "When did you take a wife?"

"This morning," Payne said, standing up as the child with his arms around his neck still clung to him. "This is Astria, Lady Matheson. Astria, this is Lady Athdara Munro, wife of The Leviathan, and Lady Elisiana de Reyne, married tae one of my dearest friends, Sinclair. Just the ladies I wished tae see, in fact."

He specifically didn't mention his new title, or any of Astria's titles, because he hadn't told any of his friends yet and he didn't want them to hear it from their wives. Elisiana was the first one to approach Astria. "Welcome, Lady Lismore," she said, smiling. "We had no idea Payne had taken a wife or we would have welcomed you with more fanfare."

Astria smiled in return, though it was hesitant. "It is a pleasure, my lady," she said. "And I am a gift from his mother."

Elisiana's smile faded and she looked for an explanation at Payne, who shook his head. "A tale for later," he said. "For now, Lady Matheson requires yer assistance. I realize ye have children tae tend, but mayhap one of ye could help my wife clean my cottage and mayhap prepare a meal. I've duties tae attend tae this morning, a class that is already waiting for me, so I was hoping tae leave Astria in yer good care."

Elisiana didn't hesitate. "Of course," she said, holding out a hand to Astria. "Come with me, Lady Matheson. I'll put the baby down to sleep and we will go and see how much work Payne's cottage needs."

There was genuine warmth in her eyes. Astria could see it. But she'd just spent five months in captivity with a woman who held her life in her hands, so she was reluctant to follow Elisiana. She was reluctant to deal with any woman right now, no matter how kind. In fact, she didn't really want to be separated from Payne because she was coming to equate him with safety. That was something she very much needed, but she hadn't even realized it until now. She'd spent months pretending she wasn't scared and that her situation didn't matter, but the truth was that she was and it did. Now, she faced separation from the man who'd essentially saved her and was trying to pretend as if that didn't matter, either.

But it was a struggle.

The women must have sensed that. As Elisiana gently took her hand, Athdara came alongside her and smiled encouragingly. "Come, my lady," she said. "You look as if you could use some sustenance. I have fresh bread and butter and porridge for my children, but if you like porridge, you are welcome to have some as well."

They were trying to lead her away, however kindly, but Astria balked. "Please," she said. "I must speak with my... my husband. Please grant me a moment."

With that, she quickly moved away, but she was motioning for Payne to follow her. He did, lowering his head so he'd be closer to her when she began to speak.

"I cannot go with them," she whispered.

He put a gentle hand on her cheek, a gesture meant to comfort. "I promise they are good and kind ladies," he said. "Please dunna fret. I wouldna leave ye with anyone I thought might not be trustworthy."

The touch on her face startled her. Astria had never had anyone touch her so sweetly or gently. It only served to emphasize the cold and unfeeling home she'd grown up in and the cold and unfeeling world she lived in. No comfort, no kindness, no love. She'd told Payne that her captivity with Maude had been about survival.

So had her entire life.

And survival could be a cold mother, indeed.

"I... I simply meant that we have a duty to... to consummate the marriage," she said, stammering over her words. "I was married once. I know how important it is. Should we not get it over with?"

Get it over with.

Payne wasn't sure he liked the way she said that, but he understood why. She was looking at the situation pragmatically, but pragmatism with a hint of fear. He could hear it in her voice. Frankly, that had crossed his mind also, but he didn't think this was a good moment for such a thing because he really did have an entire class waiting for him and he didn't want to do something quick and businesslike and then leave her alone afterward. There was that weakness again in him, the man with empathy who wanted to be kind and gentle to a woman he was increasingly coming to realize hadn't known much of it in her life. Everything over the past eight months had been hell for her, and he didn't want to add to it with a lusty and quick consummation.

He wanted it to mean something.

He was to be married to this woman, this beautiful woman, for the rest of his life, and he didn't want to get off on the wrong foot with her. He'd always hoped his marriage would be a pleasant one and was willing to do what he needed to do to make that happen. This may have been an unexpected union, but he accepted it. He had to.

It would do no good to make either of them miserable.

"We will," he said after a moment. "But I dunna think this is the right time for it. My cottage is not appropriately clean for a woman and I am not so eager tae bed ye that I would do it just anywhere. I want it tae be a moment of discovery and hopefully even pleasure for both of us. Now, if ye disagree, then I'll take ye over tae my cottage at this very moment and get it over with, as ye've said. If it means nothing more tae ye than that, then we'll go ahead with it."

She gazed at him, her expression full of confusion. "But… it is not meant for discovery or pleasure," she said. "Is it? I've been married before and, I assure you, there was no discovery and certainly no pleasure. It was uncomfortable and painful and… What more is there to it?"

He could see the bewilderment, and given she'd married an

old man who had more than likely not taken any time with her, no tenderness or joy, she knew nothing else. She knew a duty and nothing more.

It was his job to show her the possibilities.

"There *is* a good deal more," he muttered. "I am sorry yer husband never showed ye that, but ye have a new husband now and, God willing, yer last. I will show ye what more there is tae it and I promise ye'll like it. And we start by giving the duty the respect it deserves—in a clean bed in our home. But if that's not something that appeals tae ye, just say so. I dunna have tae be kind or gentle about it. I can treat it like a duty if ye wish."

There was something hard in his voice as he spoke. Astria could hear it. His expression suggested that he wanted to be kind and considerate, but something in his eyes was… defensive. As if the man didn't want to be hurt. Truth be told, she didn't want to be hurt, either.

Her guard went down, just a little.

"That is all I know of it," she murmured. "I was not trying to be harsh about it, but truthfully, that is all I know of it. If there is something more to it… I would like to know."

"Are ye at least willing tae trust me?"

"Without question."

She said it with no hesitation at all, which made him feel better about the situation as a whole. Perhaps all wasn't lost. Perhaps she wasn't lost.

Perhaps he could change her opinion after all.

"Then let Athdara and Lisi help ye with the cottage," he said. "I have a class waiting for me, but I'll return tae ye, I promise."

The warmth was back in his tone and it somehow did her heart good to hear it. She hardly knew the man, but she was quickly coming to know him, and she was most definitely learning how he made her feel.

Good.

"As you wish," she said. "I will do all I can to ensure you have a pleasant home to return to."

He gave her lopsided smile. Then he bent over and kissed her on the cheek before turning to Athdara and Elisiana.

"I leave her in yer care, ladies," he said. "I'll return later."

With that, he headed off toward the end of the village, where there was another road and big stables in the distance. Astria watched him go, still feeling that kiss, not even realizing that Athdara and Elisiana had crept up on either side of her, watching him go too.

"Come along, Lady Matheson," Elisiana said, reaching out to take her hand. "We have a big day ahead of us."

Astria let the woman pull her along. Athdara was calling to the boys, who were still running around, falling down and then piling on each other like puppies. But Astria wasn't paying any attention to the children. Her focus, her thoughts, were on the big Scotsman she'd just married, intrigued that he should be so concerned about the consummation of their marriage.

Perhaps that was a good thing.

She was about to have a baptism by fire at the Blackchurch Guild.

CHAPTER TWELVE

"WE'VE DELIVERED THE bride," Declan said, yawning. "Why do we remain? We should be heading back tae Combwich and our vessels. We're not getting rich lingering at this place, are we?"

He had a group of men cheering behind him, the same men who had spent the night in the encampment behind the Black Cock and the same men who had been told not to raid the village. The problem was that there were almost two hundred of them and they outnumbered the villagers, but add the Blackchurch army and they would be decimated. That was the only thing keeping them from giving in to their normal pirate behavior.

Annihilation.

It was a fine line that Maude was walking.

"You stole enough on our way here that ye are amply supplied with food, horses, and anything of value from here tae Combwich," she said loudly. "We'll leave when I say we'll leave."

That was a direct shot at Declan, who had grown impatient. Watching his oldest brother marry that morning, taking the bride he wanted and carrying the title he wanted, had only exacerbated his restlessness. Maude was well aware of it, but she was also quite protective of her eldest son.

Truthfully, the one she was most proud of.

Watching Payne marry that morning had been something of a spiritual experience for Maude. She'd never thought that event would affect her so, but it had. Perhaps it was the fact that Payne was now the Earl of Lismore, the title no longer held by her husband.

It was the passing of the guard, as it were.

But Payne was more than ready for the position, and he was certainly more than qualified. He was everything his brothers weren't, and there were times when Maude regretted not forcing Declan and Francis to foster in England. Declan had been too much of a Highlander and there was too much hatred for England in his heart to effectively learn from English trainers, but Francis, on the other hand, had never wanted to be a warrior in the first place. His chosen vocation would have been as a priest, hence the nickname of Pope Francis. He'd never cared much for warfare, and even now, as a pirate, he didn't do much fighting or killing. He stood back with his mother and let the others do it, only acting if he was called upon. In Maude's mind, Francis was the biggest waste of talent because he could have been a good priest, but his father would have disowned him had he tried.

Somehow, being a pirate was better than being a priest.

Now, the wedding was over, Payne was the new earl with a new bride, and there really wasn't any reason for Maude and her men to remain at Blackchurch. Even Declan knew that. But Maude wasn't so eager to depart, mostly because she wanted to spend a little more time with Payne, whom she hadn't seen in ten years. Seeing him again had awakened that part of her heart that belonged only to him, only to the first child she'd given birth to and held in her arms as her very own. One would have thought that over the years, her vocation would have hardened her heart, but that wasn't the case. She still had a heart, and most especially for her children, but she was hesitant to tell Declan why she wanted to remain. Given the fact that he resented his brother so much, she knew it would be a constant battle with him.

"We're men of the sea, Maudie," Declan said, breaking into her train of thought. "Look around ye—no one wants tae stay in this cursed place. If we wanted tae live on land, we'd be farmers."

The men laughed and Maude smiled, pretending to be in on the joke or, at the very least, agree with them. But she also knew she had to placate men who constantly needed to have their purses fed. That was simply the nature of what they did and a potentially dangerous nature at that, so she had to play along. She had to walk that line between command and camaraderie.

"I want tae spend a day or two here tae ensure the new earl and his wife are settling in," she said. "Payne wasna expecting any of this and I dunna want tae see discord between them, so we will remain a few days. Meanwhile, so ye'll not grow too restless, ye can head west and find a village over in that direction that may have something tae yer liking. I only agreed not tae raid this village. I dinna agree not tae raid others."

A collective roar of approval went up from the men, who turned for their tents, intending on preparing for a short jaunt to the west. Declan went with them, encouraging their excitement, but Francis remained with his mother. The two of them watched the men filter back into the encampment, feeding off the electric atmosphere.

"Francis," Maude said, "what if I were tae order Declan tae take the men back tae the ships and wait for me? Would that stop this impatience they seem tae have about remaining here for any length of time?"

Francis looked at her. "If ye send Declan with them, ye'll never see yer ships again," he said quietly. "The men love ye, Maudie, but they love Declan, too. He's a man. They understand him. And he's the exact image of Red Shane Connacht."

She sighed faintly. "Then I'll lose control if I give Declan that chance."

"I think so."

Maude pondered that for a moment. "He feels that he's lost the Lismore earldom," she murmured. "It was never his tae begin with, but I know that's how he feels. He's looking for something tae call his own."

"He wants Medusa's Disciples."

She knew that. She's known it for a while now. After a pause of contemplation, she looked at Francis. "And ye?" she said. "What do *ye* want?"

Francis put his arm around her shoulders. "I want tae make sure ye're safe," he said. "Why do ye think I stay?"

"Why?"

"Tae ensure Declan doesna move against ye," he said. "I'll kill him if he tries, Maudie. I swear it."

She smiled faintly, patting him on the cheek. "Ye're a good lad," she said. "But dunna worry about me. I can take care of Declan."

"How?"

She turned her gaze back toward the encampment and the activity of it. "I brought Declan intae the world," she muttered.

"And I can take him out of it."

Francis shook his head. "And ye'd mourn him the rest of yer days," he said. "Nay, Maudie. Let me protect ye from Declan as long as there's breath in my body. Ye dunna need tae shoulder the burden of killing yer own son."

"And ye dunna need the burden of killing yer own brother."

"Better him dead than ye."

Maude smiled sadly, patting his cheek. "He's got too much of his grandfather in him," she said. "He has a wild and ambitious spirit that takes precedence over everything. Even family."

Francis knew his brother well. "He's greedy," he said simply. "He'd be happy tae be the only son ye had. He wants everything."

Maude nodded in resignation. "I know," she said. "And ye'd better warn Payne about him. Declan has a particular hatred for the man who has everything he wants."

"I already have."

Maude looked at him, seeing shades of Payne in that face. Francis had the makings of an excellent warrior, had he chosen to pursue it. He was strong and talented and had a good moral compass in spite of the profession he found himself in.

She found herself in a rare weak moment.

"Francis," she said hoarsely, "if anything happens tae me, run tae Payne. Dunna stay with this bunch. They'll turn on ye. Go tae Payne and stay with him. I must know ye'll be safe."

Francis kissed her on the forehead to allay her fears, but that wasn't good enough. She wanted an agreement. He nodded, reluctantly, and Maude was comforted. There was a storm brewing with Declan. They could both feel it.

Maude most of all.

Something terrible was on the horizon.

CHAPTER THIRTEEN

"I WANT THAT… that *woman* off my lands."

St. Denis was speaking to St. Sebastian and Amir, the latter two having gone into the village during the night to do some reconnaissance on the pirate encampment.

St. Denis didn't like what he was hearing.

"This is not a simple situation," St. Sebastian said. "Payne tells us they mean us no harm, so we cannot order them away if they behave themselves. For Payne's sake, there must be some measure of trust."

"Trust?" St. Denis said, incredulous. "We are speaking of pirates. There *is* no trust."

He looked at Amir, silently asking the man to speak, and Amir took the hint.

"Then if there is no trust, there should at least be a measure of respect for the fact that they are not tearing up the countryside," Amir said. "You do not have to trust or even like your adversaries, but you must respect them for their strength. You must respect good behavior. If you order them away when they've done nothing wrong, then that is as good as attacking them. They'll look at it that way."

St. Denis hated it when his advisors were right. Unfortunately, he simply wasn't comfortable with pirates on his doorstep. It wasn't a matter of defense, because Blackchurch could defend itself quite ably. It was simply a matter of his personal preference. That was the truth. He already had his cousin who was a pirate, and he wasn't quite sure what St. Abelard would think if he found out his loyal cousin had allowed a rival pirate faction to camp upon his lands and, quite truthfully, he was hoping the man never found out. St. Abelard had a habit of showing up at Blackchurch from time to time, unannounced, so he hoped his cousin was far to sea these days.

He didn't want his cousin to think he was betraying him.

But even he knew it was a complicated situation. They were dealing with the parent of Blackchurch trainer, and at Blackchurch, the trainers were family. That was the truth of it. St. Denis viewed all of his trainers as relatives and treated them as such. That was what made this situation with Payne so difficult. There was the added complication that if he were to order the pirates away, he would offend someone he valued greatly, and he had no desire to do that.

It was a difficult situation all around.

"Then if they are going to remain, I want to know for how long," St. Denis finally said. "Find Payne and ask him how long his mother and her band of thieves intend to remain, because this is not an ideal situation."

St. Sebastian nodded patiently. "I know," he said. "I will find Payne and ask him."

St. Denis shook a finger at him. "I work hard to ensure the forests around Blackchurch are free of any criminal element."

"I *know*."

"And now we've allowed pirates to camp there?"

Amir spoke up. "You do realize there is an opportunity here."

St. Denis looked at him. "What opportunity?"

Amir looked at him as if he had missed the obvious. "You have allowed Bloody Maude to camp on your lands," he said. "You have allowed her access to her eldest son and you have shown hospitality. Even the pirates have a code of honor—they will be indebted to you for this kindness."

St. Denis hadn't thought of it that way. "Do you think so?"

Amir nodded. "I do," he said. "Mayhap in return, Bloody Maude will leave our coast alone. Mayhap she will leave Triton's Hellions alone. Your kindness could spare Abelard, and that is how you should address it should he ever ask why you allowed the pirate queen on your lands. Tell him that you did it for him."

That changed St. Denis' attitude quite a bit. He was still unhappy, but he liked the thought of his hospitality making him, and his men, immune to Bloody Maude's raids. Perhaps it would even make his cousin immune, as Amir had suggested. In any case, he was less likely to order the woman away now, because Amir made sense. But he jabbed a finger at St. Sebastian anyway.

"Very well," he said. "I will continue to show hospitality. But *you* discover when she is leaving. She cannot stay indefinitely."

St. Sebastian nodded, glancing at Amir as he did so. The man's expression suggested that the crisis was averted—for now. But St. Denis had a way of changing his mind at times, and they all knew it.

With a final nod at his father, St. Sebastian quit Exmoor's keep in search of the new Earl of Lismore.

CHAPTER FOURTEEN

"How WAS LAST evening? Rough?"

The question came from Sinclair as Payne made his way onto the field as the sun began to rise. Today, he was scheduled for swordplay with Sinclair's class because his own class was transitioning into Ming Tang's teachings and they were with him this morning. That freed Payne up to assist Sinclair, who was the master swordsman of Blackchurch. Assisting one another in their respective classes was usual for the trainers, helping to cross-train every warrior who came onto their fields.

Not strangely, Payne wasn't feeling much like training this morning.

Sinclair's question made him grin.

"The whole damnable day was rough," he admitted. "Though I've not seen any of my family in ten years, no one has changed a bit. Not my mother, not my younger brother, and certainly not my middle brother. Not him."

"What is wrong with your middle brother?"

Payne snorted softly. "Declan is his name," he said. "He's still the same idiot, but a dangerous idiot."

Sinclair chuckled. "You do not get on with him, then."

Payne shrugged. "I would if he were any less of a greedy bastard," he said. "But Declan has always wanted what I have. And it hasna changed."

"What does he want now?"

"Everything," Payne said. "My title, my lands, my money. Everything I've rightfully inherited from my da."

Sinclair shook his head. "What title?"

Payne smiled weakly. "I've not spoken tae anyone but St. Denis and Creston and Cruz since meeting my mother on the road yesterday," he said. "I forgot that I've not even spoken tae ye about what's happened."

Sinclair shrugged. "We figured you'd tell us when you were ready," he said. "You know we were watching from the woods yesterday when you met up with the pirates."

Payne laughed softly. "So I was told."

"We saw a small figure hit you."

Payne pointed to his purplish left eye. "That?" he said, laughing. "A love tap."

"Quite a tap, I'd say."

Payne couldn't disagree. "True," he said. "What's happened is this—my father died recently and my mother came tae tell me that I'm now the Earl of Lismore. The person ye saw hit me yesterday was, in fact, my bride."

Sinclair's eyes widened. "Your *bride*?"

Payne nodded. "Aye," he said. "Ye'll not believe this, but she's a daughter of King Sancho of Portugal. My mother captured her off the coast of Aragon, and when my father died, she decided that I needed a princess for a wife. I married her this morning."

The second bit of stunning news in as many minutes. Sinclair was astonished. "A royal bride?" he said. "Payne, that's astonishing. And you… now you're the Earl of Lismore?"

"So it seems," Payne said. "Quite honestly, I'm still overwhelmed by it all. That was not what I was expecting yesterday when my mother came tae call. But that is what has happened and I have much tae think about now. A future tae plan."

Before Sinclair could reply, Fox and Kristian made an appearance. They came to help with the swordplay class, like Payne had, and Sinclair blurted out all that Payne had told him before Payne could even get it out of his mouth. He watched Fox and Kristian's expressions when they realized the big Scotsman in their midst was not only an earl, but had taken a royal wife. Kristian grabbed him by the arm.

"A princess for a wife?" he gasped. "*You?* But you always swore to me that you would not marry until you were too old to stand!"

Payne snorted. "I know."

"You told me you would have several wives because you would need all of them keep you warm in bed!"

"If she does her job right, one will be enough."

Kristian started laughing, as did Sinclair, but Fox remained stoic. He was the serious one out of the group, a man who had grown up in a royal household and had been a royal knight before he came to Blackchurch. He didn't seem at all jovial about the situation. In fact, he seemed quite concerned.

"Let me understand these facts as they have been presented," he said. "The woman you married is a Portuguese princess who was a captive of Bloody Maude?"

Payne nodded. "She was."

Fox put a hand on his belly, looking sick. "And you did not marry her with royal approval?"

Payne shook his head. "Her father is dead and her nephew currently sits on the throne," he said, suspecting what Fox was leading up to. "Fox, ye worry too much. She's not close tae her family. In fact, she was married tae the Duc de Tarragona until last year when he passed away. Ye may as well all know the truth of it, something my mother doesna know, so please dunna share this with anyone other than our group. It seems that the Duc de Tarragona was not only involved in legitimate trade, but also had a fleet of pirate ships. His legitimate ships would deliver goods and then the pirate ships would sweep in after the delivery was made and steal it. At least, that is how it was explained tae me. It seems that Astria—my wife—was involved with the pirates as well as the legitimate business. She's a fiery woman, fearless in manner. Tae answer yer question, Fox, she has no relationship with the royal family that she has told me of. According tae her, she is quite on her own."

That didn't seem to ease Fox much. He still looked concerned. "Marrying a woman of royal blood by force will see you executed," he said seriously. "I do not want that to happen to you."

Payne shook his head. "Please dunna worry over me," he said. "I know ye're only thinking of my life, but the situation is far more complex. I've only given ye the main facts of the matter and I'll tell ye more when we have the time, but for now, that is the situation. Denis and Sebastian are fully informed. I intend tae stay here and continue my duties, but at some point, I will need tae return tae Scotland and see tae my lands."

There didn't seem much more to say, especially since they had a class facing them. But Sinclair had something more to speak on and wanted to make sure Fox and Kristian knew.

"There's something else you should know and it does not

seem as if Payne is going to tell you," he said. "Evidently, he has a brother serving with Bloody Maude who covets Payne's titles. We must be cautious of any Matheson brother who comes around, looking for Payne."

Payne knew they were only watching out for him and he appreciated it. Was he truly concerned about Declan? Probably not, but he also hadn't seen his brother in ten years. He didn't know just how ruthless the man had become, so vigilance wasn't a wasted effort when it came to Declan. But he'd rather wished Sinclair hadn't said anything, because it made him feel as if he couldn't handle Declan on his own.

And he'd always been able to handle him.

"Speaking of being cautious," he said, pointing to the assistant who was warming up the class. "Have ye noticed that Anteaus is as good as ye are with a sword, Sin?"

He was changing the focus deliberately, and the three men glanced over at Anteaus de Bourne, an assistant trainer from a very fine northern family who was, indeed, as good as Sinclair was with a sword.

Almost, anyway.

"Of course I have," Sinclair said. "And do not change the subject. I am concerned that your brother covets your title and property. He is a pirate, Payne."

"I know."

"Killing and stealing is his vocation."

Payne put a hand on the man's shoulder. "I am well aware," he said, giving him a pat. "I love ye for worrying over me, Sin, but it is unnecessary. Declan will keep his distance. Soon, he'll be back out tae sea and I'll probably never see him again."

"He's your brother," Sinclair said. "Of course you're going to see him again."

Payne shook his head. "*Ye're* my brother," he said quietly, a twinkle in his eye. "Ye are, and Fox and Kristian and the rest are. Ye're all my brothers. Declan and I may be related by blood, but that's all. That's where it stops."

Sinclair nodded, a smile playing on his lips as he turned his attention back to the recruits. "I'm sorry that your brother is in blood only," he said. "But you have the rest of us, and we make a loyal bunch."

"Ye do," Payne said, removing his hand from the man's shoulder. "Speaking of loyalty, ye have a class tae teach and I have a wife tae return tae, so let's get on with it."

They did. Payne was about to collect a sword from the collection Anteaus had brought out, but he was distracted by someone calling his name. As Sinclair and Fox and Kristian went to start the class, Payne found himself being summoned by St. Sebastian, who was waving an arm at him.

Payne went to meet him.

"Good," St. Sebastian said. "I wanted to catch you before you started with your tasks. Do you have a moment to speak, Payne?"

Payne nodded. "Of course," he said. "How may I be of service?"

St. Sebastian seemed to grow uncomfortable. "I come with a message from my father," he said. "Not me, mind you, but my father."

"What's the message?"

"He wants to know when your mother is leaving."

Payne had been expecting a message of that sort, just not so soon. He could see that St. Sebastian, a truly likable man, was uneasy asking it. He held up a hand to relax the man's nerves.

"Very soon, I'm sure," he said. "I married the Portuguese

princess this morning and that was the only reason my mother came tae Blackchurch, so I'm certain she'll leave immediately. Tell yer father not tae worry."

St. Sebastian looked surprised. "You *married* her?" he said. "My God, Payne, that was very fast… wasn't it?"

Payne couldn't disagree. "It was," he said. "But it is done and Bloody Maude has no more reason tae remain here, so I'll make sure she leaves."

St. Sebastian nodded, but he eyed Payne hesitantly. "Are congratulations in order?" he said. "I do not wish to congratulate you on something that is not to your liking."

Payne gave him a lopsided smile. "Dunna worry yerself," he said. "I'll take yer congratulations and be grateful for it. I suppose time will tell if this is tae my liking or not, but for now, let's simply say that I'm not unhappy."

"Good," St. Sebastian said. "And I mean that sincerely. You are well liked, Payne. No one wants you to be unhappy in this mess of your mother's doing."

Payne chuckled. "It is not quite a mess—yet," he said. "Ask me again in a week and we'll see what I say."

"I hope it does not come to that."

"As do I."

Several feet away, the swordplay exercise was beginning and the sound of metal against metal rang out. St. Sebastian waved Payne off, heading back the way he had come with a message for his father. Payne returned to the swords and, selecting one, headed over to the group.

Though Payne and Fox and Kristian were fully fledged trainers, they took a secondary role in the instruction, since it was Sinclair's class. They were there to show techniques and to let the recruits test what they were learning, and that went on most of the afternoon. Only when the sun began to wane did Sinclair dismiss the recruits, who headed off to the large dormitory on the east side of the Blackchurch property.

The trainers headed home.

Payne couldn't help but feel some anticipation for the night ahead. It was natural that he did. But he was trying very hard not to feel excitement, mostly because he didn't want to be disappointed. He had no idea how this was all going to go, so he kept his expectations low. Astria looked at this moment between them as a duty, so he would too.

Or at least try to.

It was growing dark by the time he entered the village. He could see Fox far up ahead, entering his cottage where his wife and children were waiting. He'd lost track of Sinclair, but surely the man was already home by now. He caught sight of his own cottage, near the edge of the village, the windows in the front facing west. None of the cottages had precious glass in the windows, only shutters, which could be closed against the night. As he approached his home, he could see light emitting from the closed shutters.

I always thought my wife would make a nice, warm home for me.

He paused before opening the door, feeling stupid that he'd even said that to her. Somehow, it made him feel vulnerable because if she didn't want the same thing, or was incapable of creating the same thing, then he was in for a big disappointment. It had been a nice dream, anyway.

Taking a deep breath for courage, he opened the door and stepped in.

℟

IT HAD BEEN a hell of a day.

Asteria felt as if *she'd* been a trainer today, teaching an exhausting class much like her husband was, because that was how weary she felt. Weary down to her very bones.

It hadn't been easy.

For someone who had been trained as a chatelaine, and every noblewoman was, the knowledge she had was mostly theoretical. A princess of the royal house of Portugal was not expected to scrub floors or know how to prepare a meal or even wash linens herself. The theory was that she knew *how* those things were done so she could direct the servants. She knew how to manage a household budget, what were appropriate cleaning products, how puddings were made, how livestock should be housed, and things of that nature. Therefore, she wasn't a complete novice when it came to a household. But she was, indeed, a novice when it came to actually applying that theory.

That was where the exhaustion came in.

Her new friends, Athdara and Elisiana, had left their children with another Blackchurch wife, a lovely and very pregnant woman named Gisele. With Gisele managing the pack of wild animals, as Payne had called them, Athdara and Elisiana were freed up to help Astria with Payne's cottage, from top to bottom.

And what a cottage it was.

It was unfortunate that he hadn't been kidding when he had told Astria how slovenly his cottage was. It was actually quite depressing. The three women stood in the open doorway, looking over the large common room that faced the town square, and attached to that was a chamber used for a kitchen. There was a big hearth and a table and nothing else. The whole thing looked as if it had been abandoned for years, as if nobody lived there, because there wasn't a scrap of food or rubbish, or any other signs that the place was inhabited.

Until one went upstairs.

Upstairs, there were two large bedchambers and then a small alcove that was supposed to be used for storage or bathing. One chamber had nothing in it, and the small alcove had a couple of big trunks with clothing and shoes along with various weapons that were clearly carefully tended. The chamber was an armory more than anything. The largest room, which faced away from the street, had a mattress that was stuffed with grass that Athdara speculated must have come from the last century. The mattress itself was made of canvas, which was stained and dirty, and there was just a single blanket to indicate that someone was actually sleeping there.

Once the women finished their sweep of the cottage, they at least knew where to start. Athdara suggested they begin in the living chamber downstairs and then move to the kitchen before doing the floor above. As the women gathered their cleaning instruments of choice, Athdara summoned a servant by using a bell that all of the cottages possessed. The big iron bells were attached to the rear of the homes and, when rung, summoned servants from the neighboring outbuildings.

Across the road from the village were the facilities that helped keep Blackchurch running smoothly, including a laundry, kitchens, a large dining hall, and the stables. When the iron bell at the rear of Payne's home was rung, a servant appeared within a few minutes and Athdara directed the man to bring a wagonload of fresh hay for the mattress.

Fresh stuffing in the works, Athdara summoned a second servant, this time from the laundry, and sent the woman on a mission to hunt down bed linens. Since Blackchurch housed a good many people, bed linens were in supply, and they were excellent quality. Athdara also had the woman send for any unused or old kitchen implements that might be available in the large Blackchurch kitchens. She was hoping for a few pots and perhaps bowls and even spoons if they were available, anything to help stock a kitchen that was completely empty, but as she told Astria, she would have to take what she could get until they could go to the merchant's stall in Tiverton, to a man who bought and sold household goods, and purchase what they needed.

After that, the real education for Astria began.

Watered ale mixed with ashes, vinegar, and two bars of precious soap from Castile had been brought over from a neighboring cottage along with buckets of hot water, scrub brushes, and a mop made out of water reeds collected from Lake Cocytus. As Athdara cleaned out the hearth, Elisiana took the hot water and vinegar and started scrubbing the floor of the front chamber. Astria was directed to scrub the kitchen floor and table with the watered ale mixed with ashes, and she showed confidence in doing so until it actually came to scrubbing. She had to watch Elisiana and Athdara first to see how they were doing things, and even then it took a few tries before she became comfortable with it.

The scrubbing went on all morning.

Around the nooning hour, the ladies paused to rest and share some food that one of the servants had brought. The same servant had been the one who scoured the main kitchens for anything that Astria might use to set up housekeeping. She brought back three iron pots of different sizes, two fire pokers, spoons of various sizes, four wooden cups, and six wooden bowls of different shapes and in various stages of wear.

It was enough to get started.

The servant also brought knives, four of them in total. To help start the stores for the new earl and his wife, she brought various raw ingredients from the kitchens, including flour, salt, dried carrots and beans, fresh onions, butter, milk, and about a dozen eggs. Asteria was overwhelmed with gratitude, of course, but forced to admit that she'd never done any cooking in her life. Her new friends were happy to help, explaining how bread should be made and reminding her that some portion of the dough from the previous day should be held out and used in the next day's bread so the dough would rise.

It was a great change for Astria to be the one supervised as she mixed warmed water and flour and salt, and some ferment- ed dough from Athdara's kitchen, into a bowl. After setting it aside and covering it up with a cloth, she was instructed to bake it in one of the iron pots about an hour before she intended to serve Payne his supper—and she had no idea what she even intended to feed the man. Athdara suggested that she bake eggs, which were easy, and showed her how to do it. Beaten eggs with onion and salt placed in one of the iron pots and then baked in the hearth along with the bread would make a good supper.

Astria certainly hoped so.

Eventually, the ground floor was completely scrubbed from top to bottom by three very diligent women. The hearth in the large common room was lit, as was the hearth in the kitchen. With those fires going and warming up the bricks to make everything nice and cozy, the women turned their attention to the floor above.

They actually had a good time hauling out the mattress and removing the stuffing. Elisiana was a hard worker, and most enthusiastic about it, and she ended up sneezing her head off with all of the old grass and dust flying around in the air. Once everything was out of the mattress, they hung it up on the branch of a tree nearby and beat it with another branch to get rid of the dirt and the dust. After that was done, they were able to stuff it with the hay that had been brought over from the stables. But the fact remained that even though they had a mattress that was nicely stuffed, there were no linens on it and there was no bed frame.

That was when the ladies became resourceful.

Because the village at Blackchurch had once been a thriving hamlet where people had lived, there was a repository of old furniture in one of the outbuildings by the stables. The three of them headed over to that building, which had been picked over in years past, so there wasn't a lot to go through. Still, considering Payne had nothing at all, they were able to collect some of the items and put them to good use.

The mattress Payne had was rather large because, being a large man, he liked a big bed. There wasn't much they could do with that because there was no bed frame, rope or otherwise, big enough to hold the mattress, but they did come away with three chairs, a wooden bench, a very small table, and two stools. All of that was lugged backed to the cottage and distributed in the chambers.

Already, it was looking more like a home.

The last items were the bed linens brought over from the laundry. They were clean and smelled of the wild mint that grew around the cottages. Astria stood aside and watched as Athdara and Elisiana expertly put the linens on the bed, including a heavy coverlet that had come from Elisiana's own possessions.

And with that, the cottage was clean.

To Astria, all seemed so strange. It was a world away from her months in captivity, and her activity on the sea, and her life as a duchess in a palace that was filled with servants. She had come to the duc's palace as a stranger, and the truth was that living there all of those years had been a lesson in solitude. She was the lonely girl who'd never really realized she was lonely. It was simply the way of things. But in just a day, engaging in simple activities with women who were more than happy to teach her what they knew, she felt like she was on another planet. She wondered how things could be so very different from what she was used to, but the truth was that she had never spent a more enjoyable day in her life.

She was quite overwhelmed by it.

"Now," Athdara said, wiping her hands off on her apron. "Do not forget to check your bread dough. It should have risen a great deal in the past few hours, so you'll want to put that in a pot, put the lid on it, and let it bake until it has risen and is browned. Would you like for me to stay and show you how?"

Astria shook her head. "Nay, but I thank you," she said. "I have already taken you away from your children for the entire day and do not wish to take any more of your valuable time. I cannot tell you how much I have appreciated your help, however. You must have been born doing such things, because you do them so well."

Athdara grinned. "I was not," she said. "I was born a duke's daughter in a fine house. I had to learn all of this, much as you are learning it."

Astria smiled. "You are an excellent teacher," she said, looking at Elisiana. "Both of you are. Now, if you will tell me where I can draw water, I will try to do the rest of this on my own."

"You will do very well," Elisiana said. "If you need help, we are right down the road. I have yellow flowers in front of my house and Athdara has rocks. Lots of rocks."

Astria nodded gratefully. "You are so kind," she said "I... I did not expect to find such kindness here. I thought it was all men and warriors."

Athdara and Elisiana laughed softly. "It is, mostly," Elisiana said. "The women are outnumbered, so we are very glad you are here."

"Thank you."

A silence settled, but it wasn't uncomfortable. It was simply time for Athdara and Elisiana to depart and leave the newly minted wife to her duties. The sun was at such an angle that the cottage was starting to darken, so the last thing they did together was light tapers in the kitchen, fat tapers that had been brought over when the servant delivered the kitchen imple-ments. When Athdara and Elisiana finally departed, Astria felt a little intimidated. Here she was, alone in her new home, and expected to be a proper wife. She wasn't sure she knew how, but she would learn.

She found that she very much wanted to.

The afternoon started to wane and Astria went about bak-ing the eggs and the bread, watching both nervously and checking often to see how they were progressing. She didn't really know what she was looking for other than for the bread to be brown and the eggs to not be liquid. From her chatelaine training, that much she knew.

There were other things she knew.

Pulling herself away from the hearth where things were cooking, she went out the back door. Behind the cottages were gardens, cluttered ones, with wood or discarded items that probably belonged in the repository. There were also trees, small ones, and she went to the nearest one to strip off some of the lower branches with their leaves. When she had an arm full of them, she went back into the cottage and spread the rushes out in front of the hearth in the larger common room, but also under the table to catch crumbs and other rubbish falling from the table. That was customary. The green leaves also gave the cottage a fresh smell, something she inhaled deeply.

It was comforting. In fact, the clean cottage and the baking bread were both comforting. Payne had mentioned his wife making a warm home for him, and she hoped that this was what he'd meant. It was true that this was an unexpected marriage, but now that she was entrenched in it, she wanted to do it the best way she could. The way Payne wanted it.

When he came through the entry door a short time later, the expression on his face told her that, indeed, it was the way he wanted it.

And that was a surprisingly good feeling.

"Well?" she said. "What do you think? Is it clean enough for you?"

Payne was looking around the room, his jaw slack with surprise. "*Ye* did this?" he said in awe.

Astria nodded. "I did, but I wasn't alone," she said. "Your friends Lady Munro and Lady de Reyne are the ones to thank. They worked very hard for this. I just did as they instructed. Are you pleased?"

Payne was looking at the two chairs facing the blazing hearth in the large sitting room. "My God," he breathed. "Am I pleased? It is more than I had imagined. Are *ye* pleased?"

Astria looked around at the room that smelled faintly of vinegar and rushes. "I think we did a good job of it," she said.

"It looks much better than it did."

He nodded firmly. "I would agree with that," he said. Then he turned to her, grasped her by the arms, and planted a kiss right on her lips. "Well done, lass. I'm proud of ye."

Astria was shocked by the kiss, overwhelmed by the kind words. *I'm proud of ye.* Over something like this? A clean house? It seemed so trivial.

… wasn't it?

Dumbfounded by his reaction, she stood there with her tongue tied, unable to respond as he went over to the chairs in front of the hearth and inspected them.

"Where did ye find these?" he asked.

Astria cleared her throat and found her tongue. "In the outbuilding that has old things in it," she said. "Lady Munro told me that this little village used to be an actual village, with people and businesses, but Blackchurch purchased it, so old furniture and things were cleaned out and put into a store-house."

He nodded, lifting up the chair and looking at the sturdiness of the legs. "A very long time ago," he said. "But these seem steady enough."

Astria pointed into the kitchen. "We found other things, too," she said. "Enough to start a home with, anyway, but there are a few things we may need to purchase."

"Like what?"

"A bed frame," she said. "Unless you intend that we should sleep on the floor."

He set the chair down. "Nay," he said. "It doesna matter much tae me, but I dunna want ye on the floor with the cold drafts. There's a wheelwright in Exebridge who can probably build us a proper bed."

"Speaking of bed," she said, pointing toward the stairs, "we cleaned yours and put clean linens on it."

He grinned. "Good," he said. "It needed it."

"Aye, it did."

She didn't hesitate in answering, and he snorted. "Ye agreed with me too quickly," he said. "Ye could at least be… What's that smell?"

He suddenly started sniffing the air. Astria sniffed, too, realizing it smelled like smoke. With a gasp, she ran into the kitchen and tried to grab one of the pots off the coals, but she nearly burned her hand. Payne was right behind her, using the bottom of his tunic as a barrier against the hot handle of the iron pot. He swung it onto the table and went in for the second pot as well. With both of them on the table, Astria used a spoon to remove both tops, trying not to burn herself again.

What she saw distressed her.

"Oh… no," she said sadly. "It is burned, all of it."

Payne was peering into the red-hot pots. "Nay, it's not," he said, trying to be positive. "Look—what's this? 'Tis not burned in the middle. I can simply eat the middle."

To prove his point, he grabbed one of the spoons on the table and dug into the eggs, which were cooked very hard. The bottom and sides were burned. But he took a big bite of the mostly undamaged middle.

"Delicious," he said. "Did ye make this yerself?"

"Nay," she said, now pouting because her efforts had gone up in ash. "Lady Munro did, but I watched her do it."

"I'd wager that ye can do it yerself and do it better."

"Probably not," she said, sighing in despair. "I told you that I am not a cook. I am not anything useful when it comes to a house."

"That is not true," he said, digging a hand into the other pot, which contained the *very* brown bread. He tore off a hunk from the middle, hissing when it burned his fingers.

"Look—the bread is fine," he said. "We can eat it. I am certain it is delicious."

He began shoving it into his mouth as if it were the greatest thing he'd ever eaten. Astria watched in fascination as he continued to pull out more hunks of bread, some of it burned on the bottom, and took big bites of it.

"Sit down," he told her, mouth full. "This is a grand meal, lass. Sit down and we'll eat it."

Woodenly, she did as she was told. She sat down because he'd told her to, and he began to pull out more of the bread, break off the burned parts, and put it in front of her. He did the same thing with the eggs, not even using a bowl, but simply putting the more edible pieces in front of her on the table and encouraging her to eat them. Meanwhile, he sat down opposite her and used his spoon to carve out pieces of burned bread and egg.

He ate every last bite.

Astria was so surprised at what he was doing that she barely ate what he'd given her, but she managed to swallow most of it. The taste was good even if the consistency wasn't. More than anything, she was awed by Payne's determination to eat everything she'd made for him regardless of the texture. Burned parts didn't matter to him. He ate it anyway—he ate until there was nothing left in the pots, and then he burped louder than anything she'd ever heard.

All he did was grin.

"That was a magnificent first try," he told her. "Ye're going tae be an excellent mistress of the house."

He had managed to make her feel better about the cooking mishap. "I will need to practice," she said. "You know that in the noble classes, it is unseemly for a noblewoman to actually cook or clean."

He nodded. "I know," he said. "But ye did an excellent job of it. Ye'll get better and better at it."

"I hope so."

He continued to smile at her, and she was a little embarrassed at all of the attention. Perhaps not exactly embarrassed, but she was so unused to it that she didn't know where to look or what to say. This was all so new to her.

"I suppose I should clean these out so I can use them again," she said, standing up and peering into the pots. "Although you have eaten every morsel. There is nothing left to save or clean."

He burped again, loudly, before standing up wearily. "And I'll do the same tae every meal ye prepare," he said. "If ye put a pile of mud before me, I'd eat it because ye prepared it."

She paused a moment, looking up at him. "You did that tonight," she said. "There was little more than ash left of your supper, but you still ate it. You ate it as if it were the best thing you'd ever tasted, and you did not have to. You could have become angry about it."

He shrugged. "Why?" he said. "Ye tried yer best. It was a good meal."

"It was burnt."

"I like my food burnt."

She giggled because he was being so ridiculous. Sweet, but ridiculous. It was really rather wonderful.

"Then I'll burn it every night for you," she said, watching him grin. "One of the servants brought eggs and flour and some other items, but no meat. Where would I find that for tomorrow's meal?"

He pointed off to his left, toward the rear door. "Did ye see the kitchens out by the dormitory?"

She nodded. "Aye," she said. "I did see it. There were a few servants who brought us things from there."

"A big meal is served there every night," he said. "Since we work our recruits so hard, the meals are always plentiful and full of meat. I'll tell ye a secret… if ye go tae the kitchen and tell them that ye're my wife, they'll give ye all the food ye want. Ye'll never have tae cook if ye dunna want tae."

That was the best thing she'd heard all day. "Why did you not tell me this before?" she said, rather peeved. "I would not have had to serve you burnt eggs."

He smiled. "Because I wanted tae know if ye'd at least try tae be a wife," he said. "There are a great many things around here that will make it so ye hardly have tae lift a finger, but I wanted tae know if being my wife meant anything tae ye. If ye'd even try. And ye did. Thank ye."

She seemed both pleased and irritated at his explanation. "You did not have to test me," she said. "I never intended to do anything other than fulfil my obligation."

He shrugged. "I believe ye," he said. "But speaking of obligation, we have one more tae accomplish together."

He pointed to the ceiling, meaning the floor above where the bedrooms were. Astria knew exactly what he meant, and her belly was suddenly filled with quivering butterflies. She hadn't thought about it all day, but now that the moment was upon them, she realized that she was quite nervous about it. Without another word, she simply headed up the stairs.

Fighting off a grin, Payne followed.

The bedchamber was clean, smelling of the vinegar that had

been used to scrub the floor, but it also smelled of mint from the linens. Payne took one look at the very neat and clean bed and nearly stumbled through the door, so great was his surprise.

"This doesna look like my bed," he said. "Did ye steal this from someone?"

Astria couldn't help but chuckle. "You mean from someone who does not like to sleep in a pigpen?"

"Aye, that someone."

"Nay, I did not," she said. "I had a great deal of help from Lady Munro and Lady de Reyne. They helped me clean it and restuff it. It is now fit for an earl and countess to sleep upon."

He was both pleased and awed. "It most certainly is," he agreed. "I keep saying well done, but truly, what ye've done today is remarkable. Ye're a bright lass when ye put yer mind tae it."

Astria went to sit on one of the two little stools she'd put in the chamber. "The coverlet belongs to Lady de Reyne and I am certain she would like it back, so mayhap we can purchase fabric for a new one when we commission the building of a bed," she said, pulling off one of her shoes. "I do know how to sew. That is one thing I learned because all proper young women learn that skill."

He saw the other stool and, pleased, went to sit on it himself. He tested it with his weight, approving of the fact that it didn't crack or groan, before lifting a leg to remove his boot.

"Ye see?" he said. "Ye have proper wifely skills if one wishes tae live simply. Sewing is very important if I want my wife tae make me new clothing."

She smiled faintly, pulling off the other slipper. "Speaking of wifely skills..." she said, lifting her head to look at him. Her cheeks were already turning shades of red. "You are aware that I do not have any."

She was indicating the bed, referring to what they would soon be doing. He put one boot aside and began to casually remove the other.

"It doesna matter tae me," he said. "That only means I can teach ye so that ye can enjoy it this time."

Astria's face was turning redder by the moment. "It was *not* enjoyable," she said. "It was humiliating."

"This willna be humiliating."

"How would you know that?" she said. "Also, I am coming to understand that you have done this before."

"I have."

"Many times?"

"Enough so that I know what I'm supposed tae do."

She paused for a moment. "Are you always so honest about everything?"

"Does it bother ye that I am?"

She had to think about that. "Nay," she said. "I would rather have complete honesty than secrets. Secrets can be deadly."

"That is true," he said, putting his boot against the wall with the other one and standing up to remove his clothing. "Secrets can kill many things. They can kill men. They can kill trust. And I dunna wish tae kill anything between us, so I will keep it alive the only way I know how—by telling ye the truth."

She cocked her head thoughtfully, watching him undress. "Have you ever been in love?"

He pulled his tunic over his head. "There were times when I thought I was," he admitted. "Men and women are sometimes stupid that way. Confusing love for just a passing fancy."

"Is that what you did?"

He nodded. "I think so," he said. "There's no one lingering in my heart or mind. And ye?"

She shook her head. "There is no one now," she said. "When I was very young, barely a woman, I thought I was in love with a knight who served my father. He had a wife and children and was at least twice my age, but that did not matter to me. I thought he was remarkable."

Payne smiled at her memory. "What became of him?"

She smiled in return. "He went off to battle and never returned," she said. "I remember seeing his wife weep and his friends sob. I always wondered if people would weep for me when I was dead, but I do not think so."

His smile faded. "Why would ye say that?"

"Because I have no family to speak of and no friends. There will be no one left to grieve for me."

"Ye have me," he said softly. "I realize we've only known each other a short day, but it is, nonetheless, a day. The first of many. Do ye know what I know of ye so far?"

"What?"

He pulled off his undertunic, revealing his magnificent, naked torso. "That ye're lost," he said. "I've never seen someone so lost."

Her brow furrowed. "Why would you say that?"

"Because it is true," he said. "Ye had no home when ye were young. Ye were simply one of many in yer father's family. Then ye married an old man who treated ye like an object. Ye were a possession tae him and nothing more. Ye tried tae become useful by taking control of his family's business, but that really belongs tae the man's son. Ye tried tae take back what legally belongs tae him and then my mother captured ye. Now, ye find yerself in England and the wife of a Blackchurch trainer. Ye're not lost anymore, but it is going tae take ye some time tae realize that. Ye canna always be a bit of flotsam in the sea, Astria. At some point, even the flotsam settles tae the bottom and becomes part of it."

Astria.

That was the first time she'd heard him use her given name. Her first name, Maria, was something commonly given to royal women, but it wasn't meant to be used. It was simply given in tribute to the mother of Jesus. She'd gone by Astria her entire life, but she'd never heard it used in a tone that made her stomach quiver. But his words seemed to incite something in her, something confused and resistant.

"You speak as if this was an arranged marriage and it was something agreeable to both of us," she said. "Do not tell me I belong here, because I don't. I was brought here as a captive, forced into marriage, and now you are trying to tell me that I belong. I do not mean to offend you, but you are presenting a pleasant picture of an unpleasant situation. I did not ask to come here. I did not ask to be married to you. I am not lost. I simply do not belong."

She lowered her head, going back to removing her clothing and having no idea why his words had irritated her so, but they made her want to weep. Weep because she had been forced to come here against her will and Payne was trying to make it sound like everything was sunshine and roses. Well, it wasn't. It never had been. But most confusingly, she'd never had such a lovely day in her life with Payne and then Athdara and Elisiana. So perhaps there *was* some truth to what he'd said.

Perhaps she *was* lost after all.

"I understand that ye feel like that now," he said after a moment. "But be patient. It takes time tae find yer footing."

She looked at him. "Why are you so confident about this?" she said. "Your life is in upheaval, too. You've had a wife forced on you. Are you not upset about this?"

He shrugged. "I had tae marry sometime," he said. "Why not marry ye?"

That wasn't helping her angst. The shock of the captivity and marriage had worn off and now she was feeling some emotions about it. Perhaps it was the fact that this important moment was upon them and she was helpless against it. In any case, she removed her surcoat and hose, sliding them off her legs, before climbing into the bed and pulling the coverlet up to her shoulders. She simply lay there, staring at the ceiling, waiting for him to come to her.

Removing his breeches, he did. The moment he slid into the bed, she pulled the coverlet up to her chin.

"I will again remind you that I do not know too much about what we are supposed to do this night," she said. "You will have to tell me what you want me to do."

The covers were pulled up so tightly around her that he was fairly certain he'd have to pry them away with an iron bar. He lifted himself up beside her, propping himself up with an elbow upon the soft bed as he gazed down at her.

"I want ye tae simply lie there and enjoy it," he said softly. "But I canna do anything with the coverlet pulled over ye like a shield. Ye'll have tae lower it, and it would be best if ye removed yer shift."

Astria was a brave woman under most circumstances. But at the moment, her bravery was faltering. Hesitantly, she lowered the coverlet.

"Like this?"

It was barely down to her chest. "More," he said.

It went a little lower. "This?"

He couldn't help it. He snorted with mirth. "May I help ye with it?"

Astria nodded, and he climbed out of bed and walked over to her side. Astria could immediately see that he was naked, his entire pelvic region, including his flaccid manhood, exposed in her full view. Startled, she looked up at the ceiling again as he pulled the coverlet down to her knees, took hold of her arm, and pulled her into sitting position.

God help her, this put his manhood right about eye level at this point, and she was trying desperately not to look at it. It was wagging in her face! He grasped both of her arms, pulled them straight up, and made her hold them there. Then he grabbed the sides of her shift and lifted it up, over her head, nearly lifting her off the bed in the process. She gasped in surprise as the shift was yanked off her body and then placed neatly on the stool. As she sat up in the bed, naked from the waist up and her arms covering her breasts, he pushed her down by the shoulders so she was lying down again and then climbed back into the bed, resuming his spot beside her.

"May I begin?" he asked huskily.

Nervously, Astria nodded.

"Ye're afraid because ye dunna know what is about tae happen," he whispered, his gaze moving over her lovely face. "Do ye feel my body up against yers?"

Astria's heart was pounding so hard in her chest that she could hear it pulsing through her ears. But she could feel his heat against her right side, his skin warm against hers. When Armand had made love to her the one and only time, he'd kept his nightshirt on. He'd only lifted it up to his waist, so consequently, anything she felt was fabric and old-man body in her nether regions. Even when he'd penetrated her, it had been cold and uncomfortable and very, very brief. Everything about the encounter had been cold and detached.

But this…

It was all shades of hot.

Astria had never had a man this intimately close to her, and of all the things she had imagined it would be, pleasant hadn't been among them. But his flesh was against hers and the contact between them, of his body against her right side, caused her palms to sweat. She was trembling, but not from fear.

It was a giddy and overwhelming reaction.

"I… I feel you," she murmured.

Payne had a smile on his lips, amused and pleased by her reaction to him. Very carefully, he brought up his enormous arms and wrapped them around her slender body, hearing her gasp as he did so. He squeezed, but not too hard.

Just hard enough to feel her against him for the first time.

"Have ye ever been embraced like this?" he whispered in her right ear.

Astria was very quickly collapsing. Everything was collapsing—her fear, her resistance, her ability to think clearly.

"Not like this," she managed to mutter.

His smile grew. Then he dipped his head and planted a tender kiss her cheek, then her shoulder. Tremors of desire coursed through Astria so strongly that she emitted what sounded like a groan.

"That is a kiss," he murmured, kissing her shoulder again. "Has a man ever kissed ye?"

Astria groaned again, this time for real, and her eyes rolled up into her head. "God… nay," she breathed. "Never."

He kissed her upper arm, gently. "Good," he said. "I'll be

the first and last man tae ever do it. Is that clear?"

She couldn't even open her eyes, spiraling with a sensation as simple as a kiss. "It is."

Payne believed her. He kept his left arm around her as his right arm loosened and his hand went to her belly, and he ran it carefully across her velvety skin.

"This is my touch," he said softly. "Does it frighten ye?"

"Nay," she whispered.

He leaned forward, burying his face in her hair and inhaling deeply. It smelled of lavender and musk. *Her* musk. It was quite enticing.

"Yer husband's touch is nothing tae be feared, lass," he whispered. "I'm sorry that the old man never showed ye that, but I will. My touch will always be tender upon ye. Ye'll never know it in anger, I swear it."

Astria's eyes were closed as he continued to caress the skin of her stomach. But then his hand moved to hers, squeezing it, before he brought her fingers up to his mouth. He kissed every finger gently before taking her index finger and suckling on it. That brought a gasp from her, and the moment she did so, he slanted his mouth over hers, kissing her with all of the arousal that he felt. He simply couldn't help it.

His passion took flight.

His big body rolled onto her, covering her, and Astria gasped as he suckled her delicious lips. Payne's big arms went around her, holding her against his nude flesh. When his tongue gently probed her lips, she had no idea how to respond until he managed to push it into her mouth. Then it was as if the flame of passion finally ignited and her instincts took flight.

Instincts to respond to everything he was doing to her.

Just as he was tasting her, Astria began to taste him. She

responded to his kisses, which were forceful without being overbearing, erotic without being sloppy. But his mouth soon left hers, blazing a trail down her chest until he came to her full, tender breasts. Astria hissed with shock when his hot, wet mouth closed over a tender nipple and he suckled her furiously, his arms wound around her as her body arched and bucked. He was out of control at this point, lured by the taste of her flesh.

There would be no stopping him.

The harder he sucked, the stronger her bucking and twisting grew until his free hand moved to the tender center between her legs. She gasped with surprise when he wedged his big body in between her legs and fingered the dark curls. She was wet, her body preparing to receive him, and the realization had his heart pounding. His erection was demanding satisfaction. He continued to fondle her virginal lips as he nursed at her breasts, wanting his entry to be as easy as possible so she wouldn't be uncomfortable. He knew that he was basically dealing with a virgin, so he treated her accordingly, but the more he stroked her wet folds, the more her hips would thrust forward as if she were trying to capture his fingers.

It was the most arousing thing he had ever experienced.

He answered her call by inserting a finger into her to satisfy the need her body seemed to be experiencing, to mate as nature had intended. Astria grunted at the intrusion, groaning softly as he thrust in and out of her, mimicking the lovemaking they would soon be doing. He thrust another finger into her and she cried out softly, her hips meeting his hand as he moved within her. She couldn't seem to figure out what to do with her legs, because they'd been thrashing about, but now, they were spread open wide, giving him unhindered access.

Payne couldn't wait any longer. He needed his manhood

inside of her as much as she needed to feel him.

Now.

Very quickly, he removed his fingers and placed his erection at her threshold, coiling his buttocks and thrusting into her before she realized what he was doing. When Astria became aware, for the feel of his manhood was different from the feel of his fingers, she started to tighten at the unfamiliar sensation, but Payne lay atop her and coiled his buttocks again, thrusting firm and hard this time.

The second thrust seated him fully, balls deep.

Beneath him, Astria was impaled on his big body, instinctively wrapping her arms around his neck as he thrust into her warm, wet folds. Her body, so unfamiliar with a man's touch, nonetheless accepted all of him easily. No resistance, no fear. All she could do was hang on and experience her first true coupling, thinking that this was nothing like it had been before. Something hot and carnal was sparking low in her belly. Every time Payne thrust into her, sparks flew and the feeling grew.

Astria was in a haze. At one point, Payne propped himself up so that he could look at her, watching her in the faint light. Eyes closed, feeling every sensation he was creating in her, her hands began to wander over her own body. They found her breasts, touching them sexually for the first time, which made her cry out softly in ecstasy. They wandered lower, timidly touching the junction where their bodies joined, and she discovered that if she touched herself there, the heat in her loins sparked wildly. It felt good, so she expanded her touch, feeling his male member where it entered her body, exploring everything that was happening.

Payne simply let her. But when she touched his manhood again, he couldn't hold back a release so strong that he bit his tongue in the process. Astria's body was so highly aroused that when she felt him throbbing within her, it sparked the fire that roared to life and she experienced her first climax. She cried out as much in surprise as in pleasure.

Payne put his mouth over hers to quiet her cries, mostly because he found it wildly arousing to know she'd found so much gratification. Even though he'd spent himself, he continued to thrust into her, more slowly, grinding his pelvis against hers and feeling her experience at least two more releases as he did so. Each time, Astria stiffened and cried out, one hand between her legs, feeling him, and the other on his chest, her nails digging into him.

She left marks.

God, how incredibly arousing he found those nail marks. His mouth left hers, kissing her neck, her chest, her breasts, his big hands moving between her legs again as he suckled her gently. When his manhood became too flaccid, he put his fingers into her again, feeling what he'd put inside of her, imagining that she'd conceived a son already. A strapping lad with his good looks and her strength. He kept fondling her as long as she let him, and when his manhood eventually hardened again, he put it inside of her and made love to her, very slowly, as she lay beneath him and purred like a kitten. Soft, gentle groans of pleasure told him that she was enjoying it as much as he was. No pain, no humiliation.

Only warmth and discovery.

It went on all night.

CHAPTER FIFTEEN

"H AVE YE SEEN Payne since the wedding?"

Maude and Francis were standing in their encampment at the dawn of a new day. There was food cooking on an open fire, a pot of beans and some woodland creature that had been alive the day before. They were so used to eating fish that the smell of cooking meat was somewhat off-putting, but they were trying to warm to it. For the hardscrabble pirates of Medusa's Disciples, food was food.

They'd eat anything.

"Nay," Maude said. "They went back tae Blackchurch after the mass and I've not seen them since."

"How do ye think it went for them?" Francis asked. "They dinna seem too angry about the wedding. Payne dinna seem angry at all."

"Why should he be?"

They both turned to see Declan walking up, a piece of bread in his hands as he chewed loudly. When he saw that he had their attention, he took another bite.

"I mean it," he said, chewing. "Why should he be angry? He married the princess. He has the title and all of Da's wealth.

Why should he be angry?"

Francis frowned as he watched the man eat. "Where did ye get the bread?"

Declan deliberately took another big bite, looking his brother in the eye. "There was a woman in the village more than willing tae give me a loaf," he said. "Ye simply have tae know who tae ask."

Maude looked at him. "In this village?"

"Aye. Where else?"

"I told ye that we promised not tae steal from the villagers here," she said.

"I dinna steal from her," Declan insisted. "I asked nicely."

It took Maude a moment to realize more of her men were eating loaves of bread, chatting and yawning as the day began to dawn. Her jaw began to twitch as she struggled against her rising anger.

"Did ye pay the women for the bread ye took?" she finally asked, turning to her middle son. "Well?"

He was being very casual about it. "Mayhap some of them, we paid," he said. "But others, I dunna know. We may have simply taken what we wanted."

Maude grabbed the bread out of his hand and threw it on the ground, stomping on it. "This is not a game, Declan," she growled. "I swore that we wouldna raid this village or harass these villagers whilst we were here. If ye make me look like a liar, I'll take it out on yer hide."

Angry that his bread had been taken away and ruined, Declan flared. "Ye made the vow," he pointed out hotly. "I dinna. I'm hungry for bread, so I went and found some. If that makes ye look like a liar, then that is yer misfortune. Not mine."

Maude whipped out a dagger she always carried, wielding

the weapon in front of her as Declan pulled out his own weapon. Francis, unwilling to see his mother defeated in a knife fight, kicked the dagger out of Declan's hand. When Declan tried to come at him with a fist, Francis kicked him between the legs.

Declan went down like a stone.

"All of ye," Maude shouted angrily, "take the bread back where ye found it and give the woman ye stole from a pence for her troubles. I'll not have the sloppy lot of ye make me look like a liar, so do it now or face my wrath!"

She meant every word. Maude's men knew well enough that if she was displeased, she went for the first thing a man held dear—that private body part between their legs. She'd cut off more of those than the men could count and wasn't beyond cutting them off her own men, so those with the loaves began to back away, hesitantly, but willing to return to the village. They had no choice. As Maude stood there, glaring at them, a figure came through the trees behind the tavern.

Maude found herself looking at Payne.

Her eldest son was frowning at the men who were filtering past him, some carrying loaves of bread, but he frowned even more when he spied Declan on his knees.

"What is happening?" he asked. "Where are those men going? And why is Declan on the ground?"

"He's on the ground because he threatened Maudie," Francis said, going to stand with Payne. "I made it so he canna stand anytime soon."

That brought Payne's immediate condemnation. He glared at Declan before looking at his mother. "Are ye well?" he asked. "He dinna hurt ye?"

Maude shook her head. "Nay," she said. "But he'd better

learn tae obey my commands or the next time, his injuries might not heal so quickly."

"What happened?"

Maude nodded in the direction of the village. "Did ye see the men heading toward the village?"

"I did."

She returned her attention to Declan. "Evidently, they went on a foraging mission this morning and stole bread," she said. "Or mayhap they paid for it. Declan wouldna give me a straight answer, so I can only assume they stole things. I told him I gave my promise that my men wouldna steal from the village, and by stealing bread, he's made me out tae be a liar. I canna abide by that, so I sent the men tae return their ill-gotten gains."

Payne could figure the rest out. "And Declan doesna agree?"

Maude simply shrugged, but by this time, Declan was lurching to his feet. His face was red and sweaty. "Francis," he growled, "ye better hope I never catch ye alone, because ye'll pay for this."

"If ye dinna disobey me, we wouldna be having this conversation," Maude shot back. "This is yer fault, Declan. The sooner ye take responsibility for yer actions, the sooner we can let the matter lie."

Declan wasn't willing to forgive and forget. "This is the problem, Maudie," she said. "Ye always defend Francis or Payne, but never me. I'm always the one ye take tae task and I'm tired of it."

"How do I take ye tae task?" Maude asked. "If ye commit a wrong, I tell ye. If Francis commits a wrong, I tell him. I'm not persecuting ye over the others."

Declan wouldn't be placated. "No man should have tae be subject tae his mother's punishment."

"I only punish ye when ye deserve it."

"That's all the time!"

"Then that should be a lesson tae ye tae obey me!"

Declan threw out his arms in a gesture of rage. "All I do is obey ye!" he boomed. "I serve on yer ships, I do as ye ask, and I take a bit of bread because I'm hungry, and suddenly, I'm making ye out tae be a liar."

"Ye did," Payne said seriously. "If ye canna see her point, Declan, then ye're hopeless."

Declan didn't take kindly to his eldest brother piling on. "And ye," he snarled. "Ye have no say in all of this. Ye've shunned us for the past ten years, so ye have no rights at all."

Payne snorted with mirth. "I've a position that doesna require me tae steal or kill from others," he said. "I'm the educated one, Declan. I've been trained, far more trained than ye'll ever be. All ye're good enough for is tae stand on the deck of yer mammy's ship and steal from those who have more than ye do. Ye're a thief and an outlaw and that's all ye'll ever be."

By the time he was finished, Declan was shaking with rage. "Ye bastard," he growled. "I'll not forgive ye for that."

"I dunna care if ye do or not."

Declan shook his head, slowly, his jaw tight. "Da should have disowned ye," he said. "Ye think ye're too good for the family and he should have disowned ye. Now ye marry a captive. A captive! A woman who says she's a Portuguese princess, but how do we know? For all we know, she was a whore for the men on her ship and now she's a whore for ye!"

Payne moved in his direction menacingly, but Maude and Francis stopped him from charging. "Nay, lad," Maude said steadily. "He's not worth yer talent nor yer time. Ye'll not tear him apart in front of me."

Payne was furious. He let his considerably smaller mother stop his forward progression as Francis moved toward Declan and picked up a fairly large branch off the ground as he did. Declan saw him coming, stepping back just as Francis swung the branch at his head.

"Get out of here," Francis demanded. "Ye're a shame tae the entire family, Declan. Go somewhere else before Maudie lets Payne rip yer head off."

Declan was already backing away. "I'll go," he muttered. "I'll go forever. I'll not stay with the lot of ye, filthy whore-mongers and cowards. I'm finished with ye."

He stormed off, leaving his brothers and mother to watch him go. Maude took her hands off Payne's chest, taking a few steps after Declan, watching him as he headed back into the encampment. There was concern in her expression for the son who was the most volatile, and the most unpredictable, out of them all.

"Francis," she said in a low voice, "ye'd better go. He'll try tae turn the men with his lies, so make sure he doesna."

Francis nodded, following his brother's footsteps into the encampment. They could already hear his voice in the distance as Declan began to shout his case.

"Should ye go, Maudie?" Payne asked. "Those are yer men, after all."

Maude shook her head. "Nay," she said. Then she took a deep breath and faced him. "Payne, ye may as well know that I intend that Francis should succeed me. Declan… he thinks only of himself. He doesna think of his men. That was the one thing yer grandfather begged of me before he died—*take care of my men, Maudie.* He told me that, and I've done just that for ten years. But Declan doesna think like that, and it's going tae be a battle when I turn the family business over tae Francis."

Payne understood what she was saying. In fact, it occurred to him that Maude was where he got his weakness from. That weakness that saw him show more empathy or emotion than he should. Maude had it too. Both he and his mother had hearts that they couldn't quite protect, which was strange, given their chosen vocations. But Declan didn't have that problem.

As Payne had once described him, the man was dangerous.

Even to his family.

"Ye're pitting yer sons against one another," he said quietly. "But I suppose ye already know that."

"I do," Maude said. "Francis is strong, Payne. In his heart and mind, he is strong."

"Is he?" Payne asked. "Because ten years ago, he was my weak little brother."

"He's grown since then. He's matured."

"I hope it is enough."

"It is," Maude said. "Speaking of maturing, how are ye and Astria getting on?"

Payne averted his gaze, unable to keep the smile off his lips. "Well."

"*How* well?"

"Well enough that I dunna think she is going tae try tae escape any longer," he said. Then he paused a moment in thought before continuing. "Maudie, she's my wife now, so that makes her family. It also makes her untouchable."

"Of course it does."

"That means by anyone. Even ye."

"What are ye driving at, Payne?"

Payne drew in a long, thoughtful breath before facing her. "I'm going tae tell ye something that she told me," he said. "But

I'm telling ye as a matter of yer safety. Do ye understand that?"

Maude nodded. "I do," she said. "What must ye tell me?"

"I'm not supposed tae tell ye all of it, but I'm going tae because I think it's important for ye tae know."

"Go ahead, then. Tell me."

He lifted a hand and made a swirling motion, like the choppy motion of the sea. "When ye captured Astria's ships," he said, "what were the circumstances?"

Maude thought a moment. "We were in the Balearic Sea," she said. "We'd already had a successful visit tae Denia, a port village, when we spied the princess' ships. We overtook them, moved the cargo into our holds, threw her crew overboard, and took her with us when we left. Why do ye ask?"

"Because those were not merchant ships," Payne said. "They were pirate vessels."

"I know."

Payne looked at her in shock. "Ye *know*?"

She nodded. "I also happen tae know that yer wife was once The Sea God."

Payne's jaw dropped. "Ye knew that, too?"

Maude was amused at his surprise. "Lad, I must know everything about my enemies," she said. "I'd be a poor captain, indeed, if I dinna. I also know that her husband's son has practically taken everything from her. I dunna know how she managed tae get two ships from him, but she did. I commend her for it. But now those ships are mine."

"Do ye also know that he wants those ships returned?" Payne said, rather irritated at his mother's seeming smugness. "Astria seems tae think her stepson is following ye and intends tae take them back by force."

Maude nodded. "And that's part of the reason I took them

tae Combwich," she said. "I figured he was following when I went tae Scotland, but there are so many islands, it would be difficult for him tae find me, but not impossible. So, I came south, tae the Bristol Channel. He can look all he likes, but he'll not find them inland. He'll forget about them soon enough."

She winked at him, letting him know that she felt quite superior in this situation. Frankly, Payne was still lingering in the surprise that she already knew about Astria's secret identity, but in hindsight, perhaps he shouldn't have been surprised at all. Maude was right—as an outlaw on the seas, it would be deadly if she didn't know everything she could about those who also held her profession. She didn't seem concerned about Arnaldo San Miguel coming for his ships. Truthfully, Payne was impressed by her calm approach, but he was also enraged by it.

"Maudie," he said, "if he finds ye, he will destroy ye. He has more ships and more men than ye do."

"He'll have tae find me first."

She still didn't seem too concerned, and Payne gave up. If he couldn't impress upon her how serious this was, then there was nothing more to do. He simply threw up his hands in surrender.

"Have it yer way," he said. "But if ye were smart about this… ye'd turn those vessels over tae Declan and tell him tae go and be his own man. Ye know he'd take those ships and wreak havoc in full view. Then the San Miguel son would find him and destroy him. Not ye."

Maude cocked a red eyebrow. "Use him as a decoy?"

"Ye'd rid yerself of him once and for all."

She chuckled, putting a hand on Payne's broad shoulder. "True," she said. "But he's still yer brother. And he's still my son. Declan may be a thorn in my side, and he poses a real threat tae my command, but he's still my son. He's my flesh and blood. I canna consign him tae his fate so easily."

Payne knew that. Maude was the man's mother, and that put her in a difficult position. With a heavy sigh, he shook his head.

"Then whatever ye do, be vigilant with him," he said. "I dunna trust him, Maudie."

"I know," she said, patting him on the arm. "But we willna speak on him any longer. I dunna want tae waste my breath. I want tae know about yer plans now that ye've taken a wife. Are ye still going tae remain here, at Blackchurch?"

He nodded. "Nothing has changed," he said. "I will stay here until the class I'm currently training is complete. Then I'll go north and see tae the Lismore lands."

"And take The Sea God with ye?"

He smiled, a humorless gesture. "She's my wife," he said. "If ye want grandchildren anytime soon, I'll have tae take her with me."

Maude's mood turned serious. "She's a terror, I know," she said. "I'm sorry I had tae saddle ye with her, but yer children will be of royal blood. That's a great thing for the House of Matheson. That will make yer children in much demand for marriages. It'll outweigh the fact that their grandmother is Bloody Maude."

He looked at her curiously. "Is *that* why ye brought her tae me?" he said. "So my children would be viewed as excellent mates in spite of their grandmother's vocation?"

She shrugged. "A little, mayhap," she said. "I only wanted the best for ye, Payne. I hope ye know that. And having a mother like me... That's not an advantage."

He put his big arm around her shoulders and gave her a

squeeze. "I dunna care what people think, Maudie," he said softly. "And ye've always wanted the best for me. Even when ye disowned me, I still knew ye loved me."

She eyed him. "Nay, I dinna," she said. "Ye were disowned, ye big dolt. There was no love for ye there."

He chuckled and kissed her on the forehead. "Admit it," he said. "I'm yer favorite son."

"Ye're my most annoying son," she said, watching him laugh. But that laughter, that face, softened her. Reaching up, she gently touched his cheek. "But ye're my firstborn, my pride and my joy. I'm very proud of ye, Payne. Ye'll make an excellent earl. If ye want tae know the truth, I did all of this so ye could build a reputable and prestigious earldom beyond what yer father ever did."

His smile faded as he gazed into her pale blue eyes. "Thank ye," he said softly. "I mean that."

Maude smiled faintly. "I'm just sorry I couldna give ye a queen for a mother," she said. "That would have given ye a much better standing than a pirate for a mother."

He chuckled. "When I told Lord Exmoor about ye, he was surprised tae say the least," he said. "I'd never mentioned yer identity before, so it came as a shock. Of course, he thinks that living with such a woman was rough as a lad, but I told him that what I mostly remember of ye is when I was very young and we would walk everywhere together. Do ye remember that?"

Maude smiled faintly at the memory. "I do," she said. "Ye were so attached tae me that I thought I'd never cut ye loose from my apron strings."

"True," he said with a snort. "I never wanted tae leave yer side. I remember walking intae the harbor near Achanduin and there was a man who kept fish in a barrel, fish that he'd caught in the inlet. Do ye remember that man? He'd let me grab a fish and take it with me. The smell of the sea and the smell of fish always remind me of that man, and of those days. They were good days, Maudie. I miss them."

She nodded, remembering those days too. "Ye'll have them with her own children, someday," she said. "Take them tae the harbor and let them grab for fish. Those will be yer best memories."

He nodded, but his expression was pensive. "Maudie," he said hesitantly, "will ye promise me something?"

"If I can."

He sighed, pulling his thoughts together. "When the day comes for ye tae turn Medusa's Disciples over tae Francis, I want ye tae come and live with me and Astria," he said. "I dunna want ye tae grow old alone. I want ye tae grow old under my roof, and when the days come that ye're too old tae do for yerself, I want tae be the help ye seek. Let it be me holding yer hand and walking ye along the shore of the inlet, watching the fishing boats in the distance and speaking of the days when ye were the fearsome pirate queen. Will ye do that for me? Will ye let me be the one who holds yer hand when ye breathe yer last?"

Maude was choked up at his words. Sweet, poignant words from her son with the biggest heart of all. She wasn't surprised by them. But it took her a moment to reclaim her composure.

"Ye're asking a good deal of yer wife," she said. "Given how the two of us met, she might not want me there."

"She will, I promise," he said. "I'll tell ye a secret—I intend tae fall in love with my wife. I intend tae have a happy life with her with a love that will outlast the stars. And she'll want ye there in yer old age because she'll have ye tae thank for her happiness. Ye brought her tae me and she'll be grateful. That's how I know."

Maude blinked away her tears. "I'll think on it," she said, never one to give in to such sentimentality outwardly. "Meanwhile, since the wedding is over, I've no real reason tae stay any longer. I should get Declan back out tae sea before we have real trouble on our hands."

She was changing the subject and Payne let her. He'd said what he needed to say. "That will please Lord Exmoor," he said. "The man is not comfortable with ye here as it is, but I—"

He was cut off by a shout. Both he and Maude looked off to the north to see Francis running in their direction. It wasn't a panicked run, but a run nonetheless.

That was never a good thing.

"What is it?" Payne called to him.

Francis didn't answer until he came within speaking distance. He didn't want to shout again. "Declan took several men with him and left," he said, breathing heavily. "They took the horses with them and headed east."

Maude's brow rippled with confusion. "Where did he go?"

Francis shook his head. "I dunna know," he said. "But he was yelling at the men, telling them that it was weak tae serve a woman, even Bloody Maude. I think he means tae return tae Combwich and take control of our ships."

Payne looked at his mother in concern, but Maude shook her head calmly. "He canna," she said. "I left men on the ships loyal tae me. They willna let him have them. Moreover, did ye notice what was in the last wagon we brought along?"

Francis shook his head. "There are trunks in that wagon," he said. "What about them?"

"What else did ye see in them?"

"I dunna know. What else is there?"

"The pin for the tiller," Maude said. "I took it. It secures the tiller tae the rudder. Without it, the ships canna be steered. Did ye truly think I'd leave those ships ready tae take tae sea?"

Francis looked relieved as Payne grinned. His mother was a brilliant woman even if she was a source of constant surprise. He left his mother and youngest brother in conversation about Declan and his intentions, heading back to Blackchurch to inform St. Denis of the latest developments. Truth be told, he wasn't as unconcerned about his brother running amok in the Devon countryside as his mother was. Declan, with dozens of men at his side, could be a dangerous thing.

Especially if he didn't know where his brother was going.

Blackchurch was back on high alert within the hour.

PART TWO

THE SEA GOD

CHAPTER SIXTEEN

Three Days Later

S HE'D TAKEN THE bloody pin from the tiller assembly.

Sitting in an old tavern on the river's edge in the sleepy village of Combwich, Declan knew for a fact that his mother had taken the small piece of iron so the ships couldn't be steered. Not only that, but the men left shipboard to guard the vessels were loyal to his mother and wouldn't let him on board without her permission. Declan had been planning on over-whelming them when he realized the missing pin situation on an exterior perusal of the ships. Now, those left on board were keeping everyone off with crossbows and his entire plan to confiscate the two San Miguel vessels was in ruins.

Damnation!

Now he sat in this dirty tavern, with dirty women and dirty people, as his own men wandered around the town, probably stealing and God only knew what else. Declan wasn't one to supervise them or even keep them in line. He was only worried about himself, and that had always been the case. Today, in particular, he was only thinking about himself and, in fact, was sulking as he steadily consumed the cheap ale that had been cut with water right out of a swamp. It tasted horrible. But it was enough to make him tipsy and, strangely, that helped him think straight.

He was going to leave his mother.

More precisely, he was going to leave her command and start his own. Those ships moored in the river were going to be his as soon as he could find a smithy to make the pin that his mother had so thoughtfully taken. She always seemed to be one step ahead of him, which was thoroughly annoying, but that was going to end.

He was going to strike out on his own.

At some point, he'd gather the men who came with him and they would devise a plan to remove the guards from the vessels. There were about twenty-five of them between both ships and Declan only had eighteen men with him, but those eighteen were the toughest of the tough. Men who didn't want to serve under a woman any longer. They wanted the prestige of serving under a man who would let them do as they pleased. Declan already had a name for his group.

The Fomorians.

He grinned as he thought of that, naming his band of pirates after the most horrifying creatures of Celtic legend. He wanted to live up to the name, to become legendary in both deed and destruction. Malevolence was his middle name.

Finally, he was going to be able to live the way he wanted to live.

As he sat there and pondered his future, he had a clear view of the vessels on the river. He also had a clear view of the river itself, and he saw, very clearly, when a large, well-appointed cog came down the waterway and stopped behind his mother's ships. The ship dropped anchor in the river, right in the middle of it, blocking any traffic that might be coming up, or down, the river.

That was when things began to get interesting.

As Declan watched, he could see men coming over the rail of the boat and shouting to the men who were guarding the two Medusa vessels. There was a lot of shouting going on, and when the men from the river boat tried to board, the crossbows came out and a battle ensued.

By this time, everyone in the tavern was looking from the windows, watching the battle. There were a great many men from the big ship trying to board the two other vessels, but the Medusa men were determined to prevent them. Fascinated, as well as concerned, Declan stood up from his table and went to the window with the others, watching the scene unfold.

And what a scene it was.

A full-scale battle was happening on the river's edge of sleepy Combwich. Amazingly, the men from the larger ship were ultimately unable to board the two Medusa vessels, and when one did manage to get on board, he was stabbed through the belly and thrown into the river. As this was going on, two cannons from the larger ship were being lined up and two explosions rang out, one after the other.

The cannons shot off the rudders of both Medusa vessels.

Everyone in the tavern jumped back, away from the windows, but Declan remained, shocked at what he'd just seen. Clearly, the men from the larger vessel couldn't board the two smaller cogs and had made sure the ships couldn't leave. As he watched, the men from the large vessel began to move toward the shore, swarming on the river's edge before moving into the village.

They were heading toward the tavern.

The terrified tavernkeep rushed to the front door and threw the bolt to stop them from entering, but Declan called out to the man.

"If ye do that, they'll burn this place around us," he said. "Open the door. Let them in. If they steal from us, at least we'll emerge with our lives and ye'll emerge with yer building intact. And offer them free drink, too. Trust me on this. Ye dunna want tae make them angry."

The man was absolutely panicked, but he listened. He unlocked the bolt and yanked the door open, giving what were clearly a group of pirates access to his establishment. The patrons inside, Declan included, began pouring their coin into their cups or into their food, hopefully hiding it from those who intended to take it.

And they waited.

It wasn't a long wait, however, and soon enough, men began to pour in through the open door. The tavernkeep was there to greet them, pretending to welcome them, hoping that would mitigate any damage. He offered them free food and drink and every man accepted the offer. The tavernkeep even moved them over to a side of the common room that didn't have many people in it, telling them that it was their own private area. He did everything he could to make them feel welcome and, for the moment, it was working. No fights, no stealing.

Watching all of this, Declan sank back into his seat.

He wasn't sure who these men were, but they were organized. The ship moored out in the river was large and well appointed. These were pirates—he knew the breed—but they weren't any pirates he was acquainted with. He knew Santiago de Fernandez's group, and he also knew St. Abelard's Triton's

Hellions, but this group… He had no idea who they were.

And that made him quite curious.

Who *were* these men?

Over at the tables where the pirates were drinking and eating, one man in particular caught his eye. He was young, dark-haired, and went around making sure all of his men were having a good time, like the host of a party. It was that same young man who moved away from the group and began to shout in the middle of the common room.

"I am looking for someone and I am willing to pay!" he announced. "I am looking for the men who were aboard those ships on the shore. They are led by a woman and I want to talk to that woman. I will pay handsomely for anyone who can tell me where they are."

That statement brought a bolt of shock through Declan, but he didn't respond to it. Not right away. He simply sat there near the window overlooking the river, cup of ale in hand, and wondered what in the hell this man wanted with his mother. Not that he was protecting the woman, but he didn't want to be the focus of an attack if the man had a vendetta against Maude.

But the man didn't give up. He didn't look angry, or even peeved, that no one had responded. He began to walk around the room, pointing to the ships and asking questions. Everyone he spoke with couldn't tell him who those ships belonged to, and all the while, Declan knew the man would eventually come to him. He had to come up with a plan, and it all centered around one thing—if he truly wanted to take command of Medusa's Disciples, then he would have to get rid of his mother. Remove her somehow. Not necessarily kill her, but remove her. Her and Francis.

Perhaps this mysterious stranger would help with that plan.

So he sat and drank, waiting for the man to come to his table, which he eventually did. Declan looked up from his ale, casually, as the man stood over him.

"Have you seen the woman who commands those ships, my friend?" he asked, pointing out toward the river. "I am willing to pay handsomely for information if you have."

Declan approached his answer carefully. "A runaway wife, mayhap?" he said, trying to make light of it. "Women are nothing but trouble."

The man grinned. "Not a wife," he said. "Not my wife, anyway. But she was my father's wife and he loved her dearly. Do you live in this village? Have you seen any unfamiliar women?"

Declan indicated the seat across from him. "Sit down," he said. "Let me buy ye a meal. A drink, mayhap. Let us speak on this woman ye're looking for."

The man pulled out a chair. "Can you help me?"

"Possibly. My name is Declan, by the way. And ye?"

"Arnaldo," the man said as he sat. "I am the Duc de Tarragona. Before you call me a liar, know that it is true."

Declan smiled faintly. "The Sea God."

The man's smile vanished. "How would you know that?"

Declan waved the tavernkeep over, demanding drink, before he replied. "Because ye are looking for the Portuguese princess," he said. "But I think ye are looking for Bloody Maude most of all."

Arnaldo suddenly produced a dagger, pressing the tip at Declan's throat before he could draw another breath. "Tell me who you are and how you know that," he spat. "Tell me before my dagger cuts off your head."

"Do that and ye'll never know."

He had a point. Arnaldo pondered that for a moment before sheathing the dirk, but his expression was still suspicious.

"Tell me how you know who I am and who I seek," he demanded.

Declan remained calm. "Because I want what ye want," he said. "I want tae see Bloody Maude put in her place. I'll tell ye where she is if ye promise not tae kill her, but only take her captive. Take her far away and put her in a place she canna escape from."

Arnaldo's expression grew puzzled. "Why?" he said. "What is she to you?"

"My mother."

Arnaldo's eyes widened. "You are a son of Bloody Maude?"

Declan nodded. "I am," he said. "And her fleet should be mine."

Arnaldo was genuinely surprised. "She took my ships."

"She captured the stepmother ye speak of."

"She did!" Arnaldo said with enthusiasm. "Where is Astria?"

"Married tae my brother," Declan said. "Maudie brought her all the way tae Devon tae give her over tae my brother, who serves at Blackchurch. He's a trainer there. He also inherited my father's titles and lands, so although I dunna want ye tae kill Maude, I would be in yer debt if ye were tae kill my brother."

Arnaldo leaned on the table, clearly getting more than he'd hoped for in this conversation. "I'm listening," he said. "What about your brother?"

"He's the Earl of Lismore," Declan said. "That means Astria is the new countess. If ye kill my brother, the title goes tae me and ye can have his widow. Ye *did* want her, did ye not? Or is it Maude ye want?"

Arnaldo shrugged. "I'll take both of them," he said. "But if I kill your brother, what is in it for me?"

"Ye can moor yer ships in Scotland," Declan said. "The earldom of Lismore has four islands, and I'd give ye one of them. Ye could moor yer ships there and ye'd have an ally in Medusa's Disciples. Together, we would be a formidable force."

It was an enticing offer. Arnaldo sat back in his chair as the tavernkeep brought another cup and a big pitcher of ale. As the man scampered off, the smile returned to Arnaldo's face.

"I will consider it," he said. "The alliance, I mean. I'll kill your brother without expecting recompense because he's married to Astria and I want her. I'll also take your mother with me and make it so she will never return."

"Good," Declan said, satisfied. "But dunna think this will be easy."

"Why not?"

"Because both women are at the Blackchurch Guild," Declan said. "Ye know where that is?"

Arnaldo shook his head. "I do not," he said. "But I know that Blackchurch and Triton's Hellions are linked by blood. Everyone knows that."

"They are."

"Where is Blackchurch?"

Declan pointed west. "There is a road from this village that heads west," he said. "Follow it until ye come tae a town called Exebridge. Blackchurch is about a mile away."

"And that is where I'll find Bloody Maude and the dowager Duchess de Tarragona?"

"Aye," Declan said. He drained what was left in his cup before continuing. "In fact, I'll go with ye. Ye'll need my help finding them or the Blackchurch Guild will let loose on ye and ye'll not survive. Ye need me for this, trust me."

Arnaldo didn't have much of a choice. He wanted something. Declan said he knew where it was. If he didn't, then Arnaldo would kill him.

It was all quite simple.

Before the hour was up, they were heading west to Exebridge.

CHAPTER SEVENTEEN

One Week Later

H E WAS IN her body again.

Flat on her back, Astria was nude as she gazed up at the ceiling, eyes half-lidded, coming down from the euphoria of her second climax that morning. And the sun wasn't even up yet. But Payne was lying on her, his body still joined to hers, and her ever-curious hands wandered down his big body, stroking his smooth flesh, before finding their way between them and touching the junction between her legs where they were still joined. Her fingers touched his member and he groaned.

"I have duties tae attend tae this morning," he muttered into the side of her head. "I canna stay abed with ye all day, as much as I would love tae."

He shifted so that his weight wasn't pressing down on her, but she wouldn't let him withdraw from her body. He ended up half on, half off her. Her breasts, free of the weight he brought down on them, were now available for her to fondle. She did, one hand between her legs and the other on her breasts, until Payne's big hand joined her in her exploration of her own body.

Something she'd always avoided until just a few days ago, when she and Payne consummated their marriage and she realized that touching her body wasn't a bad thing.

Now, all she wanted to do was explore.

Payne finally pulled out of her simply so he could move to a more comfortable position and suckle her breasts tenderly. Astria closed her eyes, feeling the pleasure of his mouth on her flesh, her hand still between her legs, touching herself where it was warm and moist. When Payne couldn't stand being left out of it, he moved one hand between her legs and pushed his fingers into her, pleasuring her as she groaned softly. When she finally climaxed, he pushed himself up onto one elbow, gazing down at her flushed, lovely face.

"I told ye that I have duties," he said, leaning down to kiss her cheek. "I swear tae ye that if I get punished for being late, I'll tell them it was all yer fault."

Her eyes opened sleepily and she grinned. "Would you really?"

"I would."

Her arms abruptly came up, and she threw them around his neck, pulling him down to her seeking lips. Payne surrendered without a fight, but only until things started getting heated again and he forced himself away.

"Nay," he said, leaping out of bed before she could grab him. "Ye're a wicked, wanton woman, Lady Lismore, and I shouldna let ye seduce me."

Astria sat up, bare-breasted, watching him grab for his breeches. "Mayhap not, but you did," she said, smiling. "Are you truly so weak?"

He pulled his breeches over his hips, fastening the ties as he looked up at her. "For ye, I am," he said, eyes glimmering with warmth and affection. "I never knew I could become so attached tae someone in so short a time. Now I canna remember when ye were not by my side, lass. Everything about ye consumes me."

The smile on her face faded. "Do not say such things if you do not mean them," she said. "You do not have to say them because you think it is what I want to hear."

"I say it because it's the truth," he said. "Tell me something—have ye ever wanted yer marriage tae be more than a contract? More than marrying a stranger because yer father made a bargain with him?"

She wasn't sure what he meant. "A marriage is supposed to be many things."

"It's suppose tae be happy."

"How do you know?"

"Because my parents were happy. I saw it with my own eyes."

"But she went to sea and left him."

"Only out of duty tae her father," Payne said. "My father loved her enough tae know she had tae go. And he let her."

"And you want the same thing they had?"

He nodded before hunting around for his tunic. "I do," he said. "I sound like a woman saying such a thing, but I reason that if I'm going tae spend my life with someone, then I want tae like them. Love them, even. I dunna think that is unreasonable."

He found his tunic and Astria pulled the coverlet over her bare chest, thinking on what he'd said. "I do not think so either," she said. "But it is so very rare. I do not know if I've ever truly seen a happy royal marriage. The people who seem happy are the ones who do not have the weight of important duties hanging around their neck. Mayhap that is what makes them the happiest of all—no great responsibilities. And their marriages are happy because they can focus on one another, not the world that demands their time and attention."

He found his tunic, pulling it over his head. "That is astute," he said. "And mayhap there is some truth tae it. But I like tae think that if a man and woman like each other enough, and care about each other enough, a happy marriage will be important tae them both. Love can grow from such things."

"That's the second time you've mentioned love."

He looked at her. "Do ye think ye could love me? Just a little?"

She fought off a smile, averting her gaze shyly. "Mayhap," she said. "You are rather handsome. And you are very kind."

He plopped down on the bed, grabbing his boots from the floor. "That's a start," he said. "Do ye want tae know what I told my mother?"

"What?"

"I told her that ye and I were going tae have a love that would outlast the stars."

Astria turned to look at him. His back was to her as he put his boots on. Crawling out from underneath the coverlet, she made her way over to him, gently putting her arms around him and laying her head on his shoulder.

"Do you think so?" she whispered.

He put a hand up to clasp one of her arms. "I do," he said quietly. "I truly do."

"When will we know?"

He squeezed her arm. "That is the easy thing of it," he said. "We'll simply know. No one will have tae tell us. We'll feel it in our hearts, our minds. We'll just *know*."

He lifted her arm and kissed it, twice, before standing up. As he went out of the chamber to collect another tunic from a storage chest, Astria climbed off the bed and found a long-sleeved shift, one of the garments that Margit had given her. She pulled it over her head as Payne came back into the chamber, pulling on a padded tunic that was more like a vest. It was leather and fabric, and he began to fasten the ties on the front to secure it.

"What are ye going tae do about my mother's invitation?" he asked. "She's asked ye tae break yer fasts together at the Black Cock today. Ye've not said if ye plan tae go."

Astria sighed as he brought up a subject they hadn't discussed since Maude sent a missive the day before, one that Astria read and then put aside. But now, Payne was bringing the subject up and she wasn't sure how she felt about it.

"That is because I do not know," she said. "Although it has been about a week since she brought me here, my association with her has not exactly been friendly."

"I know," he said. "But she wants tae try tae make peace with ye, as my wife. Will ye at least give her the chance?"

"You think I should?"

He nodded. "I do think ye should give her the opportunity at some point," he said. "She's my mother, after all. She'll be in our lives forever. And the fact that she captured ye… I suppose ye could say that it was her duty as a pirate. And ye canna fault her for doing her duty. I'm not defending her actions, of course, merely pointing that out. Francis told me that she was never truly brutal tae ye as far as captives go. Would ye agree with that?"

Astria's lips twisted pensively. "I suppose she was no more brutal to me than I was to her," she said. "I fought the woman quite a bit, you know. I even kicked her in the face once. She could have punished me terribly, but she never did."

Payne lifted his eyebrows. "I'm glad tae hear that," he said. "Love, I'm not asking ye tae forgive her, but she wants tae at least make peace because of me. I dunna think she thought ye and I would become fond of one another, so that puts her in a strange position. But if ye dunna want tae leave the past behind ye, that's yer decision. I'll support ye, whatever ye choose tae do."

"I appreciate that," Astria said sincerely. "And I've thought about it. I'm not naïve, Payne. I understand the way the world works, and it is a brutal place. I understand that what she did to me was an opportunity. It wasn't personal. I know that because I've done the same thing, as The Sea God. But your mother did bring me to you, so for that alone, I suppose she warrants some forgiveness. Had it not been for her, I would have never known you."

"True," he said. "Then ye'll see her today?"

Astria shrugged. "I suppose," she said. "Truthfully, I've not seen her much over the past week. I appreciate the fact that she's left us alone."

"She's been more concerned with Declan's absence than bothering us," he said. "She sent men tae check the ships at Combwich, but they've not returned yet. She's afraid that Declan might be waiting for her on the road when she returns tae those vessels with the intention of ambushing her."

The subject turned to Declan's continuing absence, which had been weighing heavily on Maude as well as on Payne. It was never a good thing to have an unhappy man, with violent tendencies, on the loose, and Blackchurch was still on the alert because of it. It had been a long week of vigilance, but so far, no sign of the errant Matheson brother.

"I was wondering why your mother had remained here," Astria said. "And given that I know something of your brother because I've spent the past five months with him, I would say that her fears are not imagined. Declan Matheson has a vicious streak in him, Payne. I know he is your brother, but he is not a good man."

"I know," Payne said quietly. "And I'll apologize again for any insults or pain he might have inflicted on ye during yer captivity. I wish I could have prevented it."

Astria went to him, putting a gentle hand on his arm. "You need not apologize for your brother's actions," she said. "He is a grown man. He has made his own choices."

She was right, but Payne still felt guilty for his brother's behavior. "And those choices have historically been bad," he said. "And because we dunna know where he is, ye are tae be careful. Be alert of yer surroundings."

"But what about going into the village to see your mother?" she said. "I will have to travel the road between Blackchurch and the Black Cock."

"True," he grunted. "'Tis too bad Lord Exmoor willna allow her tae come tae Blackchurch, still. I think he is afraid that she'll try tae take the keep and then hoist her flag in victory."

"Would she?"

Payne shrugged. Then he chuckled, which made Astria laugh. He finished tying off his leather tunic and put his arms around her, kissing her sweetly as the woman practically collapsed into him. Whenever he embraced her, she turned to putty.

And he liked it that way.

"I'll be with Sin again today," he murmured, gently nibbling on her neck. "We lost a recruit yesterday when he nearly severed a hand, so we need tae pay attention tae those who are left. If ye decide tae answer my mother's invitation, then take a soldier with ye from the gatehouse. Have him escort ye tae the Black Cock."

Her eyes were closed as his lips gently kissed her shoulder. "I was thinking of taking Athdara," she said. "She's very much a warrior and she wants to meet Bloody Maude."

That was true. Athdara had come from a war-torn country and done her share of fighting over the years. She'd even trained at Blackchurch, which was how her husband had met her. Payne gave Astria one last kiss on the neck and let her go.

"Athdara makes an acceptable escort," he said. "But I'll see ye back here at supper."

"Indeed, you will."

With a wink, he quit the chamber, heading out to accomplish his duties for the day. Astria stood there with a silly smile on her face, already missing him now that he was out of her sight. She was mostly smiling at the question he'd asked her earlier because her instant longing for him when he was gone made her think of it.

Do ye think ye could love me?

She was fairly certain that she already did.

☙

"THERE IS A man in town who sells thread," Elisiana said. "I asked him to get me a certain color a few weeks ago, so I must see if he has it now."

Astria didn't have one escort into the village, but two.

After Payne departed and Astria donned a simple blue surcoat over the shift she wore, she'd brushed and braided her hair and set out for Athdara's cottage. What she walked into was a pack of young children running and playing as Athdara tried to feed them something before the day began. Her two older boys were fostering at Okehampton Castle nearby, but the younger three made it sound as if she had an entire pack of youngsters taking over her home.

The truth, however, was that this was a day of learning. St. Denis tutored the younger children of his trainers and had since Tay's children, the first to be born, was old enough to learn. He adored the duty. While the older children went to Exmoor's keep to begin their daily lesson with the earl, Astria told Athdara about her invitation from Maude and that Payne had requested an escort. Because Athdara did, indeed, want to meet the infamous Bloody Maude out of curiosity more than anything, she eagerly offered to escort Lady Lismore to town.

With one-year-old Lisabeth on her mother's hip, Athdara and Astria began their journey to the gatehouse. They were met halfway by Elisiana, who also had her infant son with her. When she heard about the trek into the village, she invited herself to go along, so the three ladies set out to make a morning of it in the village.

The morning was soft and bright, and rabbits dashed across the road as they walked. Literally, the road from Blackchurch led straight into the village, so those at the gatehouse could watch the women almost until they got into town. It was a pleasant morning, with pleasant conversation, and Elisiana brought up the thread issue because she was sewing something new to wear.

Lovely, normal conversation.

Worlds away from being a captive of Bloody Maude.

Truthfully, Astria found that she had to keep reminding

herself that her horrible captivity was all over. These days, she was on the verge of convincing herself that Maude had been a guardian angel and delivered her to the most perfect man imaginable. When Maude had first told her about the planned marriage, Astria well remembered her reaction. The fighting, the kicking. Maude had finally brained her with the butt end of a dagger. Everything had been chaotic up until the day she'd met Payne.

After that… well, the world just made more sense. All of it made sense.

And here she was, with lovely women on a lovely morning.

She could still hardly believe any of it.

"Astria?"

Hearing her name, Astria looked over at Athdara and Elisiana. "Aye?"

The women burst out laughing. "You did not hear a word I said, did you?" Elisiana said. "I suppose you are not to blame. Payne is quite worth dreaming over."

Astria flushed to the roots of her hair. "I suppose I was doing that," she admitted. "I am sorry. I did not mean to be an uninteresting companion."

"You're not uninteresting at all," Athdara said. "In fact, my husband told me something about you."

"What did he tell you?"

"That you are from the royal house of Portugal."

Astria nodded. "That is true."

"He said you are a princess."

Astria sighed, fighting a smile. "Did Payne tell him that?"

Athdara nodded. "He told everyone that," she said. "He was not bragging. He was simply telling them of your background, or so my husband said. Please do not be angry."

Astria shook her head. "I am not," she assured her. "And I was not trying to hide my identity. I suppose it had not occurred to me to tell you. I've been enjoying your companionship so very much and we've had so many other things to talk about. To be honest, I've never really had any friends."

"Never?" Athdara frowned. "Why not?"

Astria shrugged. "I am the youngest of many children," she said. "My life was dictated by duty and tutors and priests. I also married very young. Did you know I was married before Payne?"

Athdara nodded. "My husband told me that, too."

"It's true," Astria said. "He was very old. We had no children. But I went straight from the royal court to his household, and it was very isolating. Being a duchess means I am at the pinnacle, socially. There was never any chance for close friends, not in the San Miguel household."

"I am sorry," Athdara said, shifting her daughter to her other hip. "I told you that my father was a duke, a title that now belongs to my younger brother. I know what it is like to grow up in a political household."

"As do I," Elisiana said. "My father is the *Conte de Pondevedra.*"

Astria perked up. "That is Galicia," she said. "How did I not know that about your father?"

"Much like your royal connections, it never really came up," Elisiana said, winking at her. "We've only known each other a few short days. We cannot know everything all at once."

"That is true, but I am ashamed I did not ask you more about yourself."

Elisiana smiled. "Not to worry, my dearest," she said. "Time will have us knowing everything about each other someday.

That is what friends do. But in regards to my father, he has names and titles longer than anything you've ever heard. They fill up an entire page."

She giggled as Astria shook her head. "Not as long as mine."

"Go ahead," Elisiana encouraged her. "Tell me your full name. Let us see if it is longer than my father's."

Astria laughed softly. "You'll be sorry you asked," she said. "My full name is Maria Astria Julia, Princesa Real, Princesa of Beira, Duchess of Braganza, Duchess of Barcelos, Countess of Faria, Countess of Neiva, dowager Duchess of Tarragona, and Countess of Lismore. Now you know. Do I win?"

By the time she finished, both Athdara and Elisiana were laughing. "You have," Elisiana said. "Your name is longer than anyone's. Congratulations."

The three of them laughed all the way into town.

And it was glorious.

Once they reached the village, Elisiana wanted to go to the merchant who carried the thread and other incidentals, and Athdara elected to go with her. She reasoned that it might be better if she wasn't there when Astria and Maude first sat down to talk, since the situation was rather delicate, so she thought that perhaps she and Elisiana would come to the tavern later. Enough time for any tension between Astria and Maude to ease.

So they hoped.

As her friends headed toward the eastern side of town, Astria walked over to the Black Cock. It was early enough that it wasn't busy except for the people who had slept in the tavern the night before, so she opened the door to the usual burping and grunts of men who were rising to face the morning. Hobbes was over by the kitchen, supervising the food preparation, but he saw her enter. Having seen her when she had first arrived at

Blackchurch, and knowing she was Payne's wife from Margit, he went to greet her.

"Good morn to you, Lady Lismore," he said, using Payne's new title, something the entire village knew about now because word got around quickly. "It is early for you today."

Astria smiled at the man who had been genuinely kind to her. "I've come to see my husband's mother," she said. "Can you send word to her and tell her that I am here?"

Hobbes shook his head. "No need, my lady," he said, pointing to the semiprivate alcove frequented by the Blackchurch trainers. "She is there, breaking her fast."

Astria could see the chamber and part of the table inside, and just a hint of Maude's right side. "Thank you," she said. "Will you please bring me some food as well?"

"A pleasure, my lady."

Taking a deep breath for courage, because she truly wasn't sure how this was going to go, Astria headed over the alcove and stuck her head in. Almost immediately, she and Maude made eye contract and Maude froze for a moment, eyes wide.

"Good morn," she said. "Ye… ye came. I dinna think ye would."

Astria stepped into the chamber. "I thought it would be rude not to."

Maude smiled timidly. "Of course," she said. "Thank ye for coming."

"You are welcome."

"Will ye sit?"

Maude indicated the chair at the end of the table and Astria accepted. From that position, she had an unobstructed view of the common room and the entry door, but she wasn't paying attention to either. Mostly, she was looking at Maude.

She had a few things to say.

"I am hoping you will let me speak first," she finally said. "May I?"

"Please."

"Payne thinks you want to smooth what has been a rough relationship between us," she said. "He said you wanted peace. Is that true?"

She went right to the subject, one that had perhaps been the most important subject to settle since the day Maude and Astria first came into contact with one another, but it was much more complex with the advent of the marriage. Maude set down the cup of watered wine in her hand.

"Ye and I could not have had a more difficult beginning if we'd tried," she said. "Aye, I would like peace. I hope ye know that I never hated ye, lass. I was never angry at ye. What I did was…"

"Your duty," Astria finished for her.

Maude drew in a long, perhaps regretful, breath. "Aye," she muttered. "My duty. My duty tae take what I can, even if what I take is a person."

Astria could see that the woman was uncomfortable and quickly put up a hand to ease her. "Please let me finish what I was going to say," she said. "Maude, I know that our beginnings were difficult. But you were not any more difficult than I was. And you did not attack an innocent merchant fleet, so please put that out of your mind. What you attacked was me stealing ships from my stepson, who is the rightful Sea God. The San Miguel family is full of pirates, Maude. They are the Titans of the Deep. I want to be clear about that."

"I know."

Astria's brow furrowed. "You *know*?" she said. "How do

you know?"

Maude smiled faintly. "Because I'd be a poor pirate, indeed, if I dinna know who my enemies were," she said. "I've been around awhile, lass. I know more than ye think I do."

Astria was a little stunned. She'd fully expected her information to be a revelation in nature, but evidently, Maude already knew.

She thought she knew why.

"Did Payne tell you?" she asked.

Maude nodded. "He did," she said. "But I already knew before he told me. He told me that ye were concerned about my knowing of yer past activities as The Sea God. Truthfully, ye look more like a sea goddess tae me."

It was odd how the tension between them had suddenly eased. Truths were being spoken and honesty was preserved, which did much in dispelling whatever angst was still held between them. Truthfully, Astria felt as if a burden had been lifted from her shoulders.

She smiled weakly.

"It was all part of the family I married into," she said. "In the San Miguel family, the father managed the legitimate shipping business and the son managed the piracy business. Because my husband was quite old and his mind wandered toward the end, I was forced to manage both because his son, Arnaldo, was not as he seemed."

"What does that mean?"

"It means that he killed his father so he could assume both enterprises," Astria said bluntly. "He poisoned his father and then fled before he could be brought to justice. But I knew where he was. I knew where the fleets were moored, and that is why I stole those ships, the ones you captured. I took them from him because he was running from his punishment. He'd prematurely taken something that did not belong to him, so I took it back. Or tried to."

Maude nodded in understanding, realizing that the captive she'd taken those months ago, the one who fought like a wildcat, was evidently a woman of some spirit. Going to war against the rightful heir of a dukedom, no matter how he had acquired it, took resolve. She admired that.

Truthfully, she really wasn't surprised.

"I seem tae have a dishonorable lad myself," she muttered. "Declan the Devil, they call him. He envies all that I have, all that Payne has. I think he'd do away with all of us if he could."

"He's ruthless."

"Exactly."

A silence settled between them, but it wasn't uncomfortable. It was pensive because a new understanding had dawned. Two women who had done basically the same thing, had fought for their families in an unsavory family business, yet were facing opposition from someone close to them. They were more similar than either of them had realized, but they had one thing in common above all.

Payne.

"I suppose what I wanted to say to you is this," Astria said. "I think I want your forgiveness as much as you want mine. I was not exactly a model prisoner. I was very difficult and we had difficult moments, you and I. But you brought me to your son, who is by far one of the most honorable and kindest men I've ever met, and because he is the way he is, that tells me something about you."

Maude's gaze was surprisingly warm. "What does it tell ye?"

"That beneath that pirate queen persona, there is a remarkable woman," Astria said. "Only a woman of great character could have raised so fine a son. You and I may never be close, or the best of friends, but I want you to know how grateful I am to you for bringing me to Payne. Because of him, I've learned much about myself and about the warmth and comfort life has to offer. I've never known that before. But now I do. Because a madwoman named Bloody Maude captured me and two of my ships, my life is forever changed, and I am grateful."

By the time she was finished, Maude was smiling. "Those are words I never thought I'd hear from yer lips."

"Those are words I never thought I'd say."

"How does it feel? Do ye have a bad taste in yer mouth now?"

Fighting off a grin, Astria licked her lips. "A little."

Maude broke down into soft laughter. "The taste will go away soon," she said. "I'm going tae tell ye something, lass. I knew ye were the right woman for Payne. No ordinary woman will do for him. He's very special, as ye've seen. Ye canna know how glad I am that the marriage seems tae be pleasant for ye both."

Astria lowered her gaze, fighting off a blush. "You raised an understanding man," she said. "He has a generous heart and that is very rare."

Maude's smile faded. "Dunna ever hurt it," she said softly. "Payne is a good lad. He'll make a fine earl. But dunna ever hurt him. If ye do, ye'll have tae answer tae me, and I'll not be so patient with ye the second time around. Are we clear?"

Astria knew the threat was genuine, but she also knew it was coming from a mother speaking about her son. "We are," she said. "And I'm going to say the same thing to you."

"What?"

"Do not ever hurt him or shame him. If you do, you'll have to answer to me."

Maude stared at her for a moment before breaking into a smile. "I think we're going tae get along splendidly, lass," she said. "Ye have the same fearsomeness that I do. I recognize it and I respect it."

"You'd better."

Maude started laughing. Truly laughing. It wasn't that she didn't take Astria seriously, because she did. Very seriously. She was laughing because it was a threat she very much understood and agreed with.

"Then we have a truce, lass?"

Astria nodded. "We do."

"Good," Maude said, reaching over to grasp the pitcher of warmed wine. "Eat with me. I want tae hear more about The Sea God and where it all went wrong between the two of ye."

Astria held up her cup, and Maude poured some of the warm drink into it. "It went wrong from the start," she said. "He resented his father's marrying me and then he tried to seduce me at the wedding."

Maude set the pitcher down, frowning. "The bastard!"

"It's true," Astria said, taking a bowl from Maude and spooning out some of the boiled beef that was in a pot on the table. "And I fear that he is looking for us both. You because you took his ships and me because I took his ships first. The Titans of the Deep have a fleet of thirteen ships, Maude. That is nothing to be trifled with, so you must take care."

Maude broke off a piece of bread. "The man has had five months tae find us," she said. "If he hasna found us by now, then he's a fool. And fools are not tae be feared."

Astria spooned some of the beef into her mouth. "He's not a

fool, but he does get distracted easily," she said. "Hopefully he's found something else to focus his attention on and he'll forget bout those ships. Where are they, by the way?"

Maude had a mouth full. "That way," she said, pointing east. "They're moored in a river about two days from here."

"That was smart."

The conversation continued from there, veering back onto the subject of Payne. Maude was telling a story about a pet goose he used to have, one that constantly pinched him, when the entry door to the tavern opened up. Astria was listening to the story about the grumpy goose, not paying attention to who had just come into the tavern, but she should have.

God help her, she should have.

Maude saw it before she did because of her line of sight, straight to the front door. She stopped talking and her features tightened, which caused Astria to look over at the door, purely out of curiosity. But what she saw made her blood run cold.

Declan was standing there.

And so was Arnaldo.

The dangerous sons had arrived.

CHAPTER EIGHTEEN

"WHAT ARE YOU looking at?"

The question came from Elisiana as she stood inside the merchant's stall, looking at some durable fabric that she was considering using for a garment for her baby. But Athdara was standing in the doorway, looking over at the Black Cock.

"Athdara?" Elisiana said again. "What is it?"

Athdara shook her head vaguely. "A lot of men."

"Where?"

"The Black Cock."

Elisiana came away from the fabric and stuck her head out of the stall, seeing what Athdara was seeing. There were, indeed, dozens of men outside of the Black Cock. A small army, essentially, of men neither of them recognized.

Elisiana frowned.

"Where did they come from?" she asked.

"The road from the east," Athdara said. "I heard them, but I thought it was thunder. Did you not hear them a few minutes ago?"

Elisiana shook her head. "I did not," she said. "But who

would bring an army so close to Blackchurch? Surely the gatehouse guards see them."

Athdara suddenly ducked back into the stall, taking Elisiana with her. "What if it is that pirate that the men are speaking of?" she said. "Bloody Maude's son, the one who disappeared. What if he's returned with an army?"

Elisiana's trepidation grew. "And Bloody Maude is at the Black Cock."

"With Astria."

They could no longer control their fear after that. Athdara handed Elisiana her daughter, the child that was permanently attached to her hip. "I must go for help," she said urgently. "But you must hide. If those really are pirates, they are going to come to this stall because of all of the merchandise. Go hide with the smithy down the road. They won't raid his stall."

Elisiana took the little girl, who started to whine for her mother. "I will," she said bravely. "And I'll tell the merchant to take all of his most valuable things and hide them."

Athdara nodded quickly. "Hurry," she said. "I'll go for help."

"Be careful!"

As Elisiana dashed to the rear of the stall with the children, Athdara went to the front and peered from the front door again. Somehow, she was going to make it across the road without being seen, and her best chance of that would be to move down to the end of the avenue and dash across it into the trees. Through that bank of trees, she could get to the road that led to Blackchurch, but she'd be completely visible once she got onto the road. She had to hope she could run to Blackchurch faster than those at the Black Cock when they realized there was a lone woman on the road.

And a lone woman was vulnerable.

But she had to go.

Slipping into the back as Elisiana had done and hearing her daughter crying as Elisiana carried her away from the merchant stall, toward the town smithy's, Athdara paused a moment before heading off to her right, in the direction of the Black Cock. She thought she might be able to see Astria and possibly get her away from any danger. As she drew closer, slinking along a small alleyway that ended in the livery area of the Black Cock, she suddenly caught sight of someone. But it wasn't Astria.

It was Hobbes.

"Hobbes!" Athdara whisper-yelled, waving at the man. "*Hobbes!*"

Hobbes had been standing just inside the alleyway as it led from the livery yard, watching the tavern, but he heard Athdara's hissing.

Quickly, he made his way over to her.

"Hobbes, who are those men?" Athdara demanded, grasping the man's hand. "What are they doing?"

Hobbes was distressed. "It's Payne's brother," he said. "I recognized him because he stayed here for a few days. He's come back and he's brought someone who knows Lady Lismore. There's going to be a battle, my lady. Everyone is armed. I must go to Blackchurch and tell them!"

"Nay," Athdara said quickly. "I will go. Get your wife and servants out of the tavern. Get anyone you can out of the tavern. I will run to Blackchurch and tell them."

"Very well," Hobbes said, relieved that a young woman was willing to run, because he wasn't in the best of health. "You must hurry!"

Athdara simply nodded and ran back the way she'd come. She ran past the merchant's stall, in the direction of the smithy's, only she stopped short of reaching the area that smelled of fire and hot steel. This was the easiest place to cross the road, so she made sure it was clear before making her break to the other side.

By the time she hit the trees, she was flying, sailing through the foliage, scratching her legs and arms. But she continued to run. At one point, she stumbled in a hole, but she picked herself up and continued on until she was paralleling the road that led to the main Blackchurch gatehouse. The trees were thick here, so she couldn't run very fast, which meant she had to get out onto the road.

Where she could be seen.

But she burst out of the trees and started running at top speed.

She was afraid the men at the tavern would see her and, being that they were on horseback, catch up to her before she could reach Blackchurch's gatehouse. She ran the mile as fast as she could, and given she had long legs and was generally athletic, it wasn't too difficult for her. But she was terrified the entire time. The closer she came to the gatehouse, the more relief she felt.

Safety was just a few feet away.

In fact, she could see the gatehouse guards coming out of the gate, watching her run. A few of them were coming out to meet her, so by the time she reached them, they grabbed hold of her so she wouldn't collapse in an exhausted heap. One of the men, an old sergeant who had served St. Denis' grandfather, had her by the arm.

"What's amiss, Lady Munro?" he asked with great concern.

"You just left here. Where are the other ladies?"

"My husband," Athdara managed to say, breathing heavily. "Send for my husband immediately. Send for Sinclair and Payne!"

Soldiers were already running to the fields where the trainers were working for the day. The old sergeant helped Athdara into the gatehouse, pushing her gently onto a chair that someone brought out from the guard room. Word was already getting around that something was amiss in the village, and Athdara had only been sitting for a few minutes when she saw Tay coming down the road. He was barreling toward her and, given the man's size, it was like watching a runaway horse. Athdara bolted out of her chair to meet him.

"Payne's brother has returned," she said when they came together. "He's returned with dozens of armed men and he's in the Black Cock, where Astria is. You must take men to help her!"

Tay had hold of his wife, horrified by what he was hearing. Quickly, he moved to the open gates, dragging Athdara with him, trying to see down into the village. It was far enough away that all he could make out was the village and rooftops, and little more, but he believed her. Athdara wasn't the sort to panic.

He trusted her.

"Did you run all the way from the village, love?" he asked her.

She nodded, finally slowing enough so she could catch her breath. "I did," she said. "Lisi is there, too. We went to the village with Astria, but we went to the merchant's stall while Astria went to the Black Cock to see Maude. We saw the men ride in and I gave the baby to Lisi to take to safety. She went to the smithy's while I came back here to tell you."

Tay nodded, his manner grim. He began issuing orders, one of which was to secure the gatehouse. By the time he turned around, Payne, Sinclair, Fox, Ming Tang, Cruz, and Creston were all heading in his direction. Kristian was out on the lake this morning and Amir was with St. Denis, so the available trainers had come on the run.

And no one running faster than Payne.

"What's happened?" he demanded. "Where is my wife?"

Tay answered. "Your brother has returned with a horde of armed men," he said. "They are at the Black Cock, as are your wife and mother. I've sent for an armed force, Payne. How do you wish for us to handle it?"

Payne grunted angrily, realizing Declan had come back and Astria had been caught with his mother, in the village and without his protection. There was no telling what was going to happen.

"Damnation," he growled. "That bastard. That goddamn bastard. I'm going tae cut his heart out."

"Athdara?" Sinclair said, coming up behind Payne and trying to squeeze in to the huddle to hear what they were talking about. "Where is my wife?"

"She's safe," Athdara assured him. "She went to hide with the smithy. You know he will protect her, but she has your son and my daughter with her."

Sinclair looked at Tay. "I must retrieve them," he said. "I'll take men with me. Payne, I'll come to you after I've secured my wife and the children. I'm sorry, I must get to them first."

Payne understood completely. "Go," he said, putting his hand on the man's arm and giving him a push. "Go and get them. Ye must take care of them."

Sinclair was gone, pulling men with him as he went. That left Tay and Payne and the other trainers, and Cruz and Creston were already gathering armed soldiers. Even if the Blackchurch army didn't see action too often, if at all, they still maintained a constant state of readiness, so there were gangs of armed men ready to charge into the village within minutes.

That was all it took.

Meanwhile, the trainers armed themselves as best they could. The big armory, where most of their battle armor was stored, was toward the kitchens and the big dormitory, so they grabbed what they could from the smaller armory near the gatehouse that the soldiers used. Mostly, they took swords and daggers, and all of them with the exception of Ming Tang were able to don mail coats or sleeves. Ming Tang didn't fight with any of that protection, as that wasn't how he was trained, so for him, it was only daggers and a big iron spear.

That was all he required.

"Payne," Ming Tang said as the group approached the gatehouse where the armed soldiers were gathering, "if you go charging down to the Black Cock and the women are inside, it may put them at risk. Whatever you do must be carefully thought out."

Payne knew that. "I know," he said. "And I have a plan in mind."

"Good," Ming Tang said. "How can I help?"

The Shaolin monk wasn't a battle commander, so he wasn't expected to direct troops. But he was the best soldier anyone of them had ever seen, so his help was crucial. Payne came to a halt as the others gathered around him.

"As Ming Tang has pointed out, and as we all know, we canna go charging intae the village," he said. "Right now, my mother and wife are inside the Black Cock and my brother has decided tae return. I suspect they are in enough danger at the moment, so I dunna want—"

He was cut off when one of the sentries high on the gatehouse called down to them. "There's a fight at the Black Cock!" he shouted. "Men came from the woods and swarmed the men who were in front of the tavern!"

A moment of confusion was replaced by a moment of terror. It took Payne that short a time to realize what had happened. Immediately, he turned to Tay and Fox, the men standing closest to him.

"My God," he breathed. "Medusa's Disciples."

Tay grunted with the awareness. "They must have seen them and come out of their encampment," he said. "Go. We must *go*!"

Leaving Athdara and the gatehouse sentries behind, the Blackchurch trainers and almost three hundred soldiers started running for the village.

It was an explosion of epic proportions.

And the ancillary damage could be deadly.

CHAPTER NINETEEN

"**G**REETINGS, MAUDIE," DECLAN said. "I'd hoped tae find ye here."

Maude had just watched her son and a man she didn't know enter the Black Cock and head straight for her. Astria, however, recognized both men, but she didn't run. She simply sat there as they entered the tavern with about twenty men behind them, all of them armed.

Patrons, and servants, scattered.

"Declan," Maude said evenly. "Where have ye been? We've been looking for ye."

"And you, my dearest mother," Arnaldo said, overlapping Maude as he focused on Astria with glittering eyes. "I've been so worried about you. Are you well? You've not been injured, have you?"

He was practically standing over her, and Astria didn't like the position she found herself in. Without answering him, she stood up and moved to the side of the table where Maude was sitting. At least there was a table between them now, so she felt a little better, but not much.

Frankly, seeing Arnaldo come in through the entry door

had sent bolts of fear coursing through her body. That was not a sight she had wanted to see anytime soon, if ever, and the fact that he was with Declan made no sense at all, but she could tell just by looking at them that they had colluded. Somehow, someway, the pair had found one another and undoubtedly discussed their mutual troubles.

Something very bad was about to happen.

"You are far from home, Arnaldo," she said steadily. "And if you've come to rescue me from Bloody Maude, I'm afraid you are too late. My circumstances have changed and I no longer require your assistance."

Arnaldo grinned, a handsome gesture had the man not had such a black soul. "It is not assistance I've come to offer," he said. "You've been very naughty and it is time you face your punishment."

Astria snorted. "And who is to deal out the punishment?" she said. "You? I do not think you will survive such an attempt, so for your own sake, it would be better if you left. I do not need you and, quite honestly, I do not want to see you, so go back where you came from. This is no place for you."

Arnaldo started to move around the table in a clear attempt to get to her, but Declan grasped him by the arm. "Nay," he said, his eyes on his mother. "Dunna do it. That's Bloody Maude sitting next tae her and she'll not let ye take her prize. Ye'll lose what ye treasure most dearly if ye try."

He meant the man's privates, and he even looked at his crotch, gesturing. That threat alone cooled Arnaldo, but only slightly. He was still edgy, still wanting to move. But Maude stood up, unsheathing a wicked-looking dagger from her belt, and that took the conversation to a different level when she handed the blade over to Astria.

"The lass knows how tae use it," she told Declan and Arnaldo. Then she reached behind her and unsheathed another dirk, bigger and broader than the one she'd handed to Astria. "And I know how tae use this. If ye think tae take us, ye can try. But know that they dunna call me Bloody Maude without reason."

Arnaldo wouldn't be called off. Even the threat of castration couldn't hold him back now. Furious, he motioned to his men, who began to walk around both sides of the table. The intention was clear. One man came close to Maude and she kicked him in the kneecap. When he faltered, she used her dirk and stabbed him straight in the crotch, cutting through his manhood and into his bowels.

Screaming, the man fell away.

Meanwhile, the man who came at Astria had a longer way around the table, but she was ready for him. He reached out to grab her but she fell to her knees, underneath his grasp, and then used the dirk to stab the man in the lower belly. When he fell over onto the table, she leapt to her feet and stabbed him in the back, where both lungs were.

He collapsed on the floor, unable to breathe.

Two men down in as many seconds, both of them more than likely mortally wounded. The tense meeting between family members had just turned deadly.

And it was only going to get worse.

"Now," Astria said, feeling the thrill of battle pulse through her veins, "if you think you can take me, go ahead, but I'll not make it easy."

Arnaldo almost ordered more men to rush her, but he knew she'd use that dirk, and he further knew that Bloody Maude would help her. Puzzled, he looked at Declan.

"I thought you said they hated one another?" he said. "They are allies!"

Declan didn't like being made a liar. "I dunna know what has happened in the past week, but they were not allies when I left them last," he said, turning that confusion on his mother. "Have ye failed at this, too? She is a captive!"

Maude was cool. So very cool. She'd just stabbed a man, but she hadn't even broken a sweat. Not a hint of stress or perspiration. Even if her attention was on her son, she had eyes everywhere, watching the men behind Declan, watching Arnaldo in particular.

The Sea God.

She knew exactly who he was and what he wanted.

"Declan," she said, "I dunna know where ye've been, but wherever it was, ye've collected some unsavory companions. It would be better if ye left now. Before yer brother gets here."

That seemed to bring some enlightenment to Declan. With his having been gone a week, things had evidently changed and he was struggling to figure out what, exactly, had happened between his mother and Astria. They *were* allies. That made absolutely no sense to him, but the mention of Payne did.

"Of course," he said. "The husband of yer captive. Dunna tell me that he cares what happens tae her. He only married her because ye forced him tae."

"That is true," Maude said. "But she is still his wife. And a husband protects a wife."

She deliberately didn't tell him what everyone at Blackchurch and in the Medusa's Disciples encampment seemed to know, and that was the fact that Payne and Astria were evidently growing fond of one another. Nay, she didn't want Declan to know that at all because if he did, he could use it against Payne.

Maude wouldn't give him the ammunition.

Declan sighed heavily. "He would do better tae turn her over tae Tarragona," he said, gesturing to Arnaldo. "She's stolen from him and must be punished."

"She is no longer any concern of his," Maude said, her gaze shifting to Arnaldo. "The duchess is now the wife of my son, the Earl of Lismore. She is his property now. Any offense against her, by ye, will incur his wrath and more than likely the entire wrath of the Blackchurch Guild, where he is a valued trainer. Ye may be able tae take on Medusa's Disciples, but ye canna take on Blackchurch and win."

Arnaldo knew that Astria had been married to Bloody Maude's eldest, thanks to Declan, who had freely told him everything he knew, but it never occurred to him that Blackchurch, on the whole, would be involved. Even he wasn't stupid enough to tangle with the premier training guild of warriors in the known world.

That would be suicide.

"She has greatly sinned against me," he said, his anger rising. "I have a right for justice."

"What justice?" Astria said, unable to keep silent. "If anyone should seek justice, it should be me for your sins against my husband and your father."

Arnaldo stiffened. "What sins?"

Astria held the dagger up, a menacing gesture. "You know what sins," she hissed. "You've avoided me and the tribunal in Tarragona for an entire year. Ever since your father died after he had supped with you. Alone. Everyone knows you poisoned him, Arnaldo. You wanted the empire. You wanted the money. So you took your father, who was already old and ill, and poisoned his food."

Arnaldo's eyes widened dramatically. "You make slander-ous accusations!"

"I speak the truth!" Astria shot back. "The apothecary that Armand received his usual willow potion from swore to the magistrate after your father's death that *you* had told him to include arsenic in the compound, and you paid him five gold crowns for it. We have all the proof we need that you murdered your father, and if there is any justice in the world, someday, I'll see you hanged for your crime. You killed a kind old man who loved you, Arnaldo. You are a beast!"

Dramatic accusations were flying. Even Maude and Declan seemed to be caught off guard by them. Arnaldo was preparing to fly across the table at Astria to shut her up, but he was distracted when a great commotion could be heard. The entry door to the tavern was open and they could see a clash happen-ing outside. Very quickly, it began to move inside. Men were fighting, tables breaking, and chairs shattering. In the midst of it all, Medusa's Disciples were moving through the common room, calling Maude's name.

That was all it took for chaos to reign.

The Black Cock descended into madness.

As the fight started, Astria bolted from around the table, rushing into the next chamber, where there was an enormous hearth with big iron implements. She picked up an iron rod with a pointed end, like a spear, and turned around to see that Arnaldo had followed her. He was nearly on top of her. She was able to dodge sideways, and he flew into the wall next to the hearth. As he fell past her, she lifted the dagger and stabbed him in the right shoulder. The blade stuck, driven into the bone as it was.

Arnaldo howled.

Lifting the iron rod, Astria struck him, twice, before he managed to get a grip on it. Bleeding, with a dagger sticking out of his right shoulder blade, he was still stronger than she was. He yanked on the rod, tossing her around as she held on for dear life, before finally managing to get it free. Astria tumbled to the floor, immediately ducking under the heavy table as Arnaldo beat on it with the rod.

"You little bitch," he snarled. "When I get my hands on you, you can join my father in hell!"

Astria came out from underneath the table on the other side of it. As she watched, Arnaldo reached around behind him and was able to get his hand on the hilt of the dagger. Yanking it free, he roared with agony, but now he had a weapon.

And he was going to use it.

Astria didn't panic. She remained cool, as cool as she could, trying to calculate how she could get out of that chamber. Unfortunately, she had backed herself into a corner and there was only one way in, one way out. She couldn't even look to see where Maude was because she knew the woman would help her if she could, which meant Maude was fighting her own battles, life or death, against her own son. Therefore, she picked up a chair to use as both a shield and a weapon, waiting for Arnaldo to come flying over the table at her.

She was ready for him.

And, predictably, he came.

Astria swung the chair at him, as hard as she could, and it crashed over his right shoulder. He wasn't able to move his arm very well because of the knife wound, which only served to enrage him. She scooted away from him as he barreled after her, but as she got to the doorway, an old sailor she recognized appeared.

His name was Blue Death, or Blue. He'd answer to either. He'd served the San Miguel empire for forty years and Armand had considered him a friend. He was old and nearly senile, but he was still strong. He rather liked his young mistress and even served with her shipboard for a few years. The one thing he did possess, however, was a distinct hatred for Arnaldo because he, too, had heard the rumors that the son had murdered the father. And he had liked the father. Therefore, when Blue peered inside the Black Cock and saw the fight between Arnaldo and Astria, he came in to help.

And he was armed.

"Ye young pups are all alike," he growled, holding up a heavy sword with a sharp blade. "All ye want are things that belong tae others. Like yer father. I heard ye killed him, lad. And now ye're trying to kill his wife."

Arnaldo came to a halt. He knew Blue. The man could be terrifying. Whenever they boarded an enemy vessel, Blue was the first one on the ship, cutting men's throats and taking what he wanted. Frankly, Arnaldo was surprised to see him defending Astria.

"Take her a prisoner," he said, pointing to her. "She's an outlaw and a thief and she must face my justice. Do it!"

Blue looked at Astria, standing next to him with courage in her eyes. That was all he'd ever seen from the young duchess— courage and a sense of fairness to the men. He'd liked serving her.

But he definitely didn't like serving Arnaldo.

"I dunna take commands from ye, not no more," he said. "Come any closer tae her and I'll kill ye."

Astria, realizing the old salt was on her side, could do nothing more than stay back or risk injury.

"Have it your way," Arnaldo said. "But I'll be back, and when I see you, I'll punish you, too. Don't you know she's not worth saving?"

Blue looked at Astria, instinctively, which was his mistake. In that moment, Arnaldo flew at him, dagger in hand, and stabbed the man in the chest. Astria darted away, but not before she managed to pick up the sword that Blue had dropped. As she whirled around, planning to fight her way out of the Black Cock, she ran headlong into Declan, who used the butt of his sword to knock her, hard, on the forehead.

Astria fell to the floor, unconscious.

Maude, who had been behind Astria fighting her own battle, lurched forward to grab one of Astria's arms, trying to pull her to safety, but Arnaldo was there. He grabbed Astria's torso and picked her up, creating a macabre tug-of-war with Maude. There was so much turmoil and destruction in the common room, with so many men fighting, that Maude lost her grip on Astria when Arnaldo pulled too hard.

Now he had Astria, free and clear.

In a flash, he disappeared into the crowd of fighting men, emerging outside where the fighting was more spread out. As he heaved Astria over his shoulder like a sack of grain, it occurred to him that there were more men out here than he'd originally remembered.

Hundreds more.

Where did they come from?

"I believe that is my wife ye're holding."

The statement came from someone off to his left, and he turned to see a very big man standing there.

The Earl of Lismore, and his Blackchurch brethren, had made an appearance.

☙

PAYNE COULDN'T BELIEVE the luck.

He'd just charged into a mass of fighting men and was making his way into the tavern when a tall, dark-haired man emerged with a body slung over his shoulder. It took Payne all of a split second to realize it was Astria, so he blocked the man's path.

"Ye heard me," he said in a low, threatening tone. "Give me my wife and there'll be no trouble. Deny me and I'll kill ye."

The man turned to face him fully, eyeing him unhappily. "And just who are you?"

"I'm Bloody Maude's son," Payne said. "Ye need no more explanation than that. Give me my wife. *Now*."

The man was confident. *Too* confident. But Arnaldo had all of the leverage, at least in his mind, so he refused to budge. He wanted to watch the big Highlander squirm. In fact, his lips twisted into a smirk, but before he could reply, something hit him from behind. Something hard and sharp and painful plowed into his back, severing his spine, and he immediately collapsed. Astria would have fallen to the ground had Payne not caught her. As it was, she scraped the side of her face on the dirt, but Payne swept her up and away as Cruz gored the man through the back and Creston, right behind Cruz, took off his head with his nasty, serrated blade.

And that was the end of Arnaldo de Fernandez y de San Miguel, Duc de Tarragona.

Dispatched by Blackchurch.

"Let me see her, Payne," Ming Tang said as Payne ran to the outskirts of the fighting. "Kneel down and hold her against you. Let me look at her head."

Payne was shaking. He was so distraught at Astria's state that he could hardly control his emotions. "He must have hurt her," he said, his voice quivering. "He must have attacked her and I dinna get here in time. Sweet Jesus, dunna let her be badly injured. Is she?"

Ming Tang, who had a knowledge of healing, peeled back both of Astria's eyelids to gauge her pupil reaction and then felt the pulse in her neck. He was calm and patient, doing what needed to be done, as Payne struggled not to come apart. Finally, he patted Payne on the shoulder.

"She will regain consciousness," he said. "Do not fret, my friend. She is not badly injured."

Payne nearly collapsed. He breathed a great sigh of relief, realizing tears were forming in his eyes. He blinked, trying to keep them away, but the sight of Astria with her scraped face was too much for him. He let the tears fall, just for a moment. It was a brief show of emotion that was just as quickly gone. He didn't have the luxury of wallowing over it. His mother was still inside, and now that Astria was safe, he could focus on Maude.

"Can ye see tae my wife?" he asked Ming Tang hoarsely. "My mother is still inside and I must find her."

Ming Tang nodded. "Of course," he said. "Give the lady to me. I will ensure her safety."

Carefully, Payne deposited Astria into Ming Tang's protective arms and stood up. With a deep breath for courage, he unsheathed his sword and headed back toward the fighting.

There were only pockets of fighting outside at this point. Because there had been so many Blackchurch soldiers, both pirate factions had quickly dissolved. Medusa's Disciples had gone back to their encampment for the most part, and many of the men that came with Arnaldo had gone back the way they'd come once they saw their leader in pieces in the dirt. Horses were thundering back down the road as the fight broke up.

Inside the tavern, however, it was another matter.

There was still fighting going on, and as Payne walked into the common room, something sharp caught him in his right side. Infuriated, he swung his sword around and caught Declan in the chest. Declan grunted and fell back, taking the blade he'd just put in Payne's side with him as he went. Fortunately, he'd missed vital organs when he'd stabbed his brother, but Payne's sword had cut him deeply across his belly.

Blood began to flow from both brothers as they faced off against one another.

"If I'd only been better with my aim," Declan spat, holding a hand to his bleeding wound. "Tae hell with ye, Payne, ye arrogant bastard. I hated ye as a child and I hate ye now. I wished ye dead so many times that I canna remember when I haven't."

Payne had his sword pointed at his brother. "Where's Maudie?"

Declan had a triumphant smile playing on his lips. "That's for me tae know, lad."

Payne's jaw twitched dangerously. "Declan, I swear by all that his holy, if ye dunna tell me, I'll run ye through this instant," he said. "Dunna be a fool. *Where's* Maudie?"

Declan was precluded from responding when Francis, rubbing his sleepy eyes, suddenly emerged from the corridor that led back to the sleeping rooms of the Black Cock. One look at the common room, however, and the youngest brother let out a shout.

"What happened here?" he demanded. Then he saw his brothers across the room, both of them bloodied. "What's going on? Payne?"

Payne had to back away toward the door so Declan couldn't get in behind him. "Where have ye been, lad?" he said, sounding angry. "Men are losing their lives out here!"

Francis looked stricken. "I had too much tae drink last night," he said. "I only now awoke when I heard some shouting outside my window. What's this all about?"

Payne wasn't going to take the time to explain. "Get yer weapon and find Maudie," he commanded. "Declan has done something tae her. She's here, somewhere, in this madness. Find her!"

Stricken, Francis wasn't so sleepy anymore. He ran off to collect his weapon. That left Payne returning his attention to Declan, but as he did so, Sinclair and Fox entered the tavern.

"Payne," Sinclair said in a deadly tone. "What would you have us do? What do you need?"

Payne had his eyes on Declan. "Is yer wife secure?"

"She is, thankfully," Sinclair said. "Everyone is quite well. Tell me what you need, lad. I'm at your disposal."

"Find my mother," Payne said. "Francis is going tae look for her, but Declan will not tell me where she is. I fear we may be too late tae help her, but find her. Please."

Fox immediately took off into the tavern, on the hunt for the red-haired pirate queen they'd all seen from a distance, but Sinclair came to stand alongside Payne as he faced off against his brother.

"Let me help you," Sinclair said in a low voice. "Let me take fight for you. It will be my honor."

"Nay," Payne said. "Although I thank ye, I will deal with my brother."

"If you plan to kill him, let me," Sinclair muttered in his ear.

"You do not want to have his blood on your hands. Not your brother, no matter what he's done."

Payne heard his plea. "Nay," he whispered. "He's mine. No matter what happens, he's mine. Ye'll not interfere. Promise me."

Sinclair growled. "Payne…"

"Promise me or get out."

"I promise."

Cruz and Creston entered the common room, followed by Amir and St. Sebastian, who had heard about the fight at the Black Cock and come all the way from Exmoor's keep. The classes were still going on at Blackchurch, as usual, thanks to the assistant trainers, and Kristian was still on the lake so he hadn't heard about the situation yet, but the vast majority of the training hierarchy of Blackchurch was at the Black Cock. Tay blew in finally, after making sure the fighting outside had died away, and he directed the trainers to settle down those still fighting inside because they'd already torn the place up. Reluctantly, the others moved to do Tay's bidding, but Sinclair never left Payne's side.

And he wasn't going to, no matter what he'd promised.

Not oblivious to the swordsman behind him, Payne faced off against his brother.

"Why, Declan?" he finally asked. "Why did ye do this? What devil possessed ye?"

Declan snorted. "Dunna insult me," he said. "Ye've run off and lived here for ten years, yet ye pretend tae be concerned for yer mother, yer father, and yer family. But ye're no better than me, Payne. All ye care about is yerself."

"Just because I chose a different path from ye doesna mean I dunna care," Payne said. "Who was the man ye were fighting with? The one who was carrying my wife?"

Declan gave him a look that conveyed his disgust with his brother. "Yer wife," he muttered distastefully. "Ye know that the woman tried tae steal everything from the rightful heir tae the House of San Miguel. She's a thief."

"How would ye know that?"

"Because that man is now my ally," Declan said, nearly shouting it. Irritated, he continued. "I met him in Combwich. He'd been following Maudie because he wants his ships back. He also wants that woman ye married."

Payne's brow furrowed. "How did he know tae find her in Combwich?"

Declan rolled his eyes. "The bloody Irish told him," he said. "He paid Kraken's Horde a fortune and they told him where tae find Maudie."

"But how did *they* know?"

"I wouldna know," he said. "Ask Arnaldo."

"Arnaldo," Payne repeated, confirming who the dead man outside was. "That's the Duc de Tarragona?"

"Who did ye think it was?"

Payne shook his head. "I dinna know," he said. "But the man who had my wife is lying outside with his body in one place and his head in another. I dunna think he can help ye anymore."

Declan stiffened, enraged by the news. "No matter," he said. "I've been waiting years for this, Payne. Unless ye're too much of a coward tae face me alone and ye're going tae have yer friends rush me. Face me like a man, just the two of us. Let us settle this as brothers."

Payne gazed at his brother. After a moment, he shook his head. "What have I ever done tae ye that ye'd want tae kill me?"

he said, baffled. "Other than the fact that I was born first, I've never done anything tae ye. Is it money ye want? Then take it. Take all of it. I've no need for it. But ye've a mercenary heart in ye, Declan, that's going tae be the death of ye."

Declan wouldn't, or couldn't, be reasoned with. He'd spent his whole life bitter and resentful, so it was difficult to change that way of thinking.

"It's a mercenary heart that is going tae get me what I want out of life," he said. "Not all of us had fathers who insisted we train at the finest English homes or gifted us tae kings."

Payne mulled that over, a sad expression on his face. "Is that it?" he said. "Ye envy what Da did for me?"

"He did everything for ye."

"That wasna my fault, Declan," Payne said. "I did as I was told, as ye did. And ye have had the privilege of serving with Maudie for the past ten years. I dinna. I wish I did."

Declan faltered, but only slightly. "I've spent the past ten years being told what tae do by my mother," he said. "Do ye know how humiliating that is?"

"She's Bloody Maude, for Christ's sake!"

"She's a woman!" Declan shouted in return. "A woman, my mother, and I was forced tae serve her. A grown man and his mam!"

Payne could see that there were a few issues at play here. It was the most he'd ever gotten out of his brother about the man's views. Although he'd known what they were, to hear Declan voice them was a milestone. Declan would rather ignore things, or gossip, or cast dirty expressions rather than discuss his feelings.

"Again, nothing I had control over," Payne said evenly. "Yer battle is with Maudie, not me. Or Da, but he's not here. It's not me ye're angry with, but them."

"It's *ye*," Declan insisted. "I've been the middle brother for too long. When ye're dead, I'm going tae take yer wife and sell her back tae the Portuguese. Or mayhap I'll keep her on my ship tae please the men. I told ye once she was a royal whore. Someday, it'll be the truth."

"I'll kill ye first."

"Ye can try."

Payne moved before Declan had a chance to prepare. One moment, they were standing several feet apart, but in the next, Payne was nearly on top of him. The violent storm that was The Tempest was in action as his sword moved in his brother's direction, as fast as lightning. Declan managed to step back and lift his sword to defend himself, but not fast enough. Not high enough. Payne hit the sword and then he hit Declan.

After that, the fight was on.

For the most part, the battle at the Black Cock was over. There were dead and injured men on the ground, with colleagues trying to help them. The tavern was in complete disarray, with broken windows and tables and chairs, and somewhere in the back, Hobbes and Margit were trying to keep their servants calm.

But Payne couldn't think about that. All he could think about was subduing his brother and throwing the man in the Blackchurch vault for eternity. He didn't want to kill him. He just wanted him neutralized. When all was said and done, Declan was still his brother, no matter how much the man hated him, and truth be told, the fight between them greatly saddened Payne. He'd never wanted to be at odds with his brother, but Declan had made any sort of pleasant relationship between them untenable.

And that was the saddest realization at all.

Declan wanted him dead.

But Payne wasn't going to let that happen. He was better trained, better educated, stronger, and bigger than his brother. He had everything in his favor, including a blossoming love for the woman he'd married, a woman that Declan had threatened. Therefore, Payne was pursuing Declan all over the common room, trying to disable the man or, at the very least, subdue him.

But he wasn't happy about it.

In his periphery, he could see Sinclair still standing on the edge of the room. Someone else was there, too, and it took him a moment to realize it was Amir. Both men were watching the fight, waiting to see if they were needed. In Sinclair's case, it would be breaking a vow, but Amir had made no such vow. Sinclair had whispered the situation to him and Amir was prepared to step in if things got out of hand. But Payne was handling himself beautifully, using his skill and training and talent, and Declan was mostly running from him at that point.

Until the tides changed.

Declan disappeared into the alcove that the Blackchurch trainers usually inhabited on their jaunts to the Black Cock and Payne went in after him. No sooner had he entered the chamber, there was a loud *thud* and Payne suddenly hit the floor, blood pouring from his face. Those in the common room could see the man on the ground. A broken stool ended up on the floor next to him, clearly thrown by Declan after he broke it on his brother's face. Realizing they were watching the moment when Declan would kill his brother, Sinclair and Amir rushed toward the alcove, hoping they would be in time. Right now, Payne's life was measured in seconds.

And it took several to get across the common room floor.

But then a strange thing happened.

The small corridor that led to the livery yard was adjacent to the alcove, and before Sinclair and Amir could get across the destroyed common room, Maude appeared with Francis behind her. She was beaten and bloodied, but upright and heavily armed. The first thing she saw was Payne on the ground, with blood on his face, and she charged into the alcove with Francis on her heels.

Sinclair and Amir reached the chamber a second later only to see Maude charge Declan. Seeing his mother coming, Declan thrust his sword at her, the sword meant for Payne, and Maude ran straight into it. As they watched in horror, Maude impaled herself on the sword in her haste to get to her middle son, but the sword she was holding in her right hand plowed directly into Declan's neck, pushed into him with such force that it nailed him to the wall behind him. As Declan breathed his last, impaled through the neck, Maude fell to the floor with a sword in her chest.

"My God," Sinclair gasped, leaping over Payne to get to Maude. "Easy, lady. Be at ease. I have you."

Francis, who had been trying to drag Payne away from the fighting, saw what happened to his mother and cried out in horror. He dropped Payne and rushed to Maude's side, pulling her off the floor and holding her as Sinclair tried to assess the damage. Meanwhile, Payne started coming around as Amir pulled him into a sitting position.

The world was rocking and there was blood pouring from his nose and mouth where he'd bit his cheek when Declan hit him in the face, and it took him a minute to clear the stars from his eyes. He could hardly see because of it. Not only did he *not* see Maude right away, but he didn't see Astria and Ming Tang coming in through the entry door, either. Astria had regained consciousness moments earlier, and unless Ming Tang wanted to get into a fistfight with her, he'd had no choice but to let her return to the embattled tavern in search of her husband.

She'd been desperate to get to him.

Astria saw Payne the moment she came through the door. Her ears were ringing, still, and she had a painful lump on her head, but she was alive. There was nothing more in the world that she wanted than to find Payne, so the moment she came through the entry and saw him sitting up with blood all over his face in the far alcove, she raced across the devastated common room and into the alcove. Falling to her knees, she threw her arms around him.

"I'm here, my darling, I'm here," she wept, holding him tightly. But she quickly loosened her grip to get a look at his face. "Let me see the damage. How do you feel?"

Realizing Astria was with him fed Payne's sense of relief and joy. He was still dazed, but not dazed so much that he couldn't respond to her. He pulled her into his powerful embrace, trying to shake off the fuzziness in his head.

"I'm well enough," he said. "Please dunna worry. I'm more concerned with ye. How are ye feeling?"

Astria had her hands on his face, inspecting the injuries. "I'm well, I promise," she said, a hand fluttering to the lump on her head. "It's just a bump, after all. But what's happened? I awoke and Arnaldo is in pieces and—"

"Payne," Francis called to his brother, angst in his voice. "Come quickly!"

Payne tore his eyes away from Astria, finally seeing the damage at the far end of the chamber. Declan was dead, impaled on the wall by a sword through his neck, and on the floor lay a small figure with red hair.

Maude.

Payne must have whimpered, because his reaction, or even his movement, had Astria looking over to see the same thing. Maude on the ground, bloody, with a sword in her chest. They both moved in that direction, he helping her, she helping him, both of them stagging over to see the horrific scene before them.

It was like a nightmare.

Maude was mortally wounded, but she was still conscious. Blood was spreading out underneath her and Francis was elevating his mother's head as Sinclair determined that nothing could be done. The sword was actually preventing the woman from bleeding to death in an instant, so he simply left it. But he reached up, pulling Payne down to his knees beside him.

"Speak to her," he whispered. "Her time is short. Tell her how much you love her."

Payne nearly came apart. *This canna be happening!* He took his mother's hand and held it to his lips. "Maudie," he whispered, his tears falling onto her fingers. "I'm so sorry this happened. I'm sorry I couldna protect ye."

Maude was as pale as snow. She gazed up at her son, her pale blue eyes unnaturally bright. "Dunna weep," she said haltingly. "Yer father… He's waiting for me. I'll not be alone, I promise. But I'm going tae miss ye very much."

Across from Payne, Francis broke down in quiet tears. "Oh… Maudie," he wept. "How will we go on with ye?"

Maude tried to reach up, to touch Francis as he wept, but she was too weak. Francis saw her hand, however, and grasped it tightly.

"Ye're stronger than ye know, Francis," she murmured.

"Continue the legacy. That's my wish. There's nothing more fearsome than a pirate named Pope Francis."

She smiled when she said it, teasing him gently, but Francis would have none of it. "I canna," he whispered tightly. "Not without ye. I canna do it."

"Ye must," Maude whispered.

"But I canna!"

"If ye dunna, then who will?"

"Me," Astria said, leaning over Payne's shoulder. When Maude's eyes moved to her, she smiled bravely. "Not to worry, Maudie. I understand. If the past five months have taught me anything, it is that you are a woman of strength and dedication. I'm sorry I never told you that. But I'll take care of your sons and your legacy, I swear it. Be at peace, dear lady. All will be well."

Maude's smile grew as she gazed into Astria's eyes. "My legacy," she whispered. "Who knew it would be ye?"

Astria met her smile. "It was fate," she said. "Fate the day you captured me. Fate the day you pledged me to Payne. We'll make sure you are well remembered by those who love you."

"Promise?"

"I swear upon The Sea God that Bloody Maude will live on, in hearts and in memories."

"Thank ye, lass."

Maude was fading fast. That much was clear. Still smiling, she managed to look at Payne one last time. Her beloved son. He had her hand clasped against his cheek, trying to give her some comfort, and to Maude, it meant everything.

He meant everything.

"Do ye remember what ye asked of me so recently?" she said, barely audible. "Ye wanted tae be the one who held my hand at the end. Remember?"

Payne was choked up. "I do."

"Ye were, lad," she said, her eyes closing. "In the end, ye were the one who held my hand as I breathed my last."

Payne couldn't even reply. As he watched, Maude fell silent and her breathing grew faint and unsteady before stopping completely. Even when the air left her lungs, never to return, she was still smiling.

They could all see it.

Bloody Maude died with a smile on her lips.

As Francis collapsed on his mother, his face on her neck, weeping silently, Astria wrapped her arms around Payne and held him tightly as his tears flowed. No matter who she was, or what she had done in her life, Maude was still their mother and they loved her dearly. Sinclair, Amir, and Ming Tang quietly stepped away, giving the family time to grieve, but not before Sinclair and Amir removed Declan from the wall and carried his body away. Somehow, it didn't seem right that he should be there at such a moment, the man who had killed his own mother.

The man who had wanted everything and lost.

But Maude's memory would be much different, and that was already clear. There was great grief at her death, a testament to how much she was adored. After a few moments of weeping into Astria's shoulder, Payne finally lifted his head and struggled to compose himself as his wife wiped his tears off his face.

"I am so very sorry, my love," she murmured. "In spite of our rough beginning, I had come to like your mother. And I think she liked me."

"She did," Payne said hoarsely. "I think she liked ye a great deal."

"I think so too," Astria said. "Would you like me to leave you and your brother alone with her, just the two of you?"

He looked at her, eyes watering. "Would ye mind?"

"Of course not," she said, kissing his bloodied cheek. "I will be standing just outside the chamber should you need me."

He nodded and she kissed him again, leaving him and Francis at their mother's side, mourning a tremendous loss. Astria stepped out of the alcove, seeing that all of the Blackchurch trainers had gathered there, including Kristian and St. Sebastian.

And one more unexpected person.

St. Denis had come to the tavern after hearing about the battle, now seeing the aftermath. Amir had explained everything to him, so he was aware of the situation, aware of the death of Bloody Maude. He'd never met Astria because there had never been the opportunity, but Amir led him over to her and made the introductions.

"It hardly seems appropriate for social proprieties at a time like this, but I am glad to meet you, Lady Lismore," St. Denis said. "May I extend my condolences on the loss of Payne's mother?"

Astria nodded. "Thank you, my lord," she said. She hesitated before continuing. "I realize that she was considered a fearsome individual by many and, I'm sure, there was loathing by some, but at her core, she was a mother who was much loved by her sons. Two of them, at least."

St. Denis lifted his eyebrows in understanding. "I've been apprised of the entire situation," he said. "Families can be… complicated."

Astria smiled faintly. "I would know that better than most."

"You would?" St. Denis said, his gaze moving over her, inspecting her. "Mayhap one day you will indulge me in a conversation about your family history. I do not know much about the Portuguese."

"I would be delighted, my lord."

He smiled faintly and the conversation died, though not awkwardly. Feeling weary after such an eventful morning, Astria went to find a chair that wasn't broken. Kristian found one for her and brought it out from the kitchen, where he had been discussing helping with the cleanup of the Black Cock with Hobbes. In every aspect, the Blackchurch trainers were protective of the tavern, their place of relaxation and camaraderie. Just as Astria sat down, however, Payne suddenly appeared, and Francis behind him. As Francis headed out to the encampment to inform the men of Maude's passing, Payne was faced with his friends, all of them, looking at him rather sadly. His gaze found Kristian and Sinclair and Ming Tang.

"Would ye do me the great honor of preparing my mother for transport back tae Scotland?" he asked, his voice hoarse. "I should like her treated with all due respect."

Sinclair was the first to move to him, putting his hand on the man's shoulder. "The honor is ours," he said quietly. "She was a strong woman, Payne. She raised a fine son. I am so very sorry."

Payne nodded in appreciation. It was a sentiment relayed by Kristian as well as he went to help Sinclair. Ming Tang, as a Shaolin monk, traditionally wrapped himself in *kasaya* robe, stitched together from three pieces of linen, and as a sign of respect, he removed it to wrap Maude's body in. While Sinclair and Kristian discreetly removed the sword in the woman's chest and began to wrap up her body, Ming Tang went to Payne.

"In my culture, we believe that death is not the end, but a transition to another life," he said. "We offer prayers for the dead to help them during this transition. May I offer them for your mother?"

The tears were back in Payne's eyes as he nodded. "Aye," he whispered. "Thank ye."

Ming Tang smiled faintly. "Do not be sad, my friend," he said. "Rejoice in the joy of your memories. Rejoice in the new life your mother will know. I will confess that I am torn about her rebirth, however. It is our belief that the better the life, the more positive the rebirth. Your mother was much loved by her sons, but she lived a life that some may consider questionable. Mayhap God will permit her to be reborn as a sea serpent to continue her domination of the seas."

That brought a soft laugh from Payne. "I wouldna be surprised," he said. "Or a fish with teeth that eats other fish."

Ming Tang chuckled. "Mayhap," he said. "But whatever she becomes, I shall pray for her peace and comfort."

Payne's smile faded. "It would be much appreciated."

Leaving Payne with a smile, Ming Tang went to help tend to Maude. In fact, several of the trainers went to help while Cruz and Creston were tasked with handling Declan's body, which had been taken back to the chamber he'd shared with his brother at one time. With everyone moving to help Payne in his time of need, that left Payne better able to focus on his wife.

When Astria saw him heading toward her, she stood up from the chair and opened her arms to him. He held her tightly, sighing heavily as he drew comfort from her. So much comfort.

As if he'd been doing it his entire life.

There were no more words to be spoken. Life had changed for them and they had a future to face together. A bright future.

Payne took Astria in hand, leading her out of the Black Cock, away from the chaos, away from the madness that had descended for a short time. Outside, they passed by Arnaldo's headless body, which the birds were already starting to descend on.

But Astria didn't care.

She, too, was looking ahead, not behind.

As Payne had once told her, their love would outlast the stars, and they were well on their way to that destiny. They'd weathered more than any couple should have to weather in their short marriage. It had only been a week since they'd been joined in matrimony, but in that week, they'd lived a lifetime.

And they still had a lifetime to go.

For the Black Church trainer known as The Tempest and the Portuguese princess once known as The Sea God, the possibilities of a wonderful life ahead were endless.

EPILOGUE

Four years later

I T WASN'T RAINING, although the skies were threatening. On the surface of Lake Cocytus, something was about to happen.

A great sea battle was about to take place.

Sailing north on the lake, having just come from a small inlet where it had been moored, the vessel once known as the *Mother Mary*, now rechristened the *Bloody Maude*, was looking for a secondary ship hiding somewhere on the lake shore. It was a cog belonging to the Blackchurch Guild, more specifically commanded by Kristian, and it had six recruits on it who were at the end of their seafaring module of training.

This was to be their boarding test.

Commanding the *Bloody Maude* was none other than Pope Francis, the great pirate that ruled the waters around Scotland with several ships. Seventeen in total, including thirteen that had once belonged to the Titans of the Deep. That faction was all but gone now, having merged with Medusa's Disciples, but it made for a large and imposing group of high-seas brigands.

One Francis commanded most ably. As his mother had once said:

There's nothing more fearsome than a pirate named Pope Francis.

She'd been right.

About once a year, however, Francis broke away from his pirating life and came down to Blackchurch, to the ship that he'd given the guild for the their training, and helped with the seafaring module. It was all great fun and gave him a chance to see his brother, a man he loved dearly. Even now, Payne was on board along with his three-year-old son, Bowie.

And what a son he was.

Bowie Matheson, heir to the Lismore earldom, had been born a fighter. He'd come out of his mother feet-first, howling and grabbing at anything he could get his hands on. Payne had held his infant son that first night, tears of joy running down his face, wishing his mother could see the flame-haired infant.

Perhaps she was seeing him now.

Payne held his son tightly as the boy stood on the railing of the bow, yelling in delight as the wind rushed in his face. Francis, standing next to his brother and nephew, was full of joy at the boy's reaction to being on the water.

"He's a natural, Payne," Francis said. "Look at him—he's thrilled with this."

Payne had a good grip on his child because the boy tended to be squirrely. "I know," he said with a sigh. "I'm not entirely sure how I'm going tae explain this tae his mother. She wants the lad tae be a proper knight and return tae the Portuguese royal court."

"Pah," Francis said. "She's not seen how happy he is on the water. This is what he was born tae do."

"Then ye can tell her. And run when ye do."

Francis laughed, seeing the bow of the ship that they were

meant to encounter up ahead. These sea games could be great fun, but they could also be serious, especially with the recruits trying to prove their mettle. There were only six this time, and about thirty men aboard the *Bloody Maude*, so that was why Payne had agreed to bring Bowie along for the experience. Six men against thirty would be a short fight and Bowie would have the fun of a little jaunt on the lake.

Unless Astria found out.

Then they'd all be in trouble.

"Where does Astria think her son is?" Francis asked, reading his brother's mind.

Payne was precluded from answering when Bowie threw up his arms in his excitement, clipping his father in the mouth. Payne had to rub his bruised lip before continuing.

"She thinks he's with the nurse that tends the other children during the day," he said. "The best thing we ever did was bring on that nurse. She tends Tay and Fox and Sinclair's children along with mine, and it gives the wives time they need tae do chores or other things. The woman had the children over by the gatehouse, where they were playing on the grass, and I just took him."

"Let's hope Astria doesna realize he's missing."

Payne shook his head. "After this, I'll take him back tae the nurse and she'll never know."

"You hope."

"She's just given birth," Payne reminded him. "She'll be with our new lad, who looks exactly like me, I might add."

"Aye, he does," Francis agreed. "But his name? Maximilian? 'Tis a big name for a wee bairn, Payne."

Payne grinned. "That was Astria's choice," he said. "She wanted tae name him Sancho, but no son of mine is going tae be named Sancho. Then she wanted Maximilian, a terribly grand name, and I couldna deny her. Max Matheson it is."

Francis merely chuckled.

The water at the northern end of the lake always tended to be choppier because of the shape of the lake at that end, so the boat was doing great dips in the waves, splashing water as it moved. Spray ended up on Bowie and Payne, and the little boy squealed in delight because his face was getting wet.

"Papa, faster!" he demanded. "Go faster!"

Payne grinned. "I canna make it go faster, lad," he said. "Tell Uncle Francis. Mayhap he can."

"Fanny!" the boy yelled. He couldn't pronounce Francis, so it came out as "Fanny." "Faster!"

Francis nodded quickly. "I will, lad," he said. "I'll go blow on the sails. Will ye blow with me?"

Bowie wanted to blow. Francis took him in his arms, rushing back along the deck as Payne followed to make sure Francis had a good hold on the boy. Together, Francis and Bowie blew at the sails, which were already billowing from the strong breeze. They blew and blew. Soon enough, the Blackchurch cog came closer and the time for boarding would soon be upon them. Francis handed Bowie back to his father.

"Hang tight tae the lad," he told Payne. "This shouldna take long. Ye should bring him up front so he can see his victorious uncle."

Gripping his son, who still wanted to blow on the sails, Payne followed his brother to the bow, where Francis' men were preparing to lash the ships together. The Blackchurch cog came close and the ropes began to fly, pulling the ships against one another. The men from both ships began shouting at each other, waving their swords threateningly, but the men on the

Blackchurch cog suddenly grew terribly subdued. That caused the men on the *Bloody Maude* to grow quiet purely out of confusion.

But Payne soon saw why.

Mounting the railing, with a rope in hand that was tethered to the sail above, was none other than Lady Lismore.

The Sea God had made an appearance.

The former Sea God, anyway, but no matter. Payne knew what her appearance meant. God help him. He was in so much trouble that he couldn't even fathom it. He would be in trouble for the rest of his life. He watched, with apprehension, as his wife swung from her deck to his, releasing the rope and focusing on her husband and son. Bowie screamed when he saw his mother, and Payne was forced to put down the boy, who ran gleefully to her. Astria, looking like a goddess in a fitted tunic, hose, and boots, picked her child up.

But she didn't have a word for her husband.

Only a glare.

"Francis?" she said.

Feeling as if he were somehow responsible for this situation, Francis jumped at the sound of her voice.

"My lady?"

Sword in hand, Astria pointed to the starboard rail midships. "Install the plank."

Everyone knew that that meant. As Francis ordered his men to produce the plank that would extend from the railing over the water, usually used for boarding, Astria slowly made her way over to her husband.

"I took Max for some air and thought to join his brother on the grassy area for play," she said. "And what did I find? No Bowie. The nurse was quite happy to tell me that he was safe because he was with his father, but knowing where you would be today told me that he was, in fact, shipboard with his father."

Payne sighed heavily, caught in a trap of his own making. "He was perfectly safe."

Her eyes narrowed. That wasn't the thing to say. Using her sword, she pointed to the starboard railing.

"Usually, I bind offenders and simply throw them overboard," she said. "In your case, I shall not bind you, but you will walk that plank and swim to shore. That is your punishment for taking a small child onto a boat that was to be used to train men with swords. *Sharp* swords. God's Bones, Payne, what were you thinking?"

He smiled at her, a disarming gesture. The past four years had seen their love grow in ways neither of them could have imagined, something so deep and fulfilling that it was part of them as much as blood or lungs or heart. She was part of him and he was part of her, and even looking at her now, in as much trouble was he was in, all he could feel was deep, enduring adoration.

She took his breath away.

"I was thinking how much I love my wife," he said softly. "How much I worship her. How much I love my children and my life. And how happy my mother would be if she could see us now. How proud she would be tae see Red Bowie Matheson on the bow of a ship, safe in his father's arms."

The statement was like throwing water on a fire. Astria rolled her eyes. "How dare you invoke your mother's name."

"'Tis true, my love."

With an expression of pure exasperation, Astria handed Bowie off to Francis, who took the boy eagerly. Perhaps even thinking about using him as a human shield against his mother if necessary. But Astria didn't go after Francis. She grabbed her husband by the arm and pulled him over to the railing where the boarding plank had been placed over the water.

"Get on that and walk until you fall into the lake," she said. "Swim to shore and stay out of sight. My anger may be abated by tonight, but I cannot be sure. For your sake, I hope it is."

He dutifully stepped up on the plank. He had the look of a man going to his execution. But then something changed.

He wasn't going to go alone.

Fast as lightning, he snatched up his wife into his arms and ran across the plank, leaping into the water with her still in his embrace. Astria lost her grip on her sword and it went flying. The men of both ships ran to the sides of their respective vessels that gave them the best view of Payne and Astria, now surfacing, and listening to Astria threaten Payne with great bodily harm when she caught up to him. The threats, however, were peppered with laughter, so they were far less effective that way.

But Payne swam for his life back to shore.

Days like that would be legendary at the Blackchurch Guild and something Bowie, who had witnessed the event, would tell his own children someday. Tales of a pirate grandmother, a pirate mother who retired from the seas after she had children, and a Blackchurch trainer for a father who bound them together in ways they could have never anticipated. Such stories were passed down through generations, becoming legend as the centuries went on. As Astria had promised, Bloody Maude lived on, and so did the marriage she created.

Astria and Payne's love did, indeed, outlast the stars.

And that was the way Maude would have wanted it.

CB THE END BD

Children of Payne and Astria

Bowie

Maximilian

Maude (*note: Maude took command of Medusa's Disciples when Pope Francis retired*)

Tyrus

Damara

Brisia

Shane

Ronan

KATHRYN LE VEQUE NOVELS

Medieval Romance:

De Wolfe Pack Series:
Warwolfe
The Wolfe
Nighthawk
ShadowWolfe
DarkWolfe
A Joyous de Wolfe Christmas
BlackWolfe
Serpent
A Wolfe Among Dragons
Scorpion
StormWolfe
Dark Destroyer
The Lion of the North
Walls of Babylon
The Best Is Yet To Be
BattleWolfe
Castle of Bones

De Wolfe Pack Generations:
WolfeHeart
WolfeStrike
WolfeSword
WolfeBlade
WolfeLord
WolfeShield
Nevermore
WolfeAx
WolfeBorn
WolfeBite

The Executioner Knights:
By the Unholy Hand
The Mountain Dark
Starless
A Time of End
Winter of Solace
Lord of the Sky
The Splendid Hour
The Whispering Night
Netherworld
Lord of the Shadows
Of Mortal Fury
'Twas the Executioner Knight
Before Christmas
Crimson Shield
The Black Dragon

The de Russe Legacy:
The Falls of Erith
Lord of War: Black Angel
The Iron Knight
Beast
The Dark One: Dark Knight
The White Lord of Wellesbourne
Dark Moon
Dark Steel
A de Russe Christmas Miracle
Dark Warrior

The de Lohr Dynasty:
While Angels Slept
Rise of the Defender
Steelheart

Shadowmoor
Silversword
Spectre of the Sword
Unending Love
Archangel
A Blessed de Lohr Christmas
Lion of Twilight
Lion of War
Lion of Hearts
Lion of Steel
Lion of Thunder

The Brothers de Lohr:
The Earl in Winter

Lords of East Anglia:
While Angels Slept
Godspeed
Age of Gods and Mortals

Great Lords of le Bec:
Great Protector

House of de Royans:
Lord of Winter
To the Lady Born
The Centurion

Lords of Eire:
Echoes of Ancient Dreams
Lord of Black Castle
The Darkland

Ancient Kings of Anglecynn:
The Whispering Night
Netherworld

Battle Lords of de Velt:
The Dark Lord
Devil's Dominion
Bay of Fear

The Dark Lord's First Christmas
The Dark Spawn
The Dark Conqueror
The Dark Angel

Reign of the House of de Winter:
Lespada
Swords and Shields

De Reyne Domination:
Guardian of Darkness
The Black Storm
A Cold Wynter's Knight
With Dreams
Master of the Dawn
One Wylde Knight

House of d'Vant:
Tender is the Knight (House of
d'Vant)
The Red Fury (House of d'Vant)

The Dragonblade Series:
Fragments of Grace
Dragonblade
Island of Glass
The Savage Curtain
The Fallen One
The Phantom Bride

Great Marcher Lords of de Lara
Lord of the Shadows
Dragonblade

House of St. Hever
Fragments of Grace
Island of Glass
Queen of Lost Stars

Lords of Pembury:
The Savage Curtain

Lords of Thunder: The de Shera Brotherhood Trilogy
The Thunder Lord
The Thunder Warrior
The Thunder Knight

The Great Knights of de Moray:
Shield of Kronos
The Gorgon

The House of De Nerra:
The Promise
The Falls of Erith
Vestiges of Valor
Realm of Angels

Highland Legion:
Highland Born
Highland Destroyer

Highland Warriors of Munro:
The Red Lion
Deep Into Darkness

The House of de Garr:
Lord of Light
Realm of Angels

Saxon Lords of Hage:
The Crusader
Kingdom Come

High Warriors of Rohan:
High Warrior
High King

The House of Ashbourne:
Upon a Midnight Dream

The House of D'Aurilliac:
Valiant Chaos

The House of De Dere:
Of Love and Legend

St. John and de Gare Clans:
The Warrior Poet

The House of de Bretagne:
The Questing

The House of Summerlin:
The Legend

The Kingdom of Hendocia:
Kingdom by the Sea

The BlackChurch Guild: Shadow Knights:
The Leviathan
The Protector
The Swordsman
The Tempest

Guard of Six:
Absolution
Insurrection

Regency Historical Romance:
Sin Like Flynn: A Regency Historical Romance Duet
The Sin Commandments
Georgina and the Red Charger

Gothic Regency Romance:
Emma

Historical Fiction:
The Girl Made Of Stars

Contemporary Romance:

Kathlyn Trent/Marcus Burton Series:

Valley of the Shadow
The Eden Factor
Canyon of the Sphinx

The Eagle Brotherhood (under the pen name Kat Le Veque):
The Sunset Hour
The Killing Hour
The Secret Hour
The Unholy Hour
The Burning Hour
The Ancient Hour
The Devil's Hour

Sons of Poseidon:
The Immortal Sea

Pirates of Britannia Series (with Eliza Knight):
Savage of the Sea by Eliza Knight
Leader of Titans by Kathryn Le Veque
The Sea Devil by Eliza Knight
Sea Wolfe by Kathryn Le Veque

Note: All Kathryn's novels are designed to be read as stand-alones, although many have cross-over characters or cross-over family groups. Novels that are grouped together have related characters or family groups. You will notice that some series have the same books; that is because they are cross-overs. A hero in one book may be the secondary character in another.

There is NO reading order except by chronology, but even in that case, you can still read the books as stand-alones. No novel is connected to another by a cliff hanger, and every book has an HEA.

Series are clearly marked. All series contain the same characters or family groups except the American Heroes Series, which is an anthology with unrelated characters.

For more information, find it in **A Reader's Guide to the Medieval World of Le Veque**.

ABOUT KATHRYN LE VEQUE

Bringing the Medieval to Romance

KATHRYN LE VEQUE is a critically acclaimed, multiple USA TODAY Bestselling author, an Indie Reader bestseller, a charter Amazon All-Star author, and a #1 bestselling, award-winning, multi-published author in Medieval Historical Romance with over 100 published novels.

Kathryn is a multiple award nominee and winner, including the winner of Uncaged Book Reviews Magazine 2017 and 2018 "Raven Award" for Favorite Medieval Romance. Kathryn is also a multiple RONE nominee (InD'Tale Magazine), holding a record for the number of nominations. In 2018, her novel WARWOLFE was the winner in the Romance category of the Book Excellence Award and in 2019, her novel A WOLFE AMONG DRAGONS won the prestigious RONE award for best pre-16th century romance.

Kathryn is considered one of the top Indie authors in the world with over 2M copies in circulation, and her novels have been translated into several languages. Kathryn recently signed with Sourcebooks Casablanca for a Medieval Fight Club series, first published in 2020.

In addition to her own published works, Kathryn is also the President/CEO of Dragonblade Publishing, a boutique publishing house specializing in Historical Romance. Dragonblade's success has seen it rise in the ranks to become Amazon's #1 e-book publisher of Historical Romance (K-Lytics report July 2020).

Kathryn loves to hear from her readers. Please find Kathryn on Facebook at Kathryn Le Veque, Author, or join her on Twitter @kathrynleveque. Sign up for Kathryn's blog at www.kathrynleveque.com for the latest news and sales.

www.ingramcontent.com/pod-product-compliance
Lightning Source LLC
Chambersburg PA
CBHW071242300726
48975CB00002B/518